# LOVE OR DUTY

# LOVE OR DUTY

## ROBERTA GRIEVE

**ISIS**
LARGE PRINT
Oxford

First published in Great Britain 2011
by
Robert Hale Limited

Published in Large Print 2012 by ISIS Publishing Ltd.,
7 Centremead, Osney Mead, Oxford OX2 0ES
by arrangement with
Robert Hale Limited

**British Library Cataloguing in Publication Data**
Grieve, Roberta.
    Love or duty.
    1. Love stories
    2. Large type books.
    I. Title
    823.9'2–dc23

ISBN 978–0–7531–8940–5 (hb)
ISBN 978–0–7531–8941–2 (pb)

Printed and bound in Great Britain by
T. J. International Ltd., Padstow, Cornwall

# Prologue

# 1920

Five-year-old Louise Charlton twirled round, giggling excitedly. It seemed strange to be wearing her best Sunday dress and her shiny black patent leather shoes in the middle of the week.

"Is it a party?" she asked.

"It's a surprise," Polly said. "The master said to have you all dressed up by the time he gets home."

Louise's father had been away for a few days and she'd missed him. When she heard his key in the door she ran down the wide staircase, stopping abruptly when she saw that he wasn't alone. She knew the lady with him. She attended St Mark's Church where her father was a church warden and just lately she'd taken to sitting with them instead of in her usual pew. Perhaps Father had invited her to tea.

Stanley Charlton picked her up and kissed her cheek. "How's my little poppet? Did you miss me?"

Louise nodded and wriggled to get down, pulling at his hand. "Cookie's made a special cake for tea."

The lady spoke sharply. "Well, Stanley, aren't you going to tell her?"

1

"I'm sorry, my love." He bent down and took Louise's hand. "This is Dora — your new mother."

It wasn't quite the surprise she'd been expecting but Louise's first thought was that they would be a real family now. She didn't remember her own mother and much of her upbringing had been left to Bessie Rogers, their cook and housekeeper and Polly, the maid.

Louise stepped forward shyly, a tentative smile lighting her dark brown eyes, a faint flush on her pale face. Dora was plump, with soft waving fair hair. How pretty she was in her silky dress, which perfectly matched eyes the colour of a summer sky. Dora returned the smile and bent down, offering a soft pink cheek for Louise to kiss. The scent of rosewater wafted towards her and she thought Dora looked and smelt just how a mother should. Maybe this was what her real mother had been like.

"You may call me Mother," Dora said, straightening and slipping her hand through her new husband's arm. She turned to him. "Come, dear, you must show me my room."

When Louise made to follow them up the broad stairs, Dora turned to her. "Go and wash your hands, child. Then wait for us in the drawing room. You may join us for tea today — as it's a special occasion."

Louise was disappointed, but, anxious to please, she did as she was told. In the drawing room, she perched on the edge of a chair, swinging her legs and savouring the experience of being in the large, high-ceilinged, over-furnished room. She usually took her meals in the kitchen with Cookie and Polly. Perhaps her new mother

2

would let her eat in the dining room. And surely, now that Father was married, he'd spend more time at home. A real family, she thought once more, just like her friend Peggy Fryer, who had a mother and father as well as two little brothers. Perhaps she'd have a little brother now, she thought.

The door opened and they came in, holding hands, Father smiling at his new wife, Dora gazing up at him, her cheeks dimpling, her blue eyes sparkling. He bent and kissed her, but she pushed him away playfully. "Now, now, Stanley. Not in front of the child."

She turned to Louise. "Don't stare, child," she said. "Go and tell Polly to bring the tea in. And don't run," she admonished, as Louise scampered towards the door.

Unused to being spoken to so sharply, she looked back in alarm.

Dora glanced quickly at Father before saying in a softer tone, "It's not ladylike, dear. Now, run along."

Louise's hopes of real family life didn't materialize. That remained a pleasant fantasy. It wasn't that her stepmother was unkind, more indifferent. And Dora had her own ideas on the upbringing of children. Stanley always deferred to her and Louise learned that it was useless to protest when the inevitable response was, "Your mother knows best."

Father never took sides, but she soon realized he would do almost anything to avoid Dora's tears and complaints about "her poor head".

She wasn't unhappy, just disappointed that being a "real family" hadn't lived up to her expectations. The worst thing about it was that she could no longer take refuge in the kitchen as she used to. She longed for those carefree days when Father used to come in by the back door and, after throwing his hat and coat on a chair, would join them at the big scrubbed table in the centre of the room. Cookie always had something fresh out of the oven — soft floury scones spread with butter and strawberry jam, or little fairy cakes with icing and hundreds and thousands on top.

Now, the kitchen was strictly out of bounds. Father had to use the front door and hand his hat and coat to Polly. Then, he had to join Dora in the drawing room. Sometimes Louise was allowed to sit and take tea with them but more often than not she was sent upstairs to have tea in the nursery. How she missed the companionship of Cookie and Polly in the warm intimacy of the kitchen.

When Mother's delicate condition was first mentioned in her hearing, Louise wondered what it could possibly mean. She didn't look in the least delicate. In fact she was rosy-cheeked with sparkling eyes. And she was getting fatter too.

"Is Mother ill?" Louise asked Polly, when she came to clear away the tea things one day.

Polly looked embarrassed. "No — not exactly ill, Miss Louise." She piled the things on the tray, pausing at the door with it balanced on her hip. "Don't you worry yourself. She'll be all right in a few months, you'll see."

Louise was slightly reassured, even when Dora took to lying down in the afternoons with a cold flannel over her eyes. And she couldn't really be sorry that her stepmother spent so much time in her room. It meant she herself wasn't under so much pressure to conform to the strict ladylike behaviour that was expected of her.

And the best thing about Mother's illness was that she had Father all to herself on their Sunday afternoon walks, although they were somewhat marred by a slight feeling of guilt. As she skipped along the promenade, holding Father's hand, Louise wondered if it was wrong to feel so happy when Mother was lying at home in a darkened room in such obvious discomfort.

# CHAPTER
# ONE

## Spring 1937

Louise was twenty-two when Sarah won the talent competition. She wasn't jealous — not much anyway. Hadn't Dora always impressed on her how much prettier and more talented her half-sister was?

I'm pleased for her — really I am, she told herself, as the petite dark-haired sixteen-year-old girl, her violet eyes shining, took her bow with all the assurance of a seasoned performer. She might have been at the Royal Opera House rather than the Winter Gardens in a small seaside town.

Louise loved her sister dearly. It wasn't Sarah's fault that *she* was so plain and awkward. With an inward sigh, she joined in the storm of applause.

Her father squeezed her arm. "I told you she'd do it." His eyes were moist with pride.

Louise told herself once more that she wasn't really jealous. Stanley Charlton loved both his daughters. It was just that Sarah seemed to have that little extra something that drew people to her, casting her older sister in the shade.

She smiled back at her father, returning the pressure of his hand on her arm as the MC urged Sarah forward for an encore. And as her sister took a deep breath and the first clear notes of *The Wings of a Dove* soared towards the roof of the Winter Gardens Theatre, she realized that Sarah was a true star.

"What a pity Dora was too ill to come tonight," Stanley whispered.

Louise's smile faded, replaced by a tightening of the lips and a flicker of anger. Trust her stepmother to spoil things. If I had a daughter half as pretty and talented as Sarah, Louise thought, I'd give her every encouragement — be there to share her triumphs, comfort her if things went wrong.

As Sarah, hands clasped in front of her, head tilted to one side, sang her heart out, the magic of the music was lost on Louise. Her thoughts were on Dora Charlton, Father's pretty, spoilt wife, a woman so determined to be the centre of attention that she would disappoint her own child by feigning illness. And Louise was quite sure by now that Dora's ill health was largely a figment of her imagination. She had a feeling that Dr Tate thought so too. His nephew certainly did.

Andrew Tate had acted as locum for his uncle the previous autumn when the old doctor had been ill with bronchitis. He'd been called to the house several times when Dora had been indulging in one of her frequent bouts of illness — brought on, Louise was now sure, whenever her wishes were thwarted, or when she wasn't getting the attention she so desperately craved.

Louise bit back a smile as she remembered the conspiratorial look that had passed between them on his last visit. She'd been impressed by the young doctor's manner. He had dealt with Dora firmly, not indulging her whims, yet managing to appear sympathetic. He had probably been well briefed by his uncle, she thought, with a smile. Old Dr Tate had been dealing with Dora's tantrums for years.

Since then Andrew Tate had returned to Holton Regis several times. Louise had met him again at church and was looking forward to seeing him when he came to dinner the following week. She told herself it was his skill as a doctor she admired but, as Sarah's song came to an end, she found her thoughts straying to the way his blue eyes sparkled when he was trying not to laugh, the lock of blond hair he was continually pushing back from his forehead. If only he were sitting beside her now, instead of James Spencer, the son of her father's business partner, she thought.

A burst of applause brought her back to the present and she joined in enthusiastically. Her father stood up, clapping loudly, his face shining with pride. Thank goodness that, tonight at least, Father had resisted Dora's attempts to keep him at her side. "Sarah will be so disappointed if one of us isn't there, dear," she'd heard him say gently. "Besides, there's nothing I can do if I stay. You'll be asleep soon, now that you've taken your pills."

"But suppose I wake up. I hate being alone," Dora pleaded, her blue eyes bright with the hint of tears.

"You won't be alone. Polly will be here," Stanley said, and Louise had silently applauded the hint of hardness in his voice. It was about time Dora began to realize that the world didn't revolve around her.

Louise sighed. She really couldn't see Dora allowing her daughter to pursue the career that would surely open up after this evening's triumph.

Sarah, she knew, had no such doubts. Her half-sister had always loved to perform, whether it was singing a solo in church, showing off the latest steps she'd learned at dance class or playing the piano, which Stanley, for once overriding his wife's protests, had installed in the drawing room at Steyne House. But it was singing that had proved to be Sarah's greatest talent. "The voice of an angel" the staid matrons of St Mark's had been heard to murmur when the little girl sang the solo at the Christmas carol service.

"You sing very well, dear," Dora had told her countless times. And then she would bring Sarah down to earth. "But there are other things in life, you know."

"I want to be a famous singer — I'll keep practising till I'm perfect," Sarah declared. "I'm going to sing at Covent Garden. I'll travel all over the world."

"You're much too young to be thinking of that." Dora lifted the scented handkerchief to her eyes. "I just don't want you to be hurt, darling," she said, with a catch in her voice.

"So long as I can sing, I'll do anything. I'll even play the clubs and variety palaces."

Dora gave a horrified moan. "No daughter of mine . . ." she began, her voice becoming lost in strangled sobs.

Sarah was sent to her room and Louise followed, trying to warn her against stating her intentions so openly. "If she sees you're really keen, she'll find a way to stop you," she said.

"She wouldn't withdraw me from the competition?" Sarah asked.

Louise knew her sister was pinning all her hopes on the talent contest at the Winter Gardens and winning the prize of singing in a concert to be broadcast on the wireless in celebration of the Coronation of the new king, George VI.

"I wouldn't put it past her. But don't worry, if she tries, Father will talk her out of it," she said.

And he had. Dora's revenge was to stay home, pleading illness. But she hadn't been able to prevent Louise and her father from attending the concert and witnessing Sarah's triumph.

As they stood up and pushed past the parents and families of the other contestants, Louise wondered how Sarah would cope with the disappointment if their mother now refused to allow her to take up the prize.

As the applause reached a crescendo, Sarah stood for a moment, her hands clasped in front of her. Then she threw out her arms, bending her knee in a curtsy as her dancing mistress had instructed her.

Beyond the footlights the faces of the audience were a pale blur and she strained forward, looking towards the seats that had been reserved for her family. There they were — Father and Louise, standing up, clapping and cheering along with the rest of the crowd. But where was Mother? Surely she hadn't meant it when she refused to come?

Sarah's excitement drained away, replaced by bitter disappointment tinged with resentment. Why did she always have to spoil things? But then she remembered that when Mother had one of her headaches she couldn't bear the slightest sound. Guilt at her selfishness replaced the resentment.

Later, when her father was signing the forms that would allow her to take up her prize, the euphoria returned. She wouldn't let anything mar the pleasure of this evening.

It was late when they finally left the little office at the back of the concert hall. Father tucked the contract into his inside pocket and patted Sarah's hand. "You mustn't let this go to your head, sweetheart," he said. "Remember, we're only allowing you go to accept this prize as a special treat."

"But it's my chance to be a real singer," Sarah insisted, taking his hand and swinging on it as they emerged through the gates of the Winter Gardens on to the promenade.

Father's business partner William Spencer and his son were waiting for them. Sarah smiled at James, blushing when he complimented her on her performance. He seemed much nicer now than when they'd been at school together. He'd always been teasing her and pulling her plaits. Now that he was almost grown up he was rather good-looking too. She was quite annoyed when Father refused a lift in the Spencers' Daimler. It would have been fun to sit in the back seat next to him.

As they drove off he turned and blew a kiss. Sarah giggled. "Did you see that, Lou? I think he likes me."

12

"Sarah, you're too young to be thinking about young men. Besides, I thought you were more interested in a career."

"I am. Still it's nice to be admired." She ran on ahead, giggling. She wasn't really interested in James Spencer. He'd just started work in Father's business and would probably turn out to be one of those dull men whose heads were full of profit and loss — just like her father.

She did a little skip and laughed. She was going to London to sing at the BBC. She'd meet other singers, musicians, actors. It was all going to be such fun. Her ticket away from dull old Holton Regis by the sea.

Louise called out to her. "Wait for us," and ran to catch up with her.

"I think it was you James was blowing that kiss at," Sarah said with a mischievous smile.

"Nonsense. I'm far too old for him."

Sarah didn't answer. She was probably right. Poor Louise, stuck at home at Mother's beck and call. What chance did she have to meet anyone? Since young Dr Tate had returned to London the only unmarried men she ever saw were his uncle and the curate.

She linked arms with Louise and her father and they hurried along the seafront. It had got much colder and she could see their breath on the frosty air and hear the waves crashing on the shingle. She wanted to run, anxious to get home and tell her mother of her triumph. But Dora would be in bed by now and besides, she didn't really care, did she?

As they reached the end of the promenade and crossed the road towards Steyne House, Sarah refused to think about Mother. She was imagining tomorrow in church when she would describe her success in great detail to her friends.

The next day, to her surprise, Mother seemed quite enthusiastic about her win. As she'd anticipated, Dora had been in bed when they arrived home. But the next day at breakfast she kissed Sarah and congratulated her ungrudgingly. For once, there was no reference to her own earlier musical aspirations.

As they got ready for church Dora was more animated than she'd been for weeks. "Now dear," she said as she brushed a speck of lint off Sarah's coat and straightened her hat, "if any of those snooty old dears at church say anything to you about you entering the contest, you must tell them firmly that singing on the wireless is perfectly respectable."

Sarah caught Louise's eye and grinned. Only yesterday Mother had doubted the wisdom of allowing her daughter to take part in the talent contest. She *would* worry so about what other people thought. And she was very conscious of her position as the wife of one of the town's most prominent businessmen.

The service seemed interminable and Sarah thought the Reverend Ayling was rambling even more than usual. Even the hymns couldn't cheer her up today. For some reason the vicar had chosen dreary dirges to complement his even more dreary sermon.

It was hard not to fidget, especially when her feet were so cold. Thank goodness she was sitting between

Father and Louise today and, hopefully, Mother wouldn't notice her inattention. The heating pipes gave a sudden clank and gurgle, making her jump. She tried not to giggle as in the pew in front of them, Mrs Henley's shoulders jerked and she knew that the old lady had been dozing through the sermon. Who could blame her? Sarah thought. She felt Louise's movement beside her and didn't dare look round. Her sister was probably trying not to laugh as well.

The service came to an end and they filed out, pausing to shake hands with Mr Ayling and exchange greetings with their friends and neighbours. Sarah was looking forward to basking in their admiration. But there was no hanging about today. Yesterday's spring weather had turned to driving rain and, at Dora's insistence, Stanley had got the car out for the short drive to church.

Sarah sighed. If the rain didn't stop they'd have to forego their usual afternoon walk along the seafront. It would be another interminable Sunday of Bible reading, embroidery and polite conversation. She didn't care about the weather and would much prefer to brave the wind and rain to stride along the beach, climbing over the breakwaters that had recently been installed to stop the silting up of the river mouth.

"Come along, Sarah." Dora's sharp voice interrupted her thoughts and she scrambled into the back seat with Louise. She didn't want to upset Mother today. If she stayed in a good mood she might even consent to play the piano while Sarah sang her encore song. The thought cheered her up and she turned to Louise, noting that her sister looked a little downcast.

"You will come to London with me, won't you?" she asked.

"If Mother can spare me," Louise said.

Sarah bit her lip and pouted. It seemed that whenever Louise wanted to do something, Mother found a way of stopping her — usually another bout of illness, which demanded her stepdaughter's attendance at all times. Poor Louise had no life of her own, she reflected once more — she should be married or at least engaged, as most girls of her age were by now. She had no social life, apart from church functions and a weekly trip to the Picturedrome cinema with her friend Peggy. Even the guests at the dinner parties her mother occasionally held were boring old businessmen or members of the church council.

The car stopped in the front drive of Steyne House and, as Sarah got out, she saw how her half-sister turned to help Dora, offering her arm and holding the umbrella over her. She was so sweet and kind, and when she smiled she was even quite pretty. She deserved to be happy.

# CHAPTER
# TWO

The question of Louise accompanying Sarah to London didn't arise. To Sarah's surprise — and that of the rest of the household — Dora declared her intention of chaperoning her daughter on the big day.

In the weeks leading up to the London trip, Dora was as excited as her daughter as she made daily excursions to the shops in the High Street and London Road, buying everything from shoes to handbags, scarves and gloves for both of them. They even had to have new underwear and nightwear, as well as matching luggage, for the overnight stay at the Grosvenor Hotel near Victoria Station, which Dora had been assured was a respectable place for an unaccompanied lady to stay. The BBC concert wouldn't finish in time for them to make the journey back to Holton Regis the same day.

Although Sarah was pleased that Mother was taking such an interest, she really wished Louise were going with her. They'd have so much more fun.

When the big day finally arrived, Sarah could hardly contain herself. She was ready far too early and refused to eat any breakfast. When Mother clutched her head and declared that she would have to lie down if Sarah didn't stop her incessant chattering, Louise frowned at her sister with a warning shake of the head.

"I'm sorry, Mother," Sarah said, instantly contrite. "Shall I get your cologne for you?" The thought that Mother might refuse to go and would insist that Sarah stayed at home too wasn't to be borne. This was her big chance. After today the name of Sarah Charlton would be on everybody's lips. She would be the star of the show.

At last they were ready and Stanley got the car out to drive them to the station. Louise gave her a hug and wished her good luck. "I wish you were coming with us," she whispered.

"Someone has to stay and look after Father," Louise said.

Sarah wondered why. He had Polly and Cookie to look after him; that's what they were paid for. Still, he might be lonely if they all went away. But it was only for one night.

She hoped Mother would be all right. What would happen if she got one of her "heads" just as they were about to leave the hotel for Broadcasting House? But she wouldn't think about that. Everything was going to be just perfect.

They boarded the train and Father put their suitcase on the rack. They waved him goodbye and Sarah settled in her seat by the window, prepared to enjoy the unusual treat of being whisked through the Sussex countryside, while Mother opened her magazine.

As the train rattled over the points at the junction with the main line, Sarah gazed out of the window and hummed a little tune in time with the rhythm of the wheels. The hum got louder, then developed into a song. Sarah was never happier than when she was singing. Her mother tapped her arm impatiently.

"I can't concentrate on my reading, dear. Do be quiet," she said. "Besides, I think you should save your voice for later. We don't want you getting hoarse, do we?"

Sarah nodded and sat back in her seat, pulling at a loose thread in her glove. She was so excited, she just couldn't sit still. But Mother was glaring at her so she stopped fidgeting and looked out of the window again. Would they ever get to London?

At last the green fields gave way to rows of houses with large gardens backing on to the railway embankment. Gradually the gardens became smaller, the houses more grimy and dilapidated. There were vast stretches of railway line, criss-crossing and intersecting, and dilapidated buildings of blackened brick. Then the train was rattling over a bridge, the steely waters of the Thames sliding beneath, and suddenly they were pulling into Victoria Station.

A porter rushed up and took their bags and they followed him across the noisy concourse towards the hotel entrance, which was set in the corner of the vast railway station. Sarah's feet dragged as she gazed about her curiously. She had never been to London before and felt overwhelmed by the vast echoing space, the crowds of people, the pigeons fluttering about their feet and the sulphurous smell of the huge steam engines.

But it was all quite wonderful and her steps slowed as she drank it all in. If Mother hadn't been holding tightly to her hand, almost dragging her along, she would have stood and stared forever. There was so much to see.

When they reached their hotel room, Mother sank down on the bed and took off her gloves and hat. She waved a languid hand to the boy, indicating that he should put the bags down, and instructed him to send up some tea.

Sarah looked at her mother apprehensively. Maybe Louise should have come with them too. Poor Mother looked absolutely exhausted.

To her surprise Dora looked up and smiled brightly. "Well, dear, it's a long time since I was in town but I'm sure we'll manage. I'm so proud of you, my darling. I just had to come with you and share your big day."

Sarah kissed her mother's cheek. "It is exciting, isn't it, Mother?"

The maid brought tea and they sat at a small table by the window, looking out over Buckingham Palace Road. There wasn't much to see, apart from delivery carts and lorries, what seemed like hundreds of taxicabs swinging round the corner towards the front of the station and of course, hordes of people. Sarah had imagined a wide avenue lined with trees leading up to the palace.

"You're thinking of the Mall," her mother told her.

"Will we see the king?" she asked hopefully.

"I think it's highly unlikely, dear." Dora finished her tea and stood up. "Now, Sarah, we must get ready to go to Broadcasting House. A bath and a complete change of clothes I think. One gets so disgustingly filthy travelling by train."

It was true Mother's white gloves were a little grubby. They had kept the carriage windows closed but the smuts from the engine got everywhere and Sarah knew she wasn't looking as neat and tidy as when they had set out earlier. She must look her best for the performance — even though no one would see her.

And she did look nice in her new white dress with the wide blue sash, a matching ribbon in her dark curly hair, white stockings and shiny black patent leather shoes. Mother gave a final tweak to the sash and nodded approvingly. "Get your coat and gloves, dear, the car will be here soon," she said, picking up Sarah's music case. "I'll look after this. It wouldn't do to lose it now."

There was plenty of time and, as a treat, Dora asked the cab driver to take them past Buckingham Palace and along the Mall so that Sarah had a chance to see the flags and decorations that had been put up for the coronation. She seemed almost as excited as her daughter.

When the cab turned into Portland Place, the driver turned and pointed out the imposing building, which had only been completed a few years ago. Its white stone gleamed in the spring sunshine. "That's Broadcasting House, missus," he said. "Looks like one of them great big ocean liners wot you see down the docks, don't it?"

Dora nodded as he pulled to a stop in front of the main entrance. They got out and Sarah paused for a moment, looking up at the carvings over the main entrance. It still seemed like magic to her that from inside this building her singing would be heard all over the country, wherever people had wireless sets. When Sarah had won the talent contest, Father had gone out and bought one of the most up to date sets in a shiny walnut cabinet, so that he and Louise, together with Cookie and Polly could listen to the concert together.

Sarah followed her mother towards the entrance where a stout commissionaire inspected their letter of introduction. He beckoned a young man to show them through a warren of corridors to the studio. When they arrived, they were greeted by a tall thin man with glasses who introduced himself as the producer.

"We'll have a rehearsal first, then a break before the actual broadcast," he explained after a short chat with Dora. "Your mother and I will be up there," he told Sarah, pointing to a gallery behind a glass partition where several people sat wearing headphones.

The orchestra was tuning up and the conductor stopped sorting his music and turned to smile at her. She didn't feel in the least nervous, though she knew that when the accompanist played the introduction to her song, for a few seconds her hands would grow clammy and her throat dry. Then she would open her mouth and the notes would soar out, almost effortlessly, and she would be lost in the glory and wonder of the music.

The producer was talking earnestly to her mother, whose eyes were glittering with suppressed fury. Her mother's voice sounded irritable and Sarah forced her attention back to them, an apprehensive fluttering in her stomach. What was wrong?

Dora thrust the music case at the producer and turned on her heel. "I just hope you know what you're doing, that's all," she snapped, and pushed through the swing doors.

Sarah watched her go, not sure whether to follow. "It's all right, Sarah. Your mother was under the impression that she was going to accompany you at the piano. But as I explained, it wasn't in the contract your father signed. Besides, we have our own pianist." The producer smiled apologetically. "Don't worry, everything will be fine."

Well, at least she hadn't indulged in one of her fainting fits, Sarah thought with relief. Mother usually took refuge in feeling unwell when she didn't get her own way. But what had made her think she would be allowed to accompany her today? She had said nothing about it to anyone and Sarah had had no idea that she was entertaining thoughts of sharing her daughter's fame and triumph. And why should she? She'd had her chance. But she gave up her music when she decided to marry Father and have a family. Well, that's not going to happen to me, Sarah told herself. My singing career will always come first.

And with that thought she gave the producer her most dazzling smile and took her place in front of the microphone. She glanced at the pianist and launched into *Poor Wandering One* from the *Pirates of Penzance*. After the first few notes she forgot her mother sitting in the booth with the producer, forgot her father and those at home sitting in front of the wireless. She just sang her heart out, as she'd been doing since she was only three and learned her first nursery rhyme. When she reached the end without a single false note, she knew that at last she was on her way. Of course, she wouldn't be famous overnight, but soon she was sure the world would be clamouring to hear her sing. Maybe she'd even end up in films like Shirley Temple.

The thought sustained her on the drive back to the hotel when, despite the praise heaped on her by the musicians and studio workers, she lapsed into an uncharacteristic silence. Mother was in a bad mood — but it wasn't her fault, was it? Still, it was no good saying anything. She was quite capable of forbidding her to ever sing in public again. And, although her father would be sympathetic, it was always Dora who had the last word.

Louise had managed to hide her disappointment when Dora insisted that she should be the one to go to London with Sarah. She'd been so looking forward to getting away from Holton Regis, even for just one day. She was beginning to feel stifled by the narrowness of her life and envied Sarah the chance to spread her wings. If only she had a talent like Sarah's, something she was good at.

Her envy was not bitter or corrosive. She loved Sarah dearly and was truly pleased with her success. She and her father, together with Cookie and Polly, pulled their chairs close to the wireless set as the announcer spoke Sarah's name.

"Ooh, Miss — our Miss Sarah. Who'd've believed it!" Polly said, her voice high with excitement.

Cookie shushed her as the music began and the pure sweet sound of Sarah's voice swelled out of the magic box in the corner of the drawing room. Louise's heart swelled with pride and a lump came to her throat and she saw that Cookie was wiping away a surreptitious tear with the corner of her apron.

She couldn't wait for Sarah's return to hear all about it. When she and her father met Sarah and Dora at the station the following day, Louise was surprised that her sister did not leap off the train and throw her arms round them, bubbling over with excitement in her usual irrepressible way. Dora too seemed a little subdued and Louise hoped that her stepmother hadn't spoilt things by being ill.

At home Cookie and Polly were waiting to add their congratulations and during the ensuing fuss, Sarah regained a little of her sparkle, only to subside again when Dora's voice cut into the babble of conversation.

"Stanley, forgive me if I don't join you for luncheon. The journey . . . I'm exhausted." Her hand went to her head and Stanley put his arm around her.

"I'll help you to your room, my dear. Polly will bring you up a tray."

25

"Nothing, thank you." At the foot of the stairs she paused. "Perhaps some tea and toast? Louise will see to it, won't you, dear?"

Louise nodded, then smiled at Sarah. "Go and get changed for lunch, then you can tell Father and me all about it."

Polly and Cookie returned to the kitchen and Louise followed them. By the time she'd settled her stepmother with her tray, her eau-de-cologne and a magazine "in case I can't sleep, dear", her father and sister were at the dining table.

Sarah could scarcely eat for excitement as she recounted everything in great detail. She did not mention her mother at all.

After lunch Stanley went up to see how Dora was feeling. When he came down he spoke quietly. "Your Mother's quite worn out with all the excitement. I don't have to go back to the office this afternoon so I'll keep her company." He smiled at the girls. "Why don't you go for a nice walk — leave Mother to rest? The fresh air will do you good," he insisted.

As they strode along the promenade, heads bent against the wind, Louise asked her sister if there was anything wrong.

"The concert was wonderful — I already told you. They were all so kind and helpful. I wasn't nervous at all," Sarah said.

"And the agent was there as well — the one who said he might give you a recording contract?"

"Yes. He's going to come and see Father and arrange it all with him in a couple of weeks."

"I'm so pleased for you, Sarah." Louise squeezed her sister's hand. "Think how proud I'll be when you're a famous singer."

Sarah still seemed rather subdued. "Mother's not proud — I think she's jealous."

"Nonsense, of course she's proud of you. And why should she be jealous?"

"She wanted to be a famous pianist, didn't she? And ended up playing for the cinema and then at the Winter Gardens." Sarah went on to explain how Dora had tried to persuade the producer of the radio programme to let her play the piano for her. "She was in a real huff when they said she couldn't do it."

Louise told her sister not to be so silly. But she suspected there was a grain of truth in what she'd said. Dora loved to be the centre of attention, whether it was in an admiring circle of church ladies or at home with her husband and family. Perhaps she'd seen the radio broadcast as a chance to resurrect her own musical career.

They strode along in silence and Louise was glad that the strong wind made it hard to walk and talk at the same time. She was so angry with her stepmother, but it wouldn't do to let Sarah know how she felt. Louise remembered when she was little and how desperate she'd been to win Dora's approval. But, despite her efforts to please, the older woman had steadily undermined her confidence, making her feel clumsy and useless. Now she was doing the same thing to her own daughter. Fortunately Sarah had inherited her mother's determination — but, Louise hoped, not Dora's selfishness.

When they reached the bandstand, deserted at this time of year, the girls mounted the steps and stopped in its shelter to get their breath back.

"I suppose we'd better start back. Mother will be cross if we're late for tea," Louise said.

Sarah kicked a stray pebble over the sea wall. "I feel a bit flat now it's all over. Do you really think I'll be able to make a career out of singing?"

Louise hugged her. "No doubt about it. You'll go far." She frowned. "I wish I had your talent. You'll soon be off to conquer the world and I'll be stuck here in dreary old Holton."

"Poor old Lou. It doesn't have to be like that, you know." Sarah laughed. "When I'm rich and famous you can be my personal secretary, how about that?"

"Sounds like fun. One day, maybe . . ." Louise turned to face the sea, looking out at the sparkling wavelets, the ships dotted on the horizon. Much as she longed for an escape from her dull conventional life she did love living by the sea. And there was something comforting about living in a house built by her great-grandfather in a town where her family was known and respected. Yes, she would like to travel but she knew she'd always come back to her roots.

Sarah had walked on ahead and Louise ran to catch up with her.

When they got back to Steyne House, they discovered they had a visitor. The curate, Keith Willis, was in the drawing room, gravely listening to Stanley's concerns about the state of the church roof and his plans for raising money for its repair.

Louise realized she was quite pleased to see him. She hadn't many close friends and it was always a pleasure to have a conversation with someone outside her family. Besides, her stepmother was a different person in company.

When Keith stood up, a welcoming smile lighting up his rather ordinary features, Louise returned the smile and sat down beside him. But when she attempted to join in the conversation, Dora, who had come downstairs and was now lying on the couch in front of the fire, interrupted impatiently.

"Leave it to the men, dear. They know about such things." She touched her cologne-soaked handkerchief to her forehead. "And now that you're back from your walk, we can have tea. Ring for Polly — and, Sarah, make sure you wash your hands."

"It's Polly's afternoon off, Mother. I'll see to it," Louise said, getting up hastily.

When she returned with the tray the curate jumped up to help and almost succeeded in spilling everything. With a nervous laugh he sat down and Louise put the things down on a side table.

As she passed his cup she thought what a nice shy young man Mr Willis was. She felt sorry for him, knowing how embarrassed he must have been by his display of clumsiness earlier. Hadn't she suffered the same torments when, in her eagerness to please, she had knocked things over or spilled something? Dora had told her so many times how useless she was that she'd come to believe it. It was quite gratifying to meet someone who seemed to have the same problem — not like Andrew Tate who had made her feel even more nervous with his self-confident manner.

In an effort to put Keith at his ease, she devoted more attention to him than she would otherwise have done and she sensed Dora's approval. She looked away from his intense gaze. She didn't want him getting the wrong idea.

She stood up and began to stack the used tea things on the trolley. As she pushed it along the wide passage towards the kitchen she wondered what being the wife of a vicar would be like. She pictured herself living in the vast gloomy vicarage, hosting meetings of the Mothers' Union and the Young Wives' Group, her whole life devoted to the service of others — not unlike her life now, she thought.

She gave herself a mental shake. What was she thinking of? Dora would be pleased of course, but Louise dreamed of a different life, away from the little seaside town where she'd been born and brought up.

Besides, she was quite sure her liking for Keith Willis was nothing like the feelings her friend Peggy had for her fiancé, a dashing naval lieutenant who had swept her off her feet last summer. Surely there was someone like that for her somewhere in the world — if she ever got the chance to meet him. She refused to think about Andrew Tate, telling herself her feelings for him had been brought about by loneliness. Besides, if he had the slightest interest in her, he would surely have made some excuse to return to Holton before now.

With a little laugh at her foolish thoughts she returned to the drawing room in time to hear Mother's horrified gasp.

"A *missionary*. You can't be serious, Mr Willis. But why on earth should you feel compelled to go to darkest Africa when we have such need of you here?"

"I feel God is calling me to do this work, Mrs Charlton." Keith leaned forward earnestly, his eyes shining with fervour.

Behind her mother's back, Sarah raised her eyebrows and rolled her eyes dramatically. Louise couldn't help smiling at her foolish thoughts of a moment ago. It seemed she had got it all wrong.

# CHAPTER
# THREE

It wasn't often that the Charltons entertained. Although Dora loved to dress up and show off, there were very few people in Holton Regis who lived up to her ideas of suitable guests. But since Sarah's singing success she had grasped every opportunity to boast about her talented daughter. The dinner party had been planned ever since Sarah's BBC broadcast.

How Louise wished the whole thing was over. Cookie had planned a delicious meal — lamb cooked to perfection with minted baby new potatoes and fresh peas and beans from the garden. The problem was Polly, who although usually cheerful and willing, was thrown into confusion at the thought of serving so many extra people using the best silver and china.

Louise was terrified that she'd spill soup in the vicar's lap or drop the coffee tray. She tried to reassure the terrified maid and would have offered to help were she not aware what Dora's reaction would be.

She desperately wanted this evening to be perfect for she had just heard that another guest was to join them.

"Dr Tate has his nephew staying with him so I've invited him too," Dora announced. "It's short notice but I'm sure Cook and Polly will manage. I could hardly say no, could I?"

"It's only one extra, Mother," Louise said.

"Yes, but that girl gets in such a state. She can't remember the simplest instruction. And Cook isn't used to dealing with so many guests." She sighed impatiently.

Louise didn't reply. It seemed that Dora was the one getting in a state. There would only be nine — ten with Andrew Tate.

Dora's mood changed and she smiled. "Perhaps Sarah will sing for us afterwards." She shooed Louise away. "Well, run along then and tell Cook to do some extra potatoes. And Polly will have to re-lay the table."

The dinner was going well and Louise was relieved that so far there had been no disasters at the table, for Polly's sake as much as her stepmother's.

She only half-listened as, next to her, Keith Willis told her that he was leaving for Africa very soon. She was more interested in the young doctor's conversation with her father and wished she was at their end of the table.

At least Dora was in a good mood as she regaled William Spencer and her friend Mrs Howard with the tale of her visit to Broadcasting House with Sarah. As for her sister, she was in her element. She'd been allowed wine with her dinner and her violet eyes were sparkling. She was sitting next to James Spencer and Louise smiled as she saw that her sister was flirting and that James seemed to be responding to her.

She returned her attention to her father who was telling Andrew about the problems of the fishing families who lived in such poor conditions on the other side of town.

"My uncle has spoken of it. We tend to think such problems are confined to the big cities," Andrew said.

"Your uncle tells me you are trying to rectify that in your part of London," said Stanley.

"We do what we can but it's little enough. The clinic I run only scratches the surface. We can do little to combat the dirt and malnutrition."

Louise was fascinated. She knew that Dr Tate's nephew worked in a London clinic but she hadn't realized he worked with the under-privileged in the East End. The knowledge increased her admiration for the young doctor.

Dora of course was horrified. "I do realize you have to get experience before you take over your own practice," she said. "But how do you bear it — the dirt, the disease . . ." She shuddered delicately.

"Dirt and disease are something doctors have to learn to cope with," he told her.

"But surely it's only a temporary measure," Dora insisted. "I thought you'd be taking over from your uncle eventually."

"I hope that won't be for a long time yet," Andrew had said and changed the subject by complimenting Dora on the excellence of the meal.

They had finished dessert and Louise looked up to see Polly peeping hesitantly round the door. Her face was red and she looked as if she'd been crying.

Louise hastily left her seat and followed her along the passage to the kitchen. "What's wrong?" she asked.

"Oh, miss, I dropped the milk jug," she wailed.

"Is that all? Well, use a different jug," Louise told her.

"But there's no more milk left. What about the coffee?"

Louise went into the kitchen and surveyed the mess. Cook had found another jug and was re-laying the tray. "I don't know why she had to bother you, miss," she said. "We've got cream left from dessert. That will do for the coffee."

Louise smiled. "Thank you, Cookie. I'll take it in." She turned to Polly, who had begun to pick up the pieces of broken china. "Don't worry, it wasn't your fault."

As she picked up the tray, Polly let out a yelp and Louise gasped as blood gushed from the maid's hand. She grabbed a cloth and pressed it to the wound, guiding her to a chair. "Sit here for a minute. I'll take the coffee in," she said, picking up the tray and going through to the dining room.

Dora looked up in irritation. "It took you long enough," she said. "Where's Polly?"

"She's had a little accident. Sarah, would you pour the coffee, please? I'll go and see if she's all right."

"Really, that girl. She's impossible," Dora said. Her guests didn't respond and she gave a little laugh. "She's been with the family years you know, so . . ." She gave a little shrug and another laugh.

Louise bit her lip, wanting to tell her stepmother they were lucky to have such a devoted servant who'd been like one of the family ever since she could remember. She hurried back to the kitchen, where she found Polly looking quite pale. The cloth was soaked through and the cut was still bleeding.

Cook had found a roll of bandage and some antiseptic and Louise gently removed the cloth. Polly became quite hysterical when she saw how deep the cut was. As Louise coaxed her to let her have a proper look, the door opened and Andrew Tate came in.

"Can I help?" he asked.

She smiled gratefully and moved out of the way. She watched as he deftly cleaned and bandaged the wound, speaking gently and calming Polly's hysterics in moments. When he'd finished he said, "Now you must change the dressing every day, keep it dry and if it doesn't start to heal in a few days come and see my uncle at the surgery."

"But, Doctor, how am I going to do my work all bandaged up like this?" Polly said.

"No work until it's healed," he said firmly.

Polly glanced at Louise apprehensively. "Will that be all right, miss?"

"We'll manage for a few days," she said.

"It may be more than a few days," Andrew told her. "We don't want her getting an infection."

"Of course. Thank you, Doctor. Perhaps you'd like to return to the other guests. I'll finish clearing up here."

He nodded and left the room, leaving Louise feeling rather bewildered. Although she'd been monopolized by Keith Willis all evening, she had managed to hear some of Andrew's conversation with her father and wished she could have joined in. The curate's dissertation on his imminent departure for Africa had become rather boring and Polly's accident had provided a welcome diversion.

When Andrew appeared in the kitchen she'd hoped for an opportunity to ask him more about his work. She admired the way he had dealt with Polly — efficient yet gentle and caring. How different he was from the bumptious Keith Willis and the shallow James Spencer.

But then, after making sure Polly was all right, he had left the kitchen abruptly and she'd had no chance to speak with him further. When the guests started to leave his thanks for the meal had been rather curt and Louise was left wondering what she — or her stepmother — had done to offend him. What could have caused such a change in his manner? she wondered.

Andrew had not been looking forward to an evening with the Charltons. His previous encounters with Dora Charlton had left him with a hearty dislike for her and when Uncle George had told him he was included in the invitation to Steyne House he had looked for an excuse not to go. It was only the possibility of seeing Louise again and getting to know her better that had persuaded him.

He had hoped to be seated next to her and was disappointed to find he'd been placed at the end of the table furthest away. Louise, sitting beside the curate, did not seem unhappy with the place settings. Every time he looked towards her end of the table she was smiling at something Keith Willis had said. Perhaps the rumours of a romance between the pair were true, he thought gloomily.

He cheered up somewhat when Stanley Charlton mentioned that the curate was leaving for a mission overseas very soon and began to enjoy the conversation with his host. It was a pleasure to discover that he and Louise's father had so much in common — even to their choice of life partner, he thought wryly.

The break-up with Celia was still raw, and although he now realized they were totally incompatible, he was still saddened that she hadn't turned out to be the person he thought she was. At the time, a newly qualified and idealistic young doctor, he had really thought Celia was his soulmate. She was from a medical family, the daughter of a consultant at the hospital where he had done his training and he had been convinced she would be the perfect wife. He had pictured their life together, dedicated to healing the sick and improving the lives of those less fortunate themselves. When he did not fall in with Celia's plans for a Harley Street practice pandering to the whims of the rich, she had thrown him aside in favour of someone more easily manipulated.

Dora Charlton's comments on his work had reminded him so much of Celia's attitude. He had thought her stepdaughter was different.

As he and his uncle walked home through the quiet streets, George Tate commented on his silence. "You had plenty to say earlier," he said. "I thought you were having a good time."

"I wouldn't say that. It was a good meal and I did enjoy talking to Stanley Charlton. I can't say much for the rest of the family though or his other guests," Andrew said.

George gave a short laugh. "I know what you think of Mrs Charlton. I don't know what Stanley was thinking of. Still they've two lovely daughters." He nudged his nephew playfully. "I thought you were interested in the older one."

"I don't know what made you think that," Andrew said, but he felt himself flushing and was glad of the darkness. His uncle would never leave the subject alone if he thought . . . Andrew shook himself. No, Louise wasn't for him, he thought as he replayed the scene in the kitchen.

He never went anywhere without his doctor's bag and when he heard of Polly's accident he had grabbed it and rushed into the kitchen. As he calmed the frightened woman and dressed the wound he couldn't help being glad of the opportunity to speak to Louise alone.

It was when Polly had expressed concern at not being able to work that he had his first doubts. She had given that frightened glance as if apprehensive that her job might be in jeopardy. And Louise had said nothing to reassure her. He didn't think she was like her stepmother, treating the servants as if they were inferior. But the maid had definitely been worried about something.

# CHAPTER
# FOUR

The social evening in the church hall behind St Mark's was coming to an end and Louise was in the kitchen with her friend Peggy helping to wash up the crockery from the refreshments.

The evening had been a great success and, with the sale of tickets and an additional raffle, had raised a good sum for Keith Willis's African mission. Even Dora had joined in, playing the piano for the sedate country dances and accompanying Sarah's singing during the refreshment interval.

It would have been perfect if only Andrew had stayed till the end, Louise thought. A little smile curved her lips. She hadn't seen him since the dinner party and she was delighted when he turned up at the social, especially when he had asked her to dance with him. She started to hum the tune they had danced to, re-living the feel of her hand clasped in his, the other at her waist. She wondered why he had left so abruptly. It couldn't have been a medical emergency. He was on a social visit to his uncle, not standing in for him as he had on previous occasions.

Peggy came in with the last of the cups and saucers. "That's the lot. Can't wait to get home. My feet are killing me."

"Me too," Louise replied.

"It was a good evening though. You danced a lot with Mr Willis, didn't you?" Peggy grinned. "The old dears in the corner were talking about you. They definitely hear wedding bells."

"Don't be so silly, Peggy. He's off to Africa any day now and, besides, a couple of dances at a church hop don't mean anything. Those old ladies are always gossiping and matchmaking and my stepmother's the worst of the lot." It occurred to her that Dora might be keen to get rid of her but she dismissed the thought. Who would do the running round after her if she left home? Certainly not Sarah, who had her sights set on her musical career.

But much as she longed for an escape from the narrowness of her life and the increasing demands of her selfish stepmother, she could not imagine being a missionary's wife — especially if that man was the rather earnest Keith Willis.

Peggy sighed. "I can't wait to get married. When John's ship gets back to Portsmouth, we'll set the date. I wish you were engaged, then we could have a double wedding." She put the clean crockery in the cupboard and turned to her friend. "Isn't there anyone . . .?"

Louise hadn't confided her feelings for Andrew to anyone, not even her friend. She was about to answer when the door to the kitchen swung open.

"All done, ladies?" Keith asked. "Come along then and I'll lock up." Peggy's parents were waiting in the porch and Louise looked round for her family.

"They've gone on ahead," said Mrs Fryer. "Your mother was feeling tired. We'll walk you home."

Keith turned from locking the hall door. "No need for you to go out of your way, Mrs Fryer," he said. "I'll walk along with Miss Charlton."

"I'll be all right. It's not far and it's a fine night," Louise protested as she caught Peggy's knowing glance.

"Nonsense you can't walk through the streets alone." Keith pocketed the keys and took her arm.

Not wanting to make a fuss, Louise said goodnight to the Fryers. She was acutely embarrassed and resented Keith's proprietary air.

They walked along in silence for a few moments until Keith spoke. "Your stepmother relies on you a lot doesn't she?" he asked.

"I suppose so, especially when she's unwell. But to be honest with you, I often wish I had more to occupy my time." She sighed. "I used to dream of helping in my father's business but Mother won't hear of it."

"I must say I agree with her. But I do understand your need to employ yourself."

"I do the church flowers and help with the Sunday school, and I do hospital visiting but sometimes it's not enough." Louise was surprised to find herself confiding in him. She rarely acknowledged her discontent out loud.

He squeezed her arm. "I feel the same. That's why I'm so excited about the mission. I know I can do good work out there."

"Not long now," Louise said.

"I wish I wasn't going alone." He hesitated. "I need — a helpmeet, a companion . . ."

Louise stopped walking and turned towards him. "What do you mean?" He blushed and stammered. "I had dared to hope . . . Miss Charlton — Louise — I have come to care for you. I would be greatly honoured . . ."

Louise shook her head. "I didn't realize . . ." It was true. She hadn't taken Peggy's teasing or the church ladies' gossip seriously. He was gazing at her earnestly.

She should have said no straight away but Keith must have seen her hesitation as encouragement. As they reached the front gate of Steyne House she was still trying to think of a way to let him down gently. But as she was about to speak, he grabbed both her arms and said, breathlessly, "You will say yes, won't you?"

Before she could answer he lunged at her. Startled, she jerked her head away so that his lips missed their target. His mouth left a wet smear on her cheek and, trying not to show her revulsion, she laughed nervously. "Goodnight, Mr Willis." She turned and went indoors quickly.

She leaned against the closed door shaking and scrubbed at her face with a handkerchief, thankful that the kiss hadn't touched her lips. The thought of that wet mouth fastened over hers made her stomach heave. She'd been kissed before and had found the sensation pleasant, sometimes even exciting. But, she vowed, Keith Willis would not be allowed to kiss her again. The next time she saw him it would be to firmly decline his offer of marriage. Staying in Holton and being at

Dora's beck and call was infinitely preferable to marrying a man she did not love.

The house was in darkness and Louise crept upstairs to her turret room. As she passed Sarah's door, her sister called out. "Where have you been, Lou?"

"It took ages clearing up."

At Sarah's low chuckle, she opened the door and went in. In the light of the gas lamp outside the house she saw her sister sitting up in bed.

"What's so funny?" she asked.

"You didn't spend all this time just clearing up. Besides, I looked out of the window just now and saw you with Mr Willis." She giggled. "He kissed you — I saw."

Louise blushed. "So what?"

"Did he ask you to marry him, to go to Africa with him?" She giggled again. "How exciting. Did you say yes?"

"No."

"But, Lou. It's your chance to get away. You can't stay in dreary old Holton forever." She threw her arms above her head and stretched. "I'll be gone as soon as I get the chance and I hate the thought of you being stuck here."

"No, Sarah. I don't love him and I don't think I'd make a good missionary's wife either." She was reluctant to admit her real reason for hesitating. It wasn't just the revulsion his kiss had evoked, it was the thought that if it had been Andrew Tate kissing her, her reaction would have been completely different.

A few days later, as Louise watched Keith take old Miss Bunyan's arm and help her to the church door, she still hadn't had a chance to make her position clear. She was glad her father was waiting outside with the car so that she could avoid him a little longer. Since Miss Bunyan's fall on the ice on her way back from the shops the previous winter, she had been unable to walk any distance and the Charltons had taken her under their wing, inviting her to Sunday lunch after Matins each week.

As Keith solicitously assisted Miss Bunyan into the car, Louise wished she could feel more for him. Despite her admiration for his dedication, she knew that she could never consider him as a husband.

Now, as she climbed into the car next to Miss Bunyan, she thanked him gravely, careful not to smile in case he interpreted it as a further sign of encouragement. Sarah squeezed in beside her, stifling a giggle.

As they drove away, Dora spoke her mind. "I don't know what's wrong with you, Louise. He's a perfectly eligible young man." Her tone said that Louise would be lucky to get another chance.

"I don't want to marry him, Mother. And I don't see myself as a missionary's wife either." She nudged Sarah, who was about to say something. She was still annoyed with her sister for telling Dora about Keith's proposal.

"Nonsense, my dear. You'd make an excellent job of it," Dora declared.

Louise held her tongue. It was the first time she could remember her stepmother ever saying anything so encouraging. But whatever anyone said, she'd rather remain a spinster. If she ended up like old Miss Bunyan so be it. At the thought, she acknowledged once more that her determination to remain single had less to do with Keith Willis than it did with Andrew Tate. But she had not seen the young doctor since the night of the church social. So why could she not forget him?

Perhaps she should have agreed to go with Keith to Africa. What was there for her in Holton, after all?

Sarah was now well on her way to a successful singing career, while she was still at home, not allowed a career of her own. Since Sarah's success Dora's health seemed to have miraculously improved and she always seemed well enough to accompany her daughter to auditions or recording sessions. Managing Sarah's career brought a flush of excitement to Dora's cheeks, a sparkle to her blue eyes. Nowadays there were fewer complaints about her poor head and her utter exhaustion, brought on, she'd always said, by the pressures of running the household.

Instead, with Dora away chaperoning her daughter, or busy writing letters and making telephone calls, most of these duties fell to Louise. She quite enjoyed talking to Cookie about the menus and managing the household budget. But she wondered cynically why Dora had found it so "exhausting". In fact, once she'd given Cook and Polly their orders for the day and checked on Fred's progress in the garden, there was little to do in the house. And although she had also replaced her stepmother on the church flower rota and taken over her hospital visiting, in addition to Sunday school teaching, she was bored.

If only she was allowed to get a proper job like so many of her school friends. Peggy had trained to be a school teacher and now taught at a village school not far away from Holton, although she would have to give it up when she married. And some of the other girls had become nurses or worked in shops.

But Dora insisted that ladies didn't work. It wasn't as if they needed the money. Not for the first time Louise wished she'd been born a boy so that she could follow her father into the family business. She had a feeling that Stanley would like to have her working with him. But as always, he deferred to his wife and gently told Louise "Your mother needs you at home."

As usual when her household duties were done, Louise was bored and restless. What should she do with herself for the rest of the day? Sarah was at singing practice and Dora, after a busy morning writing letters confirming engagements for future concerts, was lying down. Stanley was at the office as usual and the house was quiet.

Louise sighed and decided to go for a walk. As she opened the door into the hall, Polly came running along the passage from the kitchen at the back of the house. Her face was flushed and her cap askew.

"Oh, Miss, come quick. Cook's had a fall — she's hurt real bad." The maid clutched at Louise's arm.

"What happened?"

"I'm not sure, Miss. I came in and found her lying on the floor. She's in terrible pain."

Louise gently removed Polly's clutching hand and hurried into the kitchen. A quick glance at the overturned stool, the broken jar and spilled flour told her what had happened. She knelt beside the still figure. "Cookie, tell me — where does it hurt?"

Cook opened her eyes and moved a hand. "I can't move me leg, Miss," she said between gasps of pain.

"Lie still, we'll fetch the doctor," Louise said. She pulled the tattered old cushion off the chair by the range, put it under the old woman's head and told Polly to fetch a blanket. She sat on the floor holding her hand and gently stroking strands of hair away from her face. Cook's eyes had closed again and she was breathing raggedly.

When Polly came back she tucked the blanket round the still form. "Stay with her while I telephone the doctor," she ordered.

Old Dr Tate listened while she explained what had happened. "It sounds as if she'll need to go to hospital. I'll make arrangements then pop round," he said.

He arrived at the same time as the ambulance and decided to go to the hospital with her. "I'll let you know how she is later on," he told Louise, touching her shoulder briefly before following the stretcher out of the front door.

She must tell Mother what had happened, Louise thought. But first she must make sure Polly was all right. The poor girl looked thoroughly shaken up when she returned to the kitchen and promptly burst into

48

tears before sinking into Cook's chair — a sure sign of how upset she was.

"What are we going to do, Miss?" she sobbed.

"Well, first of all, you're going to make a pot of tea while I go up and tell Mother about the accident. I'm surprised she didn't come down to see what all the fuss was about. Then we're going to sit down and work out what we're going to give the Master and Miss Sarah for their supper when they get home."

"But I can't cook, Miss. I know I 'elps Cook out but I only does what she tells me. I can't manage on me own."

"I can't cook very well either, but I'm sure we'll manage together." Louise patted Polly's arm reassuringly and left the room.

"I thought that stupid girl had gone and broken something again when I heard the noise," Dora said.

Louise explained that Cookie had been taken to hospital.

"How are we going to manage?" Dora cried, her hysterics rivalling Polly's when she realized they would have no one to cook for them. "We'll have to engage someone to take her place," she decided when at last she had calmed down.

"I'm sure that won't be necessary, Mother. It may only be for a short while and Polly and I can manage between us."

Dora gave a little snort of disbelief and Louise felt the familiar churning in her stomach. Well, she'd show Mother that she *could* manage. It was true, she hadn't much experience of cooking and she wouldn't be able to match Cook's delicious pies and pastries. But surely she could produce some sort of meal for them. Clearly Mother was in no state to do so, although privately Louise thought she probably had more knowledge of practical household jobs than she let on. She was sure that Dora, as an impoverished pianist, hadn't employed servants before she married Father.

Sarah returned home just as Louise had managed to get Polly sufficiently organized to peel some potatoes for supper. The sight of her sister standing at the big scrubbed table in the kitchen, wrapped in one of Cook's large white aprons and busily buttering thin slices of bread for Mother's tea took her aback for a moment. But she soon recovered on being told that she would be allowed to eat her tea in the kitchen — in defiance of Dora's strict injunction that Cook's accident must not be an excuse for any slackening of standards on Louise's part.

Louise took Dora's tray up herself, hoping that her stepmother would remain in her room until Father returned from business. Boredom had fled and she found she was, rather guiltily, enjoying the crisis. Sarah, eating her tea in the kitchen and listening round-eyed to Polly's dramatic description of the accident, seemed to think it was rather fun too, despite her sympathy for poor Cookie.

When Dr Tate called in on his way back from the hospital his face was grave. Miss Rogers had broken her hip, a very serious injury in a woman of her years. Louise looked startled for a moment. She hadn't heard Cookie referred to as Miss Rogers for a long time. She had lived with the family for so long, since before Louise had been born, and no one called her by her real name any more. It was sad really, Louise reflected — as if the doctor were talking about someone else. She hastily gave her attention to what he was saying, her heart sinking when he told her it was unlikely Miss Rogers would make a full recovery. She would probably not be able to work again.

"I'm sorry about the meal, Father," Louise apologized as they finished their supper of cold meat and pickles with mashed potatoes. "It was the best I could do in the circumstances."

Stanley looked up from his plate. "There's no need to apologize. It was delicious." He took another mouthful and laid his knife and fork neatly on the plate. "We must all pull together in a crisis, mustn't we, my dear?" He looked across at Dora, who was picking at her food. "How long is Cookie going to be laid up?" he asked.

Louise had already told him what the doctor had said and her earlier conviction that he hadn't really been listening was confirmed. It wasn't like Father to be so vague but she had noticed it a lot lately. His mind always seemed to be elsewhere and she had often caught him sitting at his desk in the study gazing out of the window.

When Dora answered sharply that she had already informed him of the need to look for a replacement cook, he shook his head. "Oh no, my dear, that won't do at all. We can't possibly take on someone else."

Louise smiled. Father obviously hadn't understood and thought this was only a temporary hitch in the smooth running of the household. She also knew he had rather a soft spot for Bessie Rogers, not to mention her delicious pastry. Before she could speak however, Dora put him in the picture.

"I thought I had explained, Stanley. Cook will not be coming back. It's time she retired anyway. I'll get on to the agency in the morning and start interviewing replacements."

"I'm afraid that won't be possible, Dora." Stanley's voice was firm and his wife's eyes widened. He cut off her protest with a raised hand. "I'm sorry, my dear. I hate to say this, but the time has come for us to make certain economies. I had hoped to avoid anything as drastic as cutting the staff and of course I wouldn't dream of turning Cook away from what, after all, has been her home for nearly thirty years. But in a way this accident has happened at a rather opportune moment."

Louise gasped. "Opportune? Father, have you forgotten that poor Cookie is lying in hospital in great pain?"

"Forgive me, Louise. I didn't mean to sound callous." He pushed his plate away and ran his hands through his hair. "Oh dear. I wish I hadn't had to spring this on you." He took a deep breath. "The fact is, things are not going well with the business. I'm sure it's only temporary but, until things look up — we shall have to be careful."

"I don't understand, Stanley. What about your investments?" Dora's face was white and her plump hand went to her throat.

Hesitantly, Stanley explained that the nationwide slump had begun to affect his business. And the Wall Street crash some years before, which was still affecting Britain, had sent his shares plummeting.

"But surely, Father, the building trade is thriving, despite other industries suffering from the slump? There are houses going up in Holton all the time," Louise protested.

"That's true, my dear. But building is only one aspect of my business interests and I'm afraid one can no longer afford to subsidise the other."

Dora gave a little sob and Stanley hastened to reassure her. "As I said, my love, it's only a temporary setback. Things will pick up soon. But you can understand why I cannot contemplate engaging another cook at the moment. And I've also been thinking of letting Fred go. We will just have to manage for the time being."

Louise and Sarah were walking along the seafront towards the bandstand. Since Cookie's accident and the tightening of the family purse strings, Dora had taken refuge in ill health once more. Today she was indulging in one of her "heads" and Louise had found it difficult to bite her tongue. Her stepmother's constant carping was beginning to get on her nerves and she had invented an errand in town just to get out of the house for a while.

She stopped and leaned on the promenade railing, gazing out to sea at the passing ships in the Channel. To her right the Isle of Wight was a hazy smudge of blue on the horizon. How she wished she was on one of those ships — anywhere but here in Holton Regis. Even accompanying Keith Willis to Africa would have been preferable to this boring existence, Louise told herself, flicking a stray strand of hair off her face. But even that means of escape was denied her. She had gently but firmly refused his proposal of marriage and he had left a couple of weeks ago. Besides, it had been made clear to her that her duty was at home now.

"I think Mother does it on purpose," Sarah said, echoing Louise's thoughts.

"Oh, Sarah, that's a wicked thing to say." How could she tell her sister she felt exactly the same?

"Well, it's a funny thing that she's perfectly all right when she wants to come up to London with me. But when it comes to helping you in the kitchen she's just too poorly." Sarah clapped a hand to her forehead, closed her eyes and said, "Oh, my poor head", in perfect imitation of her mother.

Louise tried unsuccessfully to hide a smile. "You're a wicked little minx. It's not poor Mother's fault that she's sickly."

"Well, anyone would think Cookie broke her hip just to inconvenience *her*," Sarah said.

"Really, Sarah, you should show more respect," Louise said, conscious of her big sister role, although she could not help inwardly agreeing.

She turned away from the railing, pulling at Sarah's arm. "Come on, we'd better get back."

They started to walk sedately along the seafront, each deep in thought. But Sarah couldn't stay subdued for long and Louise was too tired to remonstrate when the younger girl ran ahead and started to hop and skip between the pink and beige paving slabs of the promenade. Despite insisting that she was grown-up now, Sarah sometimes reverted to childish behaviour. What harm did it do, Louise asked herself. There was no one about and besides, the poor girl was constantly being reprimanded for her unladylike behaviour. Louise sometimes seriously doubted that Dora had ever been young herself.

On impulse she ran after her sister and "hopscotched" along beside her, clutching at her prim navy-blue hat and laughing. She was looking down at the paving stones and didn't see the figure until it was too late. Gasping apologies, she looked up into the laughing blue eyes of young Dr Tate.

# CHAPTER
# FIVE

When they reached Steyne House, Louise was relieved to learn that Dora was still lying down. She sent Sarah upstairs to see if Mother was awake and ready for tea, then stood in the cool dim hall taking deep breaths. She had to get her feelings under control before going to the kitchen to speak to Polly.

The encounter with Andrew Tate had left her breathless and confused. Sarah's stifled giggles hadn't helped.

What must he have thought of such a display of hoydenish behaviour in public? And, she admitted to herself, looking at her flushed face in the hall mirror and smoothing her tangled hair, his opinion did matter — very much. Not that she stood any chance at all with the tall good-looking young doctor. The nurses at his London hospital must be falling over themselves for his attention. He could take his pick so why should he take any interest in a dull homebody like her with nothing to recommend her?

With a sigh for her foolish thoughts she bit her lip, patted her hair into place once more and went into the kitchen where Polly was getting into a state over the tea. Her hand had healed but she was still a little clumsy.

"Sarah will take the mistress's tray up to her," Louise said.

"It's all right, Miss. I can manage." Polly indicated the cooling tray where several little fairy cakes displayed their blackened tops. "What shall I do about those?"

"Don't worry about it, Polly. It wasn't your fault. Just butter a couple of those scones left from yesterday and put a dish of jam on the tray. That will have to do." Polly nodded and spread a clean cloth on the tray.

Sarah came in as she finished and eyed the scones. "No cake?" she said.

The maid looked nervous but Louise interrupted. "If Mother says anything, tell her Polly hasn't had time to cook anything else." As Sarah left with the tray, she turned to Polly. "We're doing our best, aren't we?"

"Yes, Miss."

But the scared look didn't leave Polly's face and Louise heaved another sigh. They were doing their best, but Mother didn't seem to appreciate it. And poor Polly was bearing the brunt of her discontent. Like Cookie, she had been with the Charltons for years and Louise regarded her as almost one of the family. And she was a good worker, even if a bit slow and inclined to get flustered. She just needed someone to tell her what to do and she would willingly get on with it. But she seemed totally unable to make any decisions for herself. Take the cakes today — Louise had said she wouldn't be long and would take them out of the oven on her return. But she'd lingered on the seafront, totally forgetting the cakes. And Polly, fearful of a reprimand, had waited till she smelt burning before making a decision — too late.

Louise picked up one of the burnt cakes and smiled. They weren't that bad she decided and with a burst of inspiration set about cutting the black bits off. Then she got some butter and icing sugar and creamed them together, spreading the mixture over the remains of the buns and sandwiching them together. She arranged them on a paper doily on one of the pretty serving plates and stepped back to admire her handiwork.

"Thought you said there were no cakes," Sarah said, coming back into the room and grabbing one off the plate. "You're getting to be quite a good cook, Sis," she said through a mouthful.

Louise grinned and pointed to the bits she had cut off. Within seconds both girls were laughing till tears ran down their cheeks.

"Oh, Sarah, it's not that funny," Louise gasped when she could speak again.

Polly shook her head. "What's got into you two?"

Sarah pointed to the burnt cake and started to laugh again.

"I don't see what's to laugh at. Anyway you'd better stop that racket or you'll have the mistress complaining her head's aching again." Polly raised her eyes to the ceiling and pursed her lips.

"I'm sorry," Louise apologized, turning to Sarah. "How is she?"

"Not very happy. She was grumbling about Polly. I didn't stay to listen."

"Oh dear, Polly. Did she smell the cakes burning?"

"It wasn't that, Miss. She was all right till I told her that young Dr Tate called and I sent him away saying she wasn't up to receiving callers. She said it wasn't up to me to decide." Polly looked aggrieved. "Well, how was I to know, Miss? You wasn't here to ask."

Louise's heart had jumped at the mention of Andrew — Polly had specified *young* Dr Tate hadn't she? If only she'd been home when he called. But he hadn't mentioned his visit when she had quite literally bumped into him earlier on — merely asked how her mother was.

True, she had been so flustered she hadn't really taken in what he'd said. And the foolish notion that he had called to see her, not her stepmother, was quickly squashed. He had walked on quickly after exchanging the usual pleasantries demanded by good manners. No, he wasn't interested in her at all.

Andrew Tate strode along the promenade until he reached the end, descending the steps onto the shingle where several fishing boats were drawn up. He walked on, his steps crunching on the loose stones, past the boats and the dilapidated fishermen's cottages behind them until he came to the estuary, a vast expanse of sand dunes and mud flats. He usually enjoyed these walks by the sea at Holton Regis, drawing the fresh sea air into his lungs and purging them of the smoke and fetid smells of the poverty-stricken area of London where he worked. There was poverty here too, of course, but somehow it didn't seem to carry the same air of degradation and hopelessness that he encountered in the city.

Today however his thoughts were not on his surroundings. Louise had already been in his thoughts and he had been disappointed to find she was not in when he called at Steyne House. A few words with his uncle after Polly's accident had made him revise his opinion of Louise Charlton and he wanted to apologize for his earlier rudeness. The maid's nervousness had been on account of Mrs Charlton who would not tolerate any sign of what she called slacking. "Louise will do her best to help out until Polly's hand heals," he'd said.

Now, as he thought of her, brown eyes sparkling with animation, her hat askew and her hair escaping in endearing tendrils around her face, he wished he'd stayed to talk to her. But her cheeks, already flushed pink with the fresh sea air had darkened to a deeper shade of red as she bumped into him and, to spare her further embarrassment, he had walked quickly on after greeting the sisters and exchanging a few polite words.

He'd been so deep in thought that it was his fault she'd almost knocked him down. His face had creased in a spontaneous smile of pleasure when he realized who it was. But fearful that Louise might think he was laughing at her, he had schooled his expression to mere politeness, pretending he hadn't noticed her running and jumping as if she were the same age as her sister. He made his escape when he noticed the younger girl struggling to control her giggles.

60

Now, he turned back towards the town, scuffing his feet in the pebbles and cursing his own reserve. He might tell himself he didn't want to embarrass her, but deep down he knew it was fear of making another mistake that had stopped him from making more of the encounter.

Uncle George had assured him she was nothing like Celia and, hard as it was to leave those who needed him in his busy London clinic, he had jumped at the chance to return when his uncle had asked him to fill in for a few days. Last time he had looked after the practice, when Uncle George had been ill, he had begrudged the time spent away from London. As he'd told Celia during their last acrimonious exchange, he hadn't studied hard all those years to qualify as a doctor just to pander to the whims of the Dora Charltons of this world. And he had gently refused when his uncle had told him he was ready to retire and wanted Andrew to take over from him. A few days as locum was a different matter — especially as it gave him the chance see Louise Charlton.

Anxious to make amends for his hasty judgement, he'd attended the church social in the hopes of getting to get to know Louise better. But, although he'd managed one dance with her, she had been monopolized by the curate, who had not disguised his proprietary interest in her. His only consolation was that the Reverend Willis had now left Holton Regis.

Heartened by the news, he had called at Steyne House, with the excuse of inquiring after Mrs Charlton's health. It had been a disappointment to be told by the maid that Miss Charlton was not at home and that the mistress was sleeping.

Glancing at his watch he quickened his steps, realizing he would be late for evening surgery. He walked quickly along the tree-lined avenue with its substantial Victorian villas set back from the road and turned into the High Street, which ran parallel to the seafront. His uncle's house was near the end past the shops, a double-fronted Georgian town house with a separate entrance to the surgery, which had been converted from the adjacent coach house.

As she took his hat and coat, the receptionist informed him that there were already several people waiting. He smiled at her and went quickly through to his uncle's consulting room.

"Give me a minute to get my breath back, then send the first one in," he said.

By the time he had dealt with the first patient of the evening, he had succeeded in putting all thoughts of Louise Charlton out of his head. When it came to his work, the patients came first. Absorbed in their problems the surgery hours passed quickly.

Uncle George was due back tomorrow and he would have to go back to London, but he would make an effort to see Louise before he left. Who knew when he'd have a chance to return?

# CHAPTER
# SIX

# Autumn 1938

Louise was worried about her father. He was only in his early fifties but sometimes he looked like an old man, his face drawn and grey, his eyes circled with charcoal smudges. She knew there was something wrong, although he refused to discuss it. She just couldn't think what the problem was, especially as the building trade seemed to be booming. In the past few years the west end of the town had expanded to join up with the neighbouring village of Elmham. And the houses being built were large four and five-bedroomed weekend "cottages" with their own private beaches.

Charlton and Spencer had secured the contract to build another one only last week, so why did they seem to be so short of money? Stanley had started building in a small way, developing from the small brick-making business he had inherited from his father. He had trained as an architect and surveyor and, on her walks around the town, Louise was always proud that her father had been responsible, not only for much of the housing built since the great war, but for some of Holton's civic buildings too.

He and his partner, William Spencer, had designed and built the grand new town hall and, together with other businessmen had developed the ramshackle pier into a thriving place of entertainment for the summer visitors. He had also invested heavily in the Winter Gardens with its theatre, dance hall and restaurant. But that seemed to be successful and, as far as Louise knew, there was no reason to think her father would lose money on it. Still, there had been a depression over the past few years and maybe he had lost on some of his other investments.

There was no doubt something was worrying him. And since his refusal to take on a new cook, as well as the dismissal of poor old Fred, the gardener, Louise had to face up to the fact that her father had financial troubles. She'd never had to worry about money before. They had always been comfortably off, if not rich, and she had never questioned their way of life. Not that money as such was important to her — she wasn't interested in fashions or holding her own with the social elite of the town — but it meant a lot to Dora, and to a lesser degree, to Sarah.

She knew that if there was a problem, Father would try to shield his wife from any unpleasantness. She decided to go and meet him from work and try to talk to him away from the house. She went into the kitchen to tell Polly she was going out.

"But what about dinner, Miss?" Polly asked.

"It's all under control. I won't be long and besides, you'll manage. I have confidence in you, Polly," Louise said with a smile.

Polly blushed. "Thank you, Miss."

"I'm only saying what's true. I don't know how we would have managed without you these past few months," Louise said. "Now, just remember what I told you. If I'm not back in half an hour, put the potatoes on to boil. The rest of the meal is almost ready and won't hurt if it's left in the oven a little longer." She had made a beef casserole with carrots and onions and the smell from the oven was already making her mouth water.

"What shall I tell the mistress if she asks?"

"Just say I had an errand. But don't worry — she's busy writing letters about Miss Sarah's next concert. That should keep her busy till I get back."

Louise put her hat and coat on and slipped out quietly. Instead of turning towards the sea as she usually did when she needed a breath of fresh air, she walked down the avenue and turned the corner towards her father's office. As she passed the surgery, she thought of Andrew and their brief encounter all those months ago. She had hoped that he would call again but only a couple of days later she heard that he had returned to London.

With a sigh she tried to concentrate on what she was going to say to her father. It was no good dwelling on her love life — or lack of it. As she'd so often told herself, Andrew wasn't interested and now, although she knew she would never have agreed, even the prospect of a new life in a new country was denied her. When Keith Willis had left for the mission in Africa he had not even called to say goodbye. Not that I'm

**65**

bothered, Louise thought. Despite her desire to get away from the little seaside town and lead a more exciting life, she hadn't been quite desperate enough to put up with Keith's sanctimonious ways, not to mention having to endure his wet mouth on hers and his clammy hands pawing her body.

She squared her shoulders and plastered a smile on her face before going in to see her father. As she walked up the steps and entered the premises of Charlton and Spencer, a door slammed and James Spencer rushed through the reception area, barely acknowledging her.

He had been with the firm for over a year now and was supposed to be learning the business. Louise knew that, although William Spencer had hopes of James taking over from him one day, her own father wasn't too sure.

"Young James doesn't seem to understand that he can't just jump in. He has to start at the bottom and learn the ropes," Stanley had said at dinner the other day.

Louise hoped he would soon knuckle down, if only to take some of the pressure off her father, who she was sure was suffering from overwork.

Stanley looked up from the papers he was studying and his face lit up in a smile at the sight of his daughter. His heart contracted painfully as she pulled her hat off and shook her hair free, then perched on the corner of his desk. She was so like her mother it sometimes hurt just to look at her. Although he loved Dora, he had never forgotten his sweet Mary — how could he, when every day Louise was there to remind him?

Stanley loved both his daughters and would do anything to make them happy, but just recently he'd begun to worry that he had indulged Sarah too much. In her single-minded pursuit of a singing career, he feared she was in danger of turning out to be as selfish as her mother. He wasn't blind to Dora's faults; he loved her in spite of them. But it hurt him to see Sarah going the same way. Still, he was sure Louise would never be a disappointment to him.

He sighed and reached for her hand. "To what do I owe this pleasure then, my dear?" he asked.

"I needed to get out of the house. So I thought we could walk home together. We haven't had our Sunday walks lately and I miss them."

Stanley patted her hand. "I do too. Let me finish going through these papers and then we'll walk home along the seafront."

Louise smiled and got up from the desk. "Where's Miss Baines?" she asked.

"I let her go early — her mother's not well," Stanley replied.

Louise smiled sympathetically and went to sit by the window as he bent his head to his work.

But his mind wasn't on the details of the house he'd recently surveyed for a client. He was still puzzling over what had gone wrong with his business. How could they be losing money when they still had so many contracts underway? He hadn't lost that much in the stock market crash and anyway, things were recovering a little now. But surely his problems were not just due to Dora's extravagance, or to the expenses incurred in launching Sarah's musical career.

He would just have to go through the books again. But the thought depressed him. Last time he had attempted to discuss their finances with his partner, William became quite tetchy, as if he thought Stanley were accusing him of some impropriety. That was the last thing on his mind; he and William had been friends for years and, up until now, their partnership had been a happy one.

It was no good. He couldn't concentrate on the survey, couldn't summon up any interest in dry rot and cracked guttering, faulty drains and loose window catches. He threw the papers down with a sigh and stretched.

"I think I'll call it a day, Louise. Maybe this will make more sense in the morning," he said.

He shrugged himself into his jacket, helped Louise on with hers and took his hat off the stand in the corner. As he closed the office door behind them a voice from across the hall called out.

"Just off, Mr Charlton?"

Stanley put his head round the door. "Yes, make sure you lock up securely when you leave."

"Don't worry, Mr Charlton. You can depend on me," the young man replied.

As they walked down the steps, Louise took Stanley's arm. "I didn't hear James come back. He rushed out just as I came in, nearly knocked me over."

"I expect he had another row with William. They don't see eye to eye and I'm beginning to think it was a mistake, taking him on. James has his own ideas about how we should run things but William doesn't agree."

Still, it was about time the young man grew up and started accepting some responsibility. Stanley was in full agreement with his partner on that. Once more he sighed and wished that Louise had been a boy. She would have been a real asset to the business. But it was no use dwelling on that. Dora would have a fit if he so much as hinted that he'd like his daughter to work with him. And he knew his partner would never agree either.

As they walked along the seafront, enjoying the mild autumn sunshine, Louise tentatively broached the subject that had been worrying her. She couldn't bear to see that drawn, grey look on her father's face.

"I know something's on your mind, Father. I wish you'd tell me," she said, slipping her hand through his arm.

"I don't want you to worry, my dear. There's nothing you can do anyway." Stanley sighed.

"So there is something wrong?"

"Well, I must confess, things could be better — but not a word to your mother. You know how she fusses."

"I won't say anything," Louise promised. "But why can't you confide in me? Maybe it would help to talk things over."

Stanley hesitated, then patted her hand. They strolled slowly between the flowerbeds, now bereft of their colourful summer bedding, and Louise listened apprehensively as her father confided his fears for the business he had worked so hard to build up over the years.

"You don't seriously think Mr Spencer has been cooking the books, do you?" she asked.

"Of course not." Stanley sounded shocked. But Louise could see the thought wasn't new to him. He just didn't want to believe it. He tugged at his moustache. "No, no, my dear. I'm sure that's not the case. Things will start to look up soon I'm sure."

Louise hoped he was right. She didn't mind helping out in the house, had even begun to enjoy the challenge of cooking for the family, though how they would manage if they ever had to let Polly go, she couldn't imagine. But she hated to see the pinched worried look on her father's face and his struggle to control the faint flicker of irritation at Dora's frequent demands. He tried so hard to please, but she never seemed to be satisfied.

Louise squeezed his arm and smiled up at him. "Whatever happens, Father, we'll manage," she assured him.

As they neared Steyne House they saw Sarah at the front gate, excitedly waving a letter.

"It's come," she squealed. "The letter about the concert at the Albert Hall." Her violet eyes shone and her cheeks were flushed with pride.

Louise had been so taken up with running the household, not to mention worrying about her father, she had quite forgotten that Sarah had auditioned for the concert some time ago. The letter was from

Maurice Weeks, the theatrical agent who, with Dora, was promoting Sarah's career.

"Congratulations, we're so proud of you," Louise said, giving her sister an impulsive hug. "Aren't we, Father?" she added, turning to Stanley, whose worried frown disappeared at once.

"Of course, darling," he said, smiling widely as Sarah grabbed his hand and almost dragged him up the front path.

Louise was pleased that he managed to keep the smile in place when Sarah declared that she simply must have a new dress for the occasion, adding ". . . and shoes, and a hat."

As they entered the house, Polly appeared in the hall, wringing her hands. "Oh there you are, Miss. I was beginning to get worried." She glanced over her shoulder anxiously as the drawing room door opened.

Dora, her rosebud lips pinched tightly together, stood in the doorway, her blue eyes glittering. "Where on earth have you been, Louise? I thought you were supervising dinner. Polly hasn't the first idea how to go about things and here's your father home and the table not even set."

Louise's lips tightened too. "Everything is under control, Mother," she said as evenly as she could manage through clenched teeth, wondering at the strength of will which kept her from expressing her true feelings.

Stanley seemed to guess how she felt, smiling at her over Dora's head and taking his wife's hand. "I don't mind waiting, dearest," he said. "Why don't we sit down and have a drink while you tell me about Sarah's wonderful news. Louise will call us when dinner's ready."

Dora simpered up at him. "Oh, Stanley, if you only knew how trying it is, managing with only one servant. I'm sure Polly does her best . . ."

Louise escaped to the kitchen, where she proceeded to bang the pots about, much to Polly's distress. The maid hovered uncertainly behind her, gabbling apologies.

"I haven't had a chance to set the table. Besides, I wasn't expecting the mistress down yet. Last time I went up she was sound asleep."

"It's all right, Polly. I'm not cross with you. It's not your fault I was away so long. I walked home through the park with Father." She took the pan of potatoes off the range. "Now, you set the table, while I strain and mash these."

Polly hurried away, still twittering anxiously. If only Mother would keep out of the kitchen and leave things to me, Louise thought. Polly would know where she was then and wouldn't get into such a state. She forgot for a moment that it wasn't long ago she'd been annoyed with Dora for not helping more. At times like this she almost wished she'd accepted Keith Willis's proposal and gone off to Africa with him. Then the memory of his clammy hands and wet kiss overrode her discontent with her lot. I'm not that desperate she told herself. Still, she'd have to do something soon or she'd go mad.

72

Maybe she would ask her father if she could help in the office. Dora would be horrified of course, but it was worth a try.

After so many years of marriage, Dora had had enough of wedded bliss. She was quite fond of Stanley of course and it was true he was a good provider. But her marriage hadn't turned out quite the way she'd hoped.

Of course, she had Sarah — she was very proud of her daughter. And even having a stepdaughter hadn't been as bad as she'd feared. Louise was placid and dutiful, always anxious to please. And she had been a godsend lately, taking over the household and freeing her to chaperon Sarah to her concerts. But Dora was becoming disenchanted with her daughter's career. At first she'd had visions of sharing the glory, accompanying Sarah at the piano. But after her humiliation at the BBC producer's hands, she hadn't raised the subject again. Instead she had thrown herself into organizing Sarah's engagements, at least until the advent of Maurice Weeks. The man was insufferable — always thinking he knew best. But at least he knew about the financial side of things. Sarah was accumulating a nice little nest egg which would do nicely as a temptation when it came to her daughter's marriage.

The girl was going to need it, if what Dora feared was true. It seemed Stanley wasn't quite as well off as she'd thought. In the early days of their marriage he had never mentioned money. But they lived well and he never refused her anything — not often anyway. But when she'd expressed the desire to move inland to

Chichester, to leave this draughty Victorian monstrosity, with the ever present seaborne wind howling round its gothic turrets, he'd been quite firm.

Dora sighed, picturing herself in one of those elegant Georgian houses behind the main shopping centre, mixing with the cathedral set. Her church work and her friendship with the Reverend Ayling would surely be recommendation enough. Dora could see herself on the cathedral flower rota, maybe on the committee which ran the ancient almshouses connected with the church.

Her attendance at a garden party in the Bishop's Palace garden back in the summer had reawakened her ambitions and, as she sipped her pre-dinner sherry she contemplated raising the subject with Stanley again. But then he'd only get cross and upset her and that would bring on one of her blinding headaches. Dora frowned. Stanley seemed to get cross more often lately. In a way she could understand him not wanting to move away from the house his grandfather had built. He was a great one for tradition. But hadn't he promised her when they married that he would do everything possible to make her happy?

She took another sip from her glass and looked at her husband. For the first time she noticed that he wasn't looking at all well. There were lines on his forehead that hadn't been there until recently, and his thick dark hair and moustache were sprinkled with grey. A cold finger of apprehension touched her as she recalled the financial problems he had mentioned a few months before. But surely everything was all right now. At least he hadn't said anything lately. Although they'd never got around to replacing Cook after her accident, she hadn't bothered him about it because Louise seemed to be managing so well — at least until today.

It really was too much for her to have to worry about everything, she thought with a discontented sigh. And with Sarah's concert coming up she would be far too busy to deal with the household. It was no use; they would have to get another cook.

She turned to Stanley to say so but the door opened and Polly, wringing her hands and stammering in that irritating way, announced that dinner was served. Maybe they should get another maid too, Dora thought.

By the time they sat down for their meal Louise was feeling calmer. When her father told her the casserole was almost as good as Cookie's, she couldn't help a glow of pride. She *had* been trying hard after all and it was nice to be appreciated. Those visits to Cookie's little cottage in the nearby village of East Holton were starting to bear fruit. Louise thought it was very kind of the old lady to share the expertise gained over many years of working for her family.

But before she could say anything Dora spoke. "I know Louise is managing very well," she said condescendingly, "but, Stanley dear, it is most unfair to expect a young lady of good family to be doing such menial work. It was acceptable as a temporary measure and I'm sure we were very grateful for the way she coped after Cook's unfortunate accident . . ."

Stanley opened his mouth to speak, but Dora carried on without pause. ". . . But that was over a year ago. Once we learned that Cook would be unable to carry on working we really should have taken on another one."

With a clatter Stanley laid his knife and fork on the plate. Louise looked up in alarm as for once her father spoke sharply to his wife. "I thought I had already explained that it is completely out of the question. Don't you ever listen to anything I say?"

Dora gasped and put a hand to her white face. "Stanley!" she exclaimed. Then clutching her head she pushed her chair back noisily and stumbled from the room.

Stanley followed her, leaving the food which Louise had worked so hard to perfect, congealing on the plate. She looked up and saw that her sister's eyes had filled with tears. It was seldom that their parents openly quarrelled and Sarah was usually so taken up with her ambitions that she never seemed to notice the undercurrent of tension that was so often present these days.

"Why is Father in such a bad mood?" Sarah asked. "He hardly said anything about my concert."

"I think he has things on his mind," Louise said.

"Oh, business." Sarah's voice was offhand.

"Yes, business," Louise said sharply. "And if it wasn't for business, where do you think all the new dresses and trips to London would come from?"

Sarah's eyes widened in surprise and once more her eyes filled with tears. "Now you're being horrid as well.

I don't know what's the matter with everybody." And she too jumped up from her chair and rushed from the room.

When Polly came in a few minutes later to ask if she should serve the pudding, Louise was sitting with her chin resting on her hands, surveying the plates of half-eaten food. It was an effort not to snap at the maid but it wasn't poor Polly's fault. She told her quietly to clear the table and got up to help her. "It seems nobody's hungry today," she said with an attempt at a laugh.

When she too had gone to her room, after spending a little time with Sarah and smoothing her ruffled feelings, Louise had time to think about what her father had told her earlier. The Winter Gardens, with its theatre and dance hall was losing money. When it first opened it had been a popular attraction for the summer visitors. But this year, the rumours of war and the uncertainty of the political situation seemed to have put people off coming.

Stanley, along with other businessmen in the town, had invested in the venture at the very beginning and had hoped for a substantial return on their investment. William Spencer had put in more than anyone else and so had more to lose. Stanley didn't really suspect his partner of any crooked dealing but, as he'd confided to Louise, it seemed too much of a coincidence that the firm's losses had begun just when William was starting to feel the pinch.

"I think I'll get old Jones to go through the books again," Stanley had said. The accountant was an old friend who could be relied on not to make a scandal if anything was out of order.

"I'm sure you'll find it's just a mistake," Louise had said, trying to comfort her father. She liked Mr Spencer and didn't want to think ill of him either.

As she got ready for bed Louise wished she'd brought up the subject of working in the office. But with all the tensions in the family at the moment, not to mention that she really was needed at home now, it hardly seemed the right time.

Usually, the sound of the waves caressing the shingle soothed her to sleep in no time. But tonight the seeds of discontent that were growing in her would not allow her to settle. She turned over in bed, trying to get comfortable and reflected that if she'd married they would have to do without her. Not much chance of that now, she thought with a sigh. But surely marriage wasn't the only means of escape. She thought of Sarah, who was growing up into a real beauty. She would have no shortage of suitors. But she wouldn't need them. She had her talent — and with that she could do anything she wanted. Not for the first time, Louise felt a twinge of envy. She didn't begrudge Sarah her success. She just wished she had a comparable talent to give her own life more meaning.

Sarah was finding it hard to sleep too, regretting the way she'd snapped at her sister. Poor Louise had such a lot to put up with, what with having to spend most of

78

her time in the kitchen, as well as having to cope with Mother's sulks and tantrums. Thank goodness she had her rehearsals and singing lessons.

Singing was her lifeline. She didn't know what she'd do if she had to live the sort of humdrum life her sister did. Imagine living all your life expecting to get married — as if that was the only thing that mattered — then getting to an age when you realized it wasn't going to happen. Imagine ending up like old Miss Bunyan, spending your life doing "good works", then getting so old that you became a "good work" yourself, depending on others to invite you to Sunday dinner or sit and talk to you when they'd rather be doing something else.

Well, that wasn't going to happen to her. She was going to have a wonderful life full of music and fun. Of course she might fall in love and get married one day. But whoever he turned out to be, her husband would be made to realize that her singing came first.

# CHAPTER
# SEVEN

The concert at the Albert Hall was a resounding success. Only Dora and Stanley could go, for tickets were limited. But it was also broadcast on the wireless so Louise and Polly sat together, listening entranced. When the applause rang out after Sarah's song, they hugged each other and danced round the kitchen.

For a while, Louise was able to forget her own discontent and revel in her sister's success.

A few days later they were seated at the breakfast table when the post arrived. Dora opened her letter and let out a gasp. It was from Sarah's agent, Maurice Weeks, offering her a part in a musical version of *Little Women*.

"They want her to play the youngest sister, Amy," she said.

Sarah let out a squeal and leapt up, rushing round the table to snatch the letter from her mother. "When, where?" she demanded. Without waiting for a reply she sank into a chair and began to read, her face flushed.

Louise smiled patiently, knowing that Sarah would share the details in her own time. She glanced at her father who was reading his own post, seemingly unaware of his other daughter's excitement.

Sarah noticed too and jumped up again, throwing her arms round her father's neck. "Did you hear, Father? Miss Lane is going to play Jo and I'm to be Amy."

Before he could reply, Louise said, "You mean Lucia Lane?"

Sarah nodded. "She's wonderful, I'll learn such a lot from her."

Stanley only half listened as he read his own letter, a stern demand that he settle his bill immediately. He clutched at his chest as pain speared him. Just a touch of indigestion, he told himself, managing to keep his smile firmly in place as Sarah prattled on. It was only natural that she should be excited about the prospect of performing alongside the great Lucia Lane.

"I'm sure you'll do splendidly, my dear," he said. At least there was one less thing for him to worry about now. Sarah's voice was her fortune. She was already making money and with careful investment, overseen by Jones, his accountant, she should never want for anything. Dora would be well provided for too. A handsome insurance policy would take care of that.

He took a sip of his coffee, his mind now on Louise. What future was there for his elder daughter? Things should be getting better now since Charlton and Spencer were building more new houses. The estate agency side of the business had expanded too since young James Spencer had taken over. But just lately the houses they owned and rented out seemed to need so many repairs and the costs were outweighing the rents they received.

Worst of all, Stanley was still suffering from the failure of the ambitious Winter Gardens project. Far from putting Holton Regis on the map as a desirable resort, the place had become a white elephant, its buildings boarded up and neglected. Only the dance hall remained open, attracting a most undesirable element as young men from the nearby RAF station flocked into town on Saturday nights to get drunk and force their attentions on the local girls. At least that's how Dora saw it — and she had a way of putting her point of view over at parish meetings so that poor old Mr Ayling had been forced to take notice and write a strong letter to the station's commander. But, as Louise pointed out, these lads were far from home and needed somewhere to go in their off-duty hours.

Poor Louise, Stanley thought. She should be out dancing herself, not stuck in this rambling old house seeing to the imagined needs of an increasingly querulous stepmother. Once again the pain struck and with it the panic, as Stanley wondered once more what he could do for his beloved daughter. At least she would have the house; it was only Dora's for her lifetime. And in its prime position on the seafront, with its large gardens, it would be a good investment for somebody if Louise chose to sell it.

He fumbled for one of his tablets and surreptitiously slipped it under his tongue, waiting for it to dissolve and take the pain with it. He leaned back in his chair and closed his eyes, wishing once more that Louise had been a son. Then he would have no fears for her future.

That night, Louise couldn't sleep. She and Sarah had sat up late talking excitedly about the audition for the musical. Louise was sure her sister would get the part and she was thrilled for her despite the small twinge of envy. Lying in her bed wondering what the future held for her, she was aroused by a commotion in the street outside — running footsteps, shouts, followed by banging on the front door. Struggling into her dressing-gown she hurried out on to the landing.

Her father was already downstairs wrestling with the bolts on the front door as the voice outside grew more frantic. "Mr Charlton — there's a fire."

Dora's breathless gasp and Polly's frightened wails prevented Louise from hearing what exactly was amiss. By the time she had ascertained that the fire was nowhere near Steyne House and persuaded her stepmother to return to bed, Stanley had disappeared into the night.

She knew there would be no sleep for her now and she asked Polly to make some cocoa. Giving her something to do was the best thing whenever there was a crisis. Sarah, who had joined them on the landing, eyes wide with excitement, followed Louise down to the kitchen.

"I'm sure I can smell smoke," she said, pulling the curtain aside and peering out.

"Maybe, but the fire is further along the esplanade — one of the hotels I expect. We're in no danger here — the wind's in the wrong direction," Louise said.

"Why did they want Father?" Sarah asked.

"Well, he is on the town council and chairman of the fire committee."

"I don't see what they expect him to do. Couldn't they wait till the morning to let him know what happened?" Sarah yawned. "I'm going back to bed. It's not as if they'd let us anywhere near so we can see the excitement."

Louise tutted in exasperation. Sarah could be so insensitive at times. Some poor soul could be losing their home or their livelihood. But it was true, there was nothing they could do. She asked Polly to take a drink up to her stepmother. "Then you'd better get back to bed too," she told her.

"What about the master?" Polly asked.

"I'll wait up for him and make him a hot drink when he returns. It's a cold night — I hope he's not gone too long."

They shouldn't have expected him to go out on a night like this, she thought as she sat in Cookie's old rocking chair in front of the kitchen range. The warmth of the fire was sending her to sleep and she jumped as the door opened.

Her father's exhausted body drooped and he grabbed at the door jamb for support. He ran a hand over his face and Louise leapt up and took his arm, helping him to the chair she had just vacated. As she busied herself with hot milk and cocoa powder, she caught the smell of smoke on his jacket. His shoes were wet and she knelt to take them off, then hurried to the hall cupboard for his slippers.

The milk boiled and she quickly made the cocoa. He clasped his cold hands round the mug and took a grateful sip. Only then did he look up at her, his expression bleak.

"William's dead," he said, his voice a mere croak.

"William — Mr Spencer? It was his house on fire then?"

"No, no — not his house." Stanley took another sip of cocoa and gave a long shuddering sigh.

The office, then. It must have been the office, Louise thought. That's why they called for Father. But Stanley was speaking again, his voice low and husky. "It was the theatre — that's where they think it started. Then it spread to the restaurant . . ." He looked up at her. "They managed to save the dance hall but the rest is a ruin."

"What happened to Mr Spencer then?"

"He thought he saw someone in one of the buildings — dashed in before anyone could stop him. One of the firemen brought him out — overcome by the smoke they said — not burnt."

"Oh, Father. I'm so sorry. He was your oldest friend."

"Poor old William — we'd had our differences lately, with the business and all. But I'll miss him. God knows what will happen now." Stanley finished his cocoa and stood up. "I'd better go up and tell Dora what's happened," he said.

"I expect she's sleeping. She was in such a state — I got Polly to give her a sleeping pill," Louise said.

Stanley touched her cheek. "What would we all do without you to take care of us?" he said.

Sarah hardly stopped chattering at breakfast, pestering her father for details about the fire and seeming not to notice how ill he looked. Dora of course was still in bed.

At last Louise could bear it no longer and she spoke quite sharply to her sister. "For goodness' sake, Sarah, shut up. Can't you see poor Father's exhausted? He was up half the night."

Sarah had the grace to look ashamed and concentrated for a few minutes on her boiled egg. But she wasn't subdued for long. "Can we go and look later on?" she asked.

"Don't be so morbid," Louise snapped, although truth to tell she was curious to see the extent of the damage for herself. What effect would the disaster have on Father's business, she wondered. He had been part-owner of the Winter Gardens. She was sure it wasn't only the loss of his friend that was troubling him.

Louise agreed that they should walk along the seafront later on, but only if the weather let up. The rain, which had started during the night, was still falling and they could hear the waves pounding against the promenade.

"Will you go to the office, Father?" Louise asked. He didn't usually go in on a Saturday unless there was urgent business to attend to.

"I suppose I ought to — there will be things to do, the insurance and so on." Stanley ran his hand over his face and sighed. He had hardly eaten anything.

"If there's anything I can do to help, Father . . ."

"Just keep things running smoothly here — as you always do, my dear," Stanley said.

Polly came to clear the breakfast and Louise followed her to the kitchen after sending Sarah to tidy her room. There were a few sulks but in the end Sarah did as she was told, but only after Louise promised they would go out as soon as it was done.

Once the chores were finished the sisters, muffled up against the weather, strode along the esplanade towards the Winter Gardens — or all that remained of the place where Sarah had enjoyed her first singing triumph.

A small crowd huddled against the cold wind just inside the gates watching the firemen picking over the blackened ruins. The fire must have been extremely fierce as, despite the heavy rain, a curl of smoke still rose from the centre of a pile of charred timbers.

Sarah listened to the murmured speculation going on around her.

". . . Could have been one of those young air force lads dropping a cigarette that started it off . . ."

"No, no. They say it started in the theatre, not the dance hall."

"Impossible. It was all boarded up."

"A tramp then — crept in there to shelter from the rain."

"That sounds more like it — started a fire to keep warm and it got out of control."

"You mean to say poor old Mr Spencer lost his life trying to save a tramp?"

"There weren't nobody else in there, though. 'Twas only Mr Spencer's body they found."

Louise couldn't listen to any more. She grabbed Sarah's arm and hustled her away, despite her protests.

"Do you think it's right what they're saying — a tramp started the fire?" Sarah asked as they battled against the wind towards Steyne House.

Louise didn't answer. She was wondering what the disaster would mean for their family. Could Stanley carry on without William? There was James of course, but, from the little her father had said, she wasn't sure if he could fill his father's shoes. Although the young man had a certain charm and was adept at dealing with their clients, he was lazy and incompetent, and Stanley had recently confided that he did not share William's confidence in his son.

Now more than ever she wished she'd insisted on being allowed to learn more about the business.

Her concerns deepened when they reached the house and saw Stanley's car parked in the street outside. Surely he had left for the office earlier?

Sarah went into the kitchen to ask Polly for hot chocolate to warm them after their walk, while Louise, without even taking off her coat, entered the study. Her father was sitting at his desk, his head in his hands, while Dora stood by the window clutching a sodden handkerchief.

Father must have told her the news then, Louise thought. But it was more than the death of his partner troubling him as she realized when he raised his head to look at her with bleak eyes. "They practically accused me of starting the fire," he said. "How could they even think such a thing?"

Dora gave a little cry, then sank into a chair sobbing. "Oh, the shame of it . . ."

Louise ignored her and put a comforting arm around her father. "Tell me exactly what happened."

In a halting voice Stanley explained that he had gone to the office to find James already there, the insurance certificate in his hand. "And his own father scarcely cold . . ."

Stanley had snatched it away angrily and had been soundly castigating the young man when the police arrived. The inspector's glance had been cold as he saw the file clearly marked "Insurance" open on his desk, the certificate in his hand.

Their questioning had been polite but firm. It was quite clear where their suspicions lay. Why had William Spencer been on the scene so quickly? He or an accomplice must have set the fire and both partners in the firm of Charlton and Spencer stood to gain by it.

"They seem to think that when William saw the tramp, or whoever it was, his conscience struck him and he rushed in to prevent an even worse disaster. I just can't believe it of William," Stanley whispered brokenly, his head in his hands once more.

"And I'm sure no one else will either," Louise declared.

"But they think I was involved as well."

"What nonsense! You're one of the most respected men in this town — and look at all you've done for the community."

"Of course it's nonsense, my dear. But even the most respectable men have been known to succumb to temptation when the stakes are high enough. And it's well known that William and I have suffered financial difficulties recently."

Louise knelt beside her father and took his hands in hers. "You mustn't think like that. No matter what the police suspect, they must realize in time how wrong they are. When they find no evidence to support their suspicions they'll soon eat their words."

"But mud sticks, Louise. Once the rumours start flying round town, no one will want to do business with me."

Dora gave a great wail. "Oh, Stanley, what will become of us? We shall have to move right away from here. I couldn't hold my head up . . ."

Louise felt the blood rush to her head and she leapt up, ready to give Dora a piece of her mind. Did the woman never think of anyone but herself? Only her father's gentle hand on her arm and his whispered, "She's upset — take no notice" restrained her.

"We're all upset, Father," she replied through tight lips.

The next day Stanley insisted that they all attend church as usual. Dora had breakfasted in bed and was reluctant to get up at all, let alone face the parishioners of St Mark's.

Passing from the kitchen to the dining room, Louise paused at the sound of raised voices from upstairs. She smiled. Stanley could be firm when he chose and this time he wasn't letting Dora get the better of him.

"They'll all be talking about us. I can't face it, I just can't," Dora wailed.

"Yes you can, Dora. It is I who will bear the brunt of the gossip. But I have done nothing to be ashamed of and the only way I can convince people of that is by carrying on as usual and holding my head up high. I am relying on you and the girls to support me in this."

Louise was waiting at the foot of the stairs and she gave her father an impulsive hug. "Of course you can rely on us. It will be hard but we'll do it."

"I am very fortunate in my family," Stanley said. "Your stepmother will be down in a moment. Is Sarah ready?"

Louise nodded and Stanley went on. "I am sure poor Mrs Spencer and her son won't shirk going to church this morning. Be sure to greet them warmly and let people see that they have our support too. The gossip around them will surely be more intense."

What a kind man he is, to think of others when he is in such trouble himself, Louise thought, as she went to hustle her sister into joining them. She had expected Sarah to be sulking today. After all, it was soon after the London concert and she had been looking forward to all the attention when they arrived at church that morning. The disaster which had struck their father had quite eclipsed her triumph.

But Sarah was not as self-centred as she sometimes appeared and Louise felt quite proud of her as she held her head high and marched to their pew. Those who stared were treated to dazzling smiles as if Sarah thought they were congratulating her on her performance. Dora too, despite the evidence of tears and the spots of colour high on her cheeks, held on to her husband's arm and greeted their acquaintances with dignity.

Their ordeal wasn't over yet, though. When Mr Ayling mounted the pulpit for his sermon he naturally mentioned the fire and asked for those present to pray for the soul of William Spencer and to bring comfort to his family and that of his business partner, "our respected church warden, Mr Charlton".

Louise glanced round at the sound of shuffling feet and caught a few hostile stares directed at them. She felt herself grow hot. The rumour machine was already in operation then. She looked down at her hands, twisting her gloves in her fingers and hardly noticing what the vicar was saying. Then she let out a slow sigh of relief as she realized he was berating his congregation, telling them they must take no notice of vile rumours.

As she looked round again she gave a small smile at the shamefaced looks on their faces. Maybe things wouldn't be so bad after all. Of course, it would be better if the police caught the real culprit. Father had said they seemed quite sure that the fire had been set deliberately.

# CHAPTER
# EIGHT

As Stanley had predicted, with nothing to feed on, the gossip soon died down. In such a small town there was always some fresh scandal, real or imagined, for people to get their teeth into.

But Louise couldn't forget what had happened. Every time she walked along the Esplanade past the burnt-out ruins of the Winter Gardens, she was reminded that the police had never caught the culprit. The evidence pointed to arson, not an accident. And, although both Stanley and his late partner had been publicly absolved of all suspicion, the insurance company would not pay out.

While the police inquiry continued they could do nothing with the derelict buildings. Without the insurance money it was impossible to rebuild or refurbish the dance hall. Stanley suggested that, as a temporary measure, the rubble should be cleared away and the remaining building boarded up — only temporarily, he insisted. The area where the theatre had stood would be grassed over so that at least it was no longer an eyesore. His fellow investors, all prominent local businessmen, agreed, although most of them felt that, once the case was closed, the site should be sold and developed.

To Louise's surprise, as her father began to recover from his shock and grief at the loss of his partner, he began to seem more like his old self. The challenge of getting the business back on its feet had given him new energy.

On one of their Sunday walks he confided in Louise that he very much feared he had been right in his suspicion that William was embezzling from the firm.

Shocked, Louise said, "I can hardly believe it."

"There's no other explanation for our losses," Stanley said. "I knew there was something wrong. He'd been very worried these past few months. But . . ." He paused before going on. "I have no doubts whatsoever that he had nothing to do with the fire."

Louise took his arm and squeezed it. "I don't suppose we'll ever know. Perhaps it was a tramp after all."

"Maybe. Anyway, I'm not going to worry about it any more. Things are beginning to look up. Young James is proving himself at last. I think the shock of his father's death brought him to his senses. He's begun to realize he can't go swanning off to the races or to those gambling clubs in Brighton and neglecting his duties."

"I'm pleased, Father. I just wish I could do more to help."

"You do quite enough — too much, I sometimes think."

Louise shrugged it off and changed the subject. "I'm so pleased Sarah got the part. We'll miss her when she goes off to London."

Stanley sighed. "She's still very young. I hope we're doing the right thing letting her go."

"She's nearly eighteen, Father."

"Your mother's not happy about her living in London alone, although she's found some respectable lodgings not far from the theatre." Stanley walked on in silence for a few moments then turned to Louise. "Why don't you go with her? You could stay for a few days until she's settled in — make sure she's all right."

Although Louise's heart leapt at the prospect of getting away from Holton, she hesitated. "I'm not sure. Mother needs me at home."

"Nonsense. She'll still have Polly and, now that things are looking up, I'm sure we could afford to employ a daily woman to help out. I've felt for a long time that you are being taken for granted, my dear. You need a life of your own." Stanley patted her arm. "Don't worry, Lou. I'll speak to your mother."

Louise felt the urge to run down to the beach and kick up the sand but she managed to restrain herself. Why hadn't she thought of it herself? But she knew that if it had been her own idea, Dora would have done her best to stop her. Besides, until a few weeks ago she would not have dreamt of leaving her father — not while he had been looking so ill. She would have worried about him all the time she was away.

Excitement was building in the Charlton household as the girls made preparations for their departure for London. Dora had taken some persuading to allow

Louise to accompany Sarah but concern for her younger daughter had won. Sarah had to be chaperoned while mixing with those "theatre folk".

Rehearsals for *Little Women* were due to begin at the Playfair Theatre shortly after Christmas and Louise couldn't wait to get away. Her only worry was how Polly would manage but, she told herself, it would only be for a week or two until Sarah was settled. Dora would just have to pull herself together and take control of the household, Louise thought rebelliously. She wasn't going to let her stepmother spoil things for her yet again. It was her last chance for a life of her own.

Her father was a different matter, though. Louise wouldn't hurt him for the world. Despite his earlier reassurances she still wasn't sure if he really had recovered from the trauma of the fire, especially when she saw him taking a tablet from a small box he kept in his waistcoat pocket.

"Just a touch of indigestion, my dear," he said.

"Are you sure, Father? Maybe you should see Dr Tate." Even using the name of Andrew's uncle still caused a little pang. But at the moment her concern was all for her father.

"I've spoken to George of course. But he assures me it's nothing to worry about," Stanley said.

"Then why the pills?"

"As I said, indigestion. Too much of your good cooking, my dear." Stanley laughed and Louise smiled with him, hoping that was really all it was.

96

★ ★ ★

The day before Louise and Sarah were due to leave for London, the conversation at dinner turned to the plans for the former Winter Gardens.

"James feels we should try to raise the money to rebuild the theatre," Stanley said.

"Surely not, Stanley," Dora protested. "How can he think it will be a success after what happened? Has he forgotten how much you and his poor father lost in the last venture?"

"I agree, my dear. But he has a point. It's true we do have entertainment facilities for our visitors, especially since the cinema opened at the end of the pier. But other resorts have dance halls, theatres, fairgrounds . . ."

Dora raised her hands in horror. "But Holton is hardly Bournemouth or Brighton. And as for a fairground — why, we should end up attracting all sorts."

"You don't understand, my dear. Holton has very little industry — even the fishing has declined lately. The summer visitors are the lifeblood of our little town — they are what put the bread and butter on our table."

"I like it when the summer people arrive," Sarah announced. "This place is as dull as ditchwater in winter. Father's right — we ought to have something for them to do, and for the locals too. Not everyone wants to be running the Girl Guides or doing good works."

Dora's mouth set in a thin line. "Such talk is most unseemly. Stanley, speak to your daughter."

"Your mother's right, Sarah. She works very hard for the church — and someone has to do these 'good works' as you call it so slightingly. It sounded to me as if you were belittling her efforts."

"I'm sorry, Mother. Of course I didn't mean that," she said, opening her violet eyes in wide-eyed innocence.

Dora was all smiles again. "I know you didn't, dear. I suppose now that you're off to London, it's only natural you should feel a little scornful of our parochial activities."

Louise hid a smile. How was it that Sarah managed to get round her mother so easily? She recalled that as a child, she had often been sent to her room for far lesser sins than her half-sister's outspokenness.

But Sarah had always possessed a charm that drew people to her and she could get away with almost anything. She wondered how she would cope with the younger girl's waywardness when they were living in London together.

The show opened to rave revues, with particular mention of newcomer Sarah Charlton in the part of Amy, the youngest March girl. It looked as if it was in for a long run and Louise was delighted, not just for her sister's sake.

Their lodgings in Grenville Terrace, a few streets away from the theatre, had been vetted by Dora before the girls came to London. She had firmly vetoed Maurice Weeks' suggestion that Sarah should share theatrical digs with the rest of the cast. Her daughter must stay in respectable lodgings. She could find no fault with the rooms, which were cheap and comfortable, or with their landlady, Mrs Mason, who fed them well and made sure their rooms were clean.

After the first couple of weeks Louise was bored. Although she revelled in her new-found freedom, she had little to do while Sarah was busy with rehearsals. It was time she returned to Holton but the thought filled her with dismay. She wrote to her parents asking if she could stay a little longer, giving the excuse that Sarah needed her.

Without waiting for a reply she scoured the neighbourhood of the theatre, reading the advertisement cards in newsagents' windows and even asking in some of the shops if they needed an assistant. But she soon realized that, for a woman in her twenties who had never worked before, finding a job wasn't so easy. Her only experience was running the household back in Holton but she couldn't possibly go into service. That would be just like being at home again.

One morning, despondent over her lack of success, she found herself outside the theatre where Sarah was rehearsing. She slipped in by a side door and sat quietly at the back of the stalls.

She had seen the show several times but it was always a pleasure to watch Sarah in action. During her visits to the theatre she'd got to know several of the company and she smiled when one of the stagehands sat down beside her. Julian Reynolds was a young lad, barely out of school, with flyaway blond hair and a somewhat diffident manner.

When the director called for a break, he broke into spontaneous applause. "Your sister's very good, isn't she?" he whispered.

"I think so — but maybe I'm prejudiced," Louise laughed.

"Do you sing — or act?" he asked.

"Oh no. Sarah's the performer in the family."

"I wondered why you were here."

"I wanted to be with my sister — and I'm looking for a job," she said. She didn't want to embarrass Sarah by telling the young man that she was acting as a sort of chaperon. Sarah at nearly eighteen thought she was quite grown-up enough to manage on her own.

"What sort of a job do you want?" Julian asked.

"I don't know — I'm not good at anything, really," Louise confessed.

"Can you paint?"

Louise remembered how she'd enjoyed drawing and painting as a child. But she didn't think that's what he had in mind. "What sort of painting?"

"Well, I happened to hear the stage manager saying that they needed more hands backstage to paint the scenery and such like."

"Haven't they got all the scenery they need for this show?" Louise was puzzled until Julian explained that with so many set changes, the background scenery — flats as they were called — got knocked about and often needed touching up and repairing.

"I thought maybe you could help with that," he told her, "but of course it's up to Mr Baxter." Julian got up and went back to work after pointing him out.

When she'd summoned up the courage to approach Phil Baxter, the stage manager, he looked at her over his half-moon spectacles. "Do you sing? Have you ever wanted to act?" he barked.

"No, no," she stammered.

"Never?"

"No, not at all."

The man sighed with relief. "Thank God for that. Most people who claim that they'll do anything — yes anything — to work in theatre, even making the tea, only see it as a way in. They all see themselves as the next Henry Irving or Florrie Ford."

Louise had no idea who he was talking about and hastened to explain that she'd moved to London to keep an eye on her sister — he knew that anyway — but she had to earn some money. She smiled gratefully when he said in a gentler voice that they'd take her on at "fifteen bob a week" as general dogsbody.

If it hadn't been for Lucia Lane, Sarah would have been on cloud nine. Working in the theatre was all she'd dreamt it would be. But Lucia, the nominal star of the show, was jealous of Sarah's success.

Arriving for rehearsals she'd been somewhat in awe of Lucia, who had held centre stage at most of the West End theatres for the past few years. But the singer had taken her under her wing, delighting in showing her the ropes.

Basking in her friendship and kindness, Sarah had been quite taken aback by the abrupt change in her demeanour the day after the first reviews came out.

The critics waxed lyrical over Sarah's performance, predicting that the world would soon hear more of the newcomer. Lucia received only a perfunctory mention.

"I don't understand it, Lou," Sarah complained as they relaxed in their sitting room at Grenville Terrace. "She was so nice to me at first — I thought we were going to be friends."

"She's jealous of your success that's all. She's used to being the centre of attention."

"But it's not as if we're rivals. I couldn't sing the part of Jo to save my life. Lucia's perfect for it with her deep rich voice. I'm a soprano — she's never going to be in competition with me for parts."

"I expect it'll all blow over — besides, this show won't run forever. You'll both probably move on elsewhere eventually."

"Well, until we close I'll be treading on eggshells. I do try not to upset her — she takes it out on everybody if she's in a bad mood — even poor old Steve."

"But Mr Forbes is the director. He's supposed to keep her in line isn't he?"

Sarah gave a short laugh. "I don't think *anybody* could keep Lucia in line. She's too used to having her own way. Besides, she only has to bat her eyelashes and murmur something in that husky voice and everyone falls at her feet."

"Well, I shouldn't worry about her — from what I can see everyone's falling at *your* feet now."

Sarah just smiled but as she got ready for bed she was a little worried. She didn't want to make an enemy of Lucia. Her star might be waning, but she still had many influential friends in the business. Maybe she should try to be a little more sensitive to Lucia's feelings. It wouldn't hurt to butter her up a bit, maybe ask her advice — even though she didn't need it. Steve Forbes was more than happy with her performance.

As she snuggled down under the blankets she smiled at the thought of Steve and a little tremor of excitement ran through her as she recalled the way he'd looked at her that evening. Of course, he was old. She had noticed the little flecks of grey at his temples and the wrinkles around his eyes. But they only made him look more handsome — distinguished was the word. She compared him with the stagehand, Julian, who had made no secret of his admiration. But he was just a boy — how he irritated her with his stammer, and the way he went red every time she so much as glanced in his direction. Steve was a real man, one who knew all the famous singers and actresses. If he was interested in her, she must be really special, she thought as she hugged her pillow and drifted off to sleep, dreaming of what it would be like to be kissed by him.

Louise enjoyed working in the theatre. Although being a dogsbody entailed all sorts of jobs, no two days were ever the same. One day she might be painting over the cracks that had appeared in the flat that depicted the Marchs' sitting room. Another day she would be helping the wardrobe mistress, pressing the voluminous dresses before the show. The dressing rooms were tiny and cramped — apart from Miss Lane's of course —

and there was nowhere to hang the gowns between changes, so that they were constantly creased.

It was a small company and the backstage people all worked together, swapping jobs and pulling together to make the show a success. Louise hadn't realized how much work went on behind the scenes, even while the show was running.

Best of all she liked it when Steve or Phil Baxter, the stage manager, sent her on errands. She loved wandering around the narrow streets off the Strand and Charing Cross Road, the big red buses, the noise, the pigeons — it was all a world away from sleepy Holton Regis. Still, she had to admit she missed the sea and was looking forward to going home at the weekend. The theatre was closed on Sundays, of course, and there was no performance on Mondays so she had persuaded Sarah that, after several months away from home, they ought to pay a visit to their parents.

Sarah didn't want to go home. Whenever Louise suggested it, she always managed to find some excuse not to go. That part of her life was over now, she told herself. The company was her family now. Besides, after a week of performances she looked forward to a lazy lie-in on Sundays, reading the papers and theatrical magazines and pampering herself with a long bath and beauty treatment. Later she would go for a walk in the park, then join her fellow performers for a late supper. Mondays were for shopping. If Louise wanted to go back to Holton for a couple of days that weekend she was welcome to do so. But Sarah definitely wouldn't be joining her.

When Louise failed to persuade her, she said she would stay too. "I can't leave you in London on your own — Mother would never forgive me," she said.

"Don't be such an old fusspot," Sarah said. "What harm can I come to? I'll be here all day under Mrs Mason's eagle eye. Then I'll be with the theatre people in the evening — just a friendly supper like we always do."

"Well, I'll go down on the train Sunday morning and come back on Monday. I just want to make sure Polly's managing. Are you sure you'll be all right?"

Sarah wished her sister would stop worrying. "I'm not a child, Louise. Of course I'll be all right." And it'll be a nice change to be able to do what I want without you fussing, she added silently.

She was still in bed when Louise left and she turned over and closed her eyes as she heard the front door close. A whole day to herself to be as lazy as she liked — and then an evening with her friends. Behind her closed eyelids floated an image of Steve Forbes' lean, handsome face. She would do her best to make sure of a seat beside him at the restaurant.

The day passed pleasantly in anticipation of the coming evening. But as she entered the restaurant she was annoyed to see that Lucia Lane was already seated next to Steve with Max Lloyd, the leading tenor, on her other side. She brightened when Steve looked up and waved her over, indicating the free seat on his other side.

Sarah hadn't enjoyed herself so much for ages — except when she was on stage of course. Without Louise to glare at her disapprovingly, she drank two glasses of wine, enjoying the pleasantly fuzzy feel they gave her. She would have had more but Steve restrained her.

"You don't want to get me in trouble with your sister, do you?" he asked, his blue eyes twinkling.

"She isn't here, is she?" Sarah giggled. She noticed Lucia glaring at her across the table. Of course, Steve had practically ignored her all evening. Still, she had Max, didn't she? He was all over her. And it wasn't her fault if Steve liked her better than Lucia.

She leaned closer to say something to him but at that moment Lucia stood up. "We've decided to go on to a club," she announced, her hand possessively on Max's arm. The rest of the cast got ready to leave too, leaving Steve and Sarah still sitting at the table.

"Well — are you coming, Steve?" Max asked.

The thought of going on to a club was quite exciting, Sarah thought. But she would rather be alone with Steve. Surely he would stay. But he stood up and held out a hand to her. "I'm sorry, sweetie. I wish you could come too. But there's no way they'd let you in. I'll call a cab for you."

Sarah tried hard to hide her disappointment. But she couldn't argue. She didn't want to get anyone into trouble. The others had gone outside and were clustered on the pavement, waiting for Steve. He saw her into the cab and gave the driver the address. Then he leaned inside and kissed her — a brief but warm kiss on the lips.

She gasped. "See you on Tuesday," she managed to say.

"No — tomorrow," Steve said. "I almost forgot. I need to make a few changes in one of your scenes. Come to the theatre at two o'clock — don't be late."

As the taxi took her home through the quiet Sunday night streets, Sarah wondered if the extra rehearsal was just an excuse to see her alone. Her heart beat faster and she pressed her fingers to her mouth where she could still feel the warmth of his lips. Suddenly the thought of being alone with Steve Forbes was a little unnerving. Well, she didn't have to go, did she?

But she knew she would.

As she neared the theatre her steps slowed and she began to feel a little apprehensive. Would the rest of the cast be there? After all, Steve had said it was an extra rehearsal. But when she entered by a side door all was quiet. There was no sign of old Joe, the caretaker — or of Steve. She went down the narrow passage towards the dressing rooms but, finding no one there, decided to go up on stage.

The auditorium was dark but the stage was softly lit. She walked on and glanced around. It was strange being alone in the theatre which was usually a bustle of activity. Even during rehearsals there was always someone coming or going, moving furniture, hammering, making running repairs.

And during performances there was the audience — a quiet murmur, then a breathless hush as the cast swung into action — then later the applause. Sarah smiled, recalling Saturday night's performance and the curtain calls she, Lucia and Max had taken.

She walked to the front of the stage and curtsied deeply to her imagined audience — then spun round as a low chuckle broke the dusty silence. Steve was lounging in a deep armchair, almost hidden in shadow at the back of the stage.

Sarah gave a little laugh, clutching her throat. "You frightened me," she said, then, looking round, "Where are the others?"

"Come on, sweetie. You didn't really think I wanted to rehearse, did you?"

Of course she hadn't — not really. But now that the moment had arrived, she felt unsure of herself. Well, she'd have to go through with it now, if she didn't want to look a fool.

"What else did you have in mind?" she asked.

"I'm sure you know exactly what I have in mind," he replied, getting to his feet and coming towards her.

She backed away but his hands were on her shoulders, pulling her towards him and his mouth came down on hers — not the warm, gentle kiss she remembered from the night before, but hard, demanding, forcing her own lips apart. She gasped and he leaned back to look into her eyes.

"This *is* what you wanted, isn't it?" he said.

She nodded but she was still a little unsure.

He took her hand and led her offstage to one of the dressing rooms. She followed mutely, her heart beating faster. He closed the door and pulled her down on the low couch beside him.

He smiled. "You've never done this before have you?" His voice was gentle.

She shook her head but managed to smile.

His kiss this time was less demanding and she found herself responding. "That's better," he murmured and gave a low chuckle. "Don't worry, I won't do anything you don't want me to."

It wasn't quite how she'd imagined her first experience of lovemaking would be but Steve was a skilled lover. Sarah gave herself up to the feelings he aroused in her but at the last minute doubts arose. But it was too late to draw back and she called on all her acting skills to convince him she was enjoying the experience. Playing a part came easily to her now.

Afterwards she lay in his arms on the couch and he stroked her hair. Suddenly he sat up and pushed her away. "I think I heard someone outside," he said.

Sarah grabbed her clothes and dressed hastily. She wasn't ashamed of what they'd just done but the theatre was a hotbed of gossip and she dreaded Louise finding out.

Steve sensed her discomfort. "I think we'd better keep this to ourselves, sweetie, don't you?" he said. "Perhaps I'd better come to your digs next time."

"No," Sarah gasped. "My sister . . ."

"Oh, yes, your chaperon." He laughed. "You don't know how I've longed to get you alone but she's always there. Doesn't she realize you're old enough to make your own decisions?"

"She worries about me — so does my mother." Sarah felt like a child again. She stuck her lip out. "I *am* old enough. I'm not going to let them rule my life any more."

"Good for you, sweetie." He pulled her down beside him again and she trembled in anticipation. But he only took her hand and said," You're going to go far — a real star. I'm going to let you in on a little secret."

She knew the run of *Little Women* was nearing its end and she felt excitement welling up. Was he going to offer her a part in another show? What he told her was beyond her wildest dreams.

"Oh, Steve, that's wonderful." She clapped her hands, her eyes shining.

"Swear you won't mention it — even to your sister? I want to make sure of all the arrangements before I announce it to the cast."

"I promise," Sarah said. But she wondered how she could possibly stop herself from blurting out both her secrets when Louise returned from Holton that evening.

# CHAPTER
# NINE

Louise was glad she'd gone home although she hadn't really enjoyed the weekend. At least Polly was managing quite well. The extra responsibility seemed to have given her more confidence. Although she couldn't wait to get away after a just a few hours of her stepmother's constant carping, Louise felt happier about going back to London, knowing that the household was in good hands.

"Your father spends far too much time at the office," Dora said at breakfast on Monday morning. "What's the point of young James being there if he leaves most of the work to Stanley?" She wiped her mouth with her napkin and gestured at her husband who sat at the other end of the table, his face hidden by *The Times*.

Stanley looked up and said mildly, "I enjoy my work, Dora, and there's plenty to keep both of us busy. I've put James in charge of the rental properties, which leaves me more time for the surveying side of things."

Dora tutted impatiently and picked up the hand bell from beside her plate, summoning Polly to clear the plates.

Louise stood up. "I must pack," she said, anxious to escape the uncomfortable atmosphere.

"Must you go back so soon?" Dora asked.

Stanley folded his paper. "If what I read here is true, I don't feel happy about either of my girls staying in London," he said.

For the past few months, Louise had lived and breathed the life of the theatre and had taken little notice of the news. Besides, hadn't Mr Chamberlain come back from Germany last year declaring that there would be no war? Dora seemed to agree.

"Nonsense, Stanley. It's all alarmist talk," she said. "You can't expect Sarah to give up her career now that she's doing so well, just because some madman is marching across Europe. If we were going to war it would have happened in March when Hitler took over Czechoslovakia. He's got what he wanted. Besides, we're an island."

Stanley reached over and patted her hand. "I'm sure you're right, dear. We shouldn't believe everything we read in the papers." He sighed. "Well, I must be off." He turned to Louise. "It's a lovely day. Would you like to walk to the office with me? I just have to pop in and speak to Miss Baines then I'll see you off on your train."

Louise smiled and nodded. Upstairs she threw her things into her small overnight case and hurried down to where her father waited in the hall. Dora came out of the dining room and gave her a perfunctory peck on the cheek. "Make sure Sarah comes with you next time," she said. "I'd come up to London myself but I haven't been feeling too well. With you gone and no cook still"

— she threw a malicious glance at her husband — "I can barely manage this big house." She gave a big sigh.

"I'll try to come again next week," Louise said. But she knew that if it wasn't for her father she would not come back to Holton Regis at all. Although he had been quick to reassure her that he was quite well now, she still felt a little pang of guilt at leaving him. But she had to admit she was impatient to get back to the theatre.

"Let's walk along the seafront," Stanley said as they turned the corner. "You're not in a hurry to get back are you?"

"I thought you were busy at the office?"

"Never too busy to spend time with you, my dear," he said.

They strolled along in the sunshine and Louise breathed deeply of the sea air. Much as she loved her new life in London, she missed all this when she was in the big city. Hearing shouts and laughter she looked down from the promenade onto the sandy beach. A group of children, supervised by a couple of men from the council, wielded spades and shovels, filling sacks with sand.

"What are they up to?" she asked.

"This is the sort of thing your stepmother chooses to ignore," Stanley said. "The powers that be must think war is inevitable. Why else would they be making preparations? These sandbags are intended to shore up the walls of important buildings, the council offices and such, in case we get bombed."

**113**

"Bombed? Surely not?" Louise couldn't imagine it happening in their quiet little town. But Stanley pointed out that France was only just across the Channel and the Germans had a navy and an air force to match our own.

"It's best to be prepared," he said.

Louise was thoughtful, resolving to pay more attention to the news in future. When they reached the office, she greeted her father's secretary, Miss Baines, and sat down to wait for him.

A few minutes later the door opened and James Spencer came in. When he saw Louise he took off his hat and came towards her with his hand out. "Good morning, Miss Charlton. How nice to see you again," he said.

Louise was somewhat taken aback by his enthusiastic greeting. The last time she had spoken to him had been at his father's funeral more than a year ago.

Instead of going to his office across the passage, he sat down next to her and began to chat amiably about London, asking how Sarah was getting on and promising to come and see the show soon. When the door to her father's office opened, he jumped up and said a hasty goodbye, before disappearing into the other room.

"Young Spencer late again?" Stanley said to Miss Baines.

She gave a rueful nod and Stanley tutted impatiently.

"I thought you said he was pulling his weight," Louise said, picking up her suitcase.

Outside Stanley gave a rueful smile. "He's young yet. Perhaps I've given him too much responsibility." He sighed. "It's times like this I really miss William."

Louise slipped her free hand through his arm for the short walk along the London Road. The quiet street, once so familiar, now seemed alien compared with the noisy bustle of London. She wondered how much longer it would continue to be like this if her father's predictions proved right.

"Is James often late for the office?" Louise asked as they neared the station.

Stanley gave a short laugh. "Punctuality is not his strongest suit," he said, patting her hand. "But he is very useful in his way — very good with the clients especially."

Louise hoped the young man really was pulling his weight. She knew James had been a bit of a ne'er-do-well in his school and university days and she'd been surprised to hear that he had settled down in the business. But his father wasn't there to keep a rein on him now — and her own father was sometimes too easygoing for his own good. But she didn't have time to voice her misgivings. The train was already at the platform, the engine snorting quietly to itself, like a huge beast gathering itself for flight.

Louise heaved her case up onto the rack, then leaned out of the window. She reached out impulsively and touched her father's cheek.

"Look after yourself, Father," she said. "I'll come again soon."

"You look after *yourself*, my dear — and Sarah." He clasped her hand as the whistle blew and the train began to move. "Be happy — both of you," he said.

When Louise arrived back at Grenville Terrace, Sarah ran downstairs to greet her. Her cheeks were flushed and her eyes had a mischievous sparkle. She scarcely bothered to ask how her parents were or what sort of weekend Louise had had before launching into a description of how she'd spent her days off.

"It was a wonderful meal, a really elegant restaurant," she gushed. "It must have cost a fortune but Steve and Phil paid for it as thanks for all our hard work these past months."

Louise had a feeling Sarah wasn't telling her everything and she wondered what her sister had been up to while she was away. She just hoped she hadn't done anything silly. "Sounds as if you had fun. Perhaps I should have stayed here," she said, trying to sound careless.

"It was all theatre talk," Sarah said. "You probably would have been bored."

Trying not to feel hurt at her sister's airy dismissal of her own hard work on the production, Louise brought the conversation back to their imminent return to Holton Regis. "I suppose this means the run is ending then?" she said. "You'll have to get on to your agent to find you a part in something else."

"Oh, I'm not worried about that. Steve said —" She stopped and started coughing. When she'd recovered, she said, "Steve told me I'll have no problem finding

**116**

parts. He thinks I'm really talented." She flushed and giggled.

"I'm sure he's right," Louise replied, trying to hide her concern. Steve seemed to figure a lot in Sarah's conversation and she was worried that her sister might get hurt. "And I'm sure Mother and Father will love having you home for a little while between engagements."

Sarah twisted her lips. "I don't really want to go home. I'll be so bored." She laughed. "Anyway, I might not have to."

"What do you mean?"

"I could get another part straight away, couldn't I?"

"I suppose so."

As the evening wore on and Sarah continued to prattle excitedly, her conversation peppered with "Steve says …" and "Steve thinks …" Louise became worried. Something *had* happened while she was away. She settled down to sleep, praying that her suspicions were unfounded. Despite her grown-up looks, in many ways Sarah was still a naïve child. If Steve Forbes had taken advantage of her innocence, he'd have to answer to Louise.

For the next few days Louise watched her sister and the director carefully but both seemed to be behaving normally. Besides, the show only had a couple of weeks to run and then they'd both be going back to Holton.

Much as she too loved her life in London, Louise was anxious to return. She was sure something was wrong. When she'd phoned the office to speak to her father Miss Baines had told her he hadn't been in for a few days. "A summer cold, so he said, but it's not like Mr Charlton to take time off."

Miss Baines had sounded worried but Louise was reluctant to telephone the house in case her stepmother answered. She should go down soon just to reassure herself that father really was all right.

Back at their digs after a mid-week performance, she voiced her concerns.

Sarah lounged on the sofa chewing her nails. "I'm sure you're making a fuss about nothing," she said.

"You should pay them a visit at least," Louise said.

"I suppose so. But I hate Holton now — it's so dull after London."

"If there's a war we might have to go back. I heard someone say that they'll close all the theatres and cinemas. Besides, London won't be safe." Louise was remembering those children filling the sandbags on the beach. Perhaps Holton wouldn't be safe either but she wouldn't tell Sarah that.

"War — that's all anyone talks about these days," Sarah said, flapping her hand.

"Well, we must face up to it. Looks like it's going to happen." Louise stood up. "I'm off to bed. I think I'll go home tomorrow — just for the day." She turned in the doorway. "Why don't you come with me?"

"I've got better things to do."

Louise sighed as she went to their room. She couldn't help thinking that Sarah was turning out to be just as selfish as her mother.

**118**

The next day she tried to persuade her to spend the day in Holton but Sarah turned over in bed and drew the covers over her head. "I'm too tired. I need to rest," she muttered.

"Well, I'm going. I'm worried about Father."

"It's probably just a cold like Miss Baines said." Sarah sat up and brushed her hair out of her eyes. "You go if you want to waste your day off."

Louise bit back a retort and got her jacket out of the cupboard. "I'll be back this evening and we can go out for dinner," she said.

"See you later then." Sarah burrowed under the covers again.

Louise stepped off the train and breathed deeply of the sea air. She enjoyed the freedom of her life in London away from her stepmother's demands, but in many ways she missed her home town. She strode along the High Street and turned off down the narrow road that led to the seafront. A few fishing boats were drawn up on the beach near the pier but there were no children playing on the sands today.

As she neared home she saw Dr Tate's old Austin parked outside Steyne House. She broke into a run and burst through the front door just as the doctor came down the stairs.

She grabbed his arm. "Is everything all right?" she gasped.

"Louise, my dear. I didn't realize you were home." He patted her arm. "Come and sit down." He led her

**119**

into the small sitting room just off the hall and forced her into a chair.

Louise's heart beat faster and she twisted her fingers together. She knew she should have come before. What was wrong with her father?

Dr Tate smiled. "Don't be alarmed. He's been poorly, but he is recovering. Just a touch of summer flu and it's left him with a nasty cough."

"I was so worried . . ."

"I must admit I was a little concerned myself. However, so long as your father does what he's told and doesn't try to do too much, he'll be fine." The doctor patted her arm. "He can be a bit stubborn, my dear, so I'm relying on you to make sure he follows doctor's orders."

"But surely, he has Mother —"

"Mrs Charlton is not in the best of health either. I think you're needed at home."

"But, I'm working in London now at the theatre where my sister . . ."

"I know. But I hear that the show finishes soon and you'd be returning to Holton anyway. Surely they'll let you off early if you explain the circumstances."

Louise nodded. Of course she'd stay and look after her father. But she hated the thought of giving up her theatre work. She had enjoyed the comparative freedom of living in London and she dreaded a return to the narrow humdrum life she'd be forced to live under her stepmother's roof. But she felt it was her duty; she loved her father and would do anything to please him.

"I must give notice at the theatre, Doctor. But I'll be home as soon as I can."

Dr Tate patted her hand. "You're doing the right thing, my dear," he said.

As Louise put her key in the lock, Sarah ran down to greet her, a smile lighting her face.

"You'll never guess what's happened," she said, throwing her arms round her. "It's so exciting. Steve said —"

"What?" Louise asked, heart thumping at the thought of what might have been going on in her absence.

Sarah giggled. "Guess," she said, hugging Louise even tighter.

"I can't guess." She tried gently to disengage herself and get her to calm down. "Aren't you going to ask about Father?"

Sarah frowned. "He's OK, isn't he? I thought it was just a summer cold."

"It's left him with a bad cough and Dr Tate says he has to take it easy."

"I'm sure he'll be all right then."

Sarah followed Louise upstairs and started to giggle again. "I'm so excited," she said again.

"I can tell." Louise couldn't help smiling. She opened the door to their sitting room and put the case on the floor, shrugged off her jacket and turned to Sarah. "Now, sit down and tell me all about it."

Sarah threw herself down on the sofa. "Well, you know the show finishes its run in a couple of weeks? Well . . ." She paused. "Go on, guess."

"Your agent has found you another role?"

Sarah couldn't contain herself any longer. "Better than that. Steve called a meeting of the cast this morning. He's had an offer to transfer the show to America. Just fancy — I'm going to be on Broadway."

"America?"

"Isn't it exciting? Of course, I knew ages ago — Steve told me. He wanted to make sure I was up for it."

So that's what that air of suppressed excitement these past couple of weeks had been about, Louise thought. She sighed with relief that she'd been worrying over nothing and slapped her sister's arm. "You could have told me. I knew something was on your mind."

"Steve told me not to tell anyone."

Although Louise was pleased for Sarah, she knew her sister would have to be disappointed. She couldn't possibly go so far away when their father was ill. And there was the threat of war too. "You can't go, Sarah," she said.

Her sister's eyes flashed. "And why not?"

"We need you here. Father really isn't well, you know. Besides, I don't think Mother will agree."

"She would if you came too. It would be an adventure, Lou."

"Maybe I'm not cut out for adventure."

"No, I suppose not. After all, you had the chance to go to Africa and turned it down. And you wouldn't have come to London if it wasn't for me. I suppose you want to spend the rest of your life in dreary old Holton."

"Of course I don't. But if Father's ill . . ."

Sarah sighed. "You've already said it's nothing to worry about." She stood up and began pacing. "You've got to come, Lou. Mother will have to let me if you agree."

For once, Louise wasn't going to let herself be swayed by her sister. Exciting as a trip to America would be, she just couldn't contemplate going away while she was worried about her father. She grabbed Sarah's hand, pulling her down beside her again. "Please understand, Sarah. I can't go."

"Father's not really ill, is he?" For the first time, concern showed in her face. "I don't mean to be selfish, Lou, but —"

"I do understand, love. But this offer couldn't have come at a worse time." She told Sarah what Dr Tate had said. "I just feel that if I'm not there, he'll carry on over-working. I can help him with the business, keep an eye on James Spencer and make sure he pulls his weight."

"Mother won't like you helping in the office," Sarah said.

"I'll deal with that when the time comes." She patted Sarah's hand. "I'm so sorry if you're disappointed. I never dreamed of anything like this. I thought we'd go back to Holton and have a bit of time together as a family before another singing engagement turned up."

Sarah flung her hand off and stood up. "I know what it is. You were hoping I wouldn't get another part. I do believe you're jealous of my success."

"Don't be silly, Sarah. Of course I'm not jealous. I'm proud of what you've achieved. But you have to think of others sometimes."

"So, now you're saying I'm selfish." Sarah burst into tears and rushed into the bedroom.

Louise was about to follow her when she heard the click of the bedroom door key. She threw herself down on the sofa with a sigh. The truth was she did think Sarah was selfish but at the same time she could understand her disappointment. Still, she was young. There would be other opportunities.

At the theatre the next day there was an air of subdued excitement among the cast, coupled with regret that the run was coming to an end. However, most of them would be transferring to the New York theatre, together with Steve, the director.

There was still a strained atmosphere between the sisters. They'd hardly exchanged two words that morning, and had made their way to the theatre separately. Louise finished sorting out the costumes for the matinee and made her way to her usual seat at the rear of the auditorium.

Steve had assembled the cast on stage and was talking about passports, booking berths on the *Queen Mary* and arrangements for their accommodation in New York.

Sarah hung on his every word, her eyes shining and Louise sighed. She hated the thought of her sister's disappointment when she realized how impossible it was for her to go with them.

124

Julian came and sat beside her, gesturing at the group on stage. "Lucky things. Wish I could go too," he said.

"Why can't you?"

"There wouldn't be any work for me over there. They have their own theatre crew." He grinned. "Maybe I'll get the chance one day. I envy Sarah though — getting the break so young."

"Don't envy her too soon. I don't think she'll be going," Louise said, and went on to explain about her father's health. "And I'm sure my stepmother won't hear of her going all that way alone."

"But who knows when an opportunity like this might come again?"

"Try explaining that to my stepmother," Louise said. But in her heart she knew he was right. Sarah's singing and acting career meant everything to her. How could she be the one to sabotage it? She summoned a smile. "Don't worry, Julian — I'll do all I can to persuade Mother, short of agreeing to go along as chaperon myself."

Julian gave a rueful smile. "Don't know why I'm so keen to see her go. I'll miss her." He blushed a little and ran his hand over his face. "Well, you must know how I feel about her but I know I don't stand a chance. The next best thing is to see her succeed." He laughed. "At least I can tell my grandchildren that I knew the famous Sarah Charlton." He stood up abruptly. "Looks like they're taking a break. Better go and see what the boss wants me to do."

Louise glanced up at the stage where the group was breaking up, still chatting animatedly. Sarah disappeared from view and Louise stood up. She had to talk to her, say she was sorry for her harsh words and promise to speak to Dora on her behalf, hard as that would be.

As she mentally framed her apology, Sarah came towards her smiling.

"I'm sorry I said you were jealous."

"It's all right, love. We were both a bit het up." She took Sarah's hand. "We have to talk about this though."

The smile disappeared. "There's nothing to talk about — I'm going."

Louise bit her lip. "I know you've made up your mind but you must talk to Mother first. You don't want to leave with bad feeling between you — or between us."

"I don't mean to be selfish. But you must know how much it means to me."

"I do understand — really. I'm sure we can work something out."

"There's only a few more days to run, then there'll be all the preparations. I won't be able to get home until just before we sail." Sarah put her hand on Louise's arm. "You'll have to talk to her for me, Sis. I'm sure you can get round her."

Louise wasn't so sure but she promised to try. *Little Women* was due to close on the following Friday night and the theatre was fully booked for the last performance. She would be kept busy herself right up to the last minute. Then there were the costumes to be

**126**

cleaned and pressed ready to pack into trunks. She didn't think she'd be able to get down to Holton until the middle of the following week.

Sarah should be the one to tell their parents that she was going away and Louise hadn't given up hope that she would persuade her to come with her. But as usual she was just ignoring the problem, hoping that her sister would sort things out for her.

When Louise arrived at the theatre on the Wednesday she was met by Phil Baxter, the stage manager.

"Haven't had a chance to talk to you lately. It's all been a bit hectic."

"Sarah's very excited."

"I know. But it's you I want to talk about. I hear you won't be going with her. What will you do now?"

"Go home. I don't know if Sarah's told you that our father isn't well."

Phil looked thoughtful. "That's a pity. I was hoping to persuade you to stay on here. You've done such a good job —"

"No, I can't," Louise interrupted. "I'm sorry, Phil. I only came to London because my parents thought Sarah needed someone to keep an eye on her." That might have been true at first but Louise had come to love her work in the theatre and would like to have taken up Phil's offer of a permanent job. It would have been easy enough to travel up and down to London on the train. But she wouldn't give way to temptation and she went on, "With my father unwell I feel my place is

**127**

at home. It will be hard enough for them with Sarah so far away."

Phil shrugged and said, "OK then, but if you change your mind . . ."

The next few days were hectic, filled with shopping, meetings with Sarah's agent and signing contracts. When Louise once again tackled her sister about going home, Sarah shrugged her off. "Didn't I tell you? I phoned Mother yesterday. She's really pleased that I've got this chance."

"Really? She was all right about it?" Louise found it hard to believe. She grasped her sister's wrist. "You did tell her I wouldn't be going too?"

"Of course. She said she understood and that she needs you at home anyway."

"I can't believe she gave in just like that. Besides, I thought you wanted me to tell them." But Louise was relieved — she hadn't been looking forward to breaking the news to their parents. "What did Father say?" she asked.

"He's really pleased for me. He said not to worry about him. He's much better — just a summer cold like we thought. He's back at work now."

Louise was glad they seemed to have accepted that Sarah was grown-up enough now to make her own decisions. And it was a load off her mind to learn that her father was better. Perhaps she would talk to Phil about staying on at the theatre after all. But she'd go home first, make sure everything really was all right.

As the days rushed by in a ferment of preparations, some of Sarah's excitement rubbed off on Louise and she couldn't help feeling a little twinge of regret that she wasn't going too. She told herself there would be other opportunities but, as well as the fears for her father's health, the threat of war seemed even nearer. Chamberlain had announced that he was willing to go to Germany again to try to come to some agreement with Hitler. But everyone knew that it was a futile gesture. As she hurried to the theatre, only half-listening to Sarah's excited prattle, she realized it might be a long time before she could think of following her sister to America. At least if war came, Sarah would be safe on the other side of the world, she told herself.

It was the last night of the show and there was a subdued feeling among the cast and theatre crew, along with a buzz of excitement from those who were to continue the run on the other side of the Atlantic.

Louise was in her work room backstage sewing on a button when Phil came in, his face grave. "There's a phone call for you. Someone called Polly. She sounds a bit hysterical . . ."

Louise threw down her sewing and followed Phil down the narrow passage to his office. "Did she say what . . .?"

"She said to tell Miss Charlton to come home and then she started crying."

"Oh, God, it must be Father."

"I don't think so. She said something about the mistress and you'd know what to do." Phil paused at the office door and put his hand on her arm. "I do hope it's not serious, Louise. But whatever the problem, can you not tell Sarah until after the show? I can't have her upset. It's a packed house out there for our last night."

Louise nodded and pushed past him, grabbed the phone and gasped, "Polly, what is it?"

"Oh, Miss, I had to phone you. I didn't know what else to do." The maid's voice was hoarse as if she'd been crying.

Louise's stomach lurched. "Is it Father? Is he ill?"

"No, Miss. It's the mistress. She's in a terrible state. I don't know what to do. I tried her smelling salts but she threw the bottle at me." Polly burst into loud sobs.

"Where's my father? Can't he do anything?"

More sobs.

Louise shook the phone impatiently. "Polly, calm down. Tell me what brought it on. Are you sure Father's not ill? Has the doctor been?"

With a loud sniff, Polly seemed to pull herself together. "The master's at his council meeting and I tried Dr Tate but he's out too. I wish you'd come home, Miss."

"I'll try. Just tell me what got Mother in such a state." Louise thought longingly of the evening ahead; she'd been looking forward to watching Sarah's last performance as well as the party afterwards. She'd go down to Holton on the first train tomorrow. But Polly's next words soon changed her mind.

**130**

"She read it in the paper, Miss. About Miss Sarah going off to America."

"But, didn't Sarah . . .?" Louise sagged against the desk as she realized her sister had lied to her. How could she? And how could Louise herself have been taken in? She should have known Dora wouldn't meekly accept her daughter going so far away with no one to keep an eye on her.

"I told her it was the chance of a lifetime and begged her not to spoil things and she gave in," Sarah had said, smiling. "I knew she would."

And Louise had believed her. After all, hadn't Sarah always managed to get her own way, right from when she was small child? Louise had meant to phone and make sure her parents were agreeable but in the bustle of preparations and the excitement of the show's run coming to an end, she simply hadn't found time.

She sighed. She'd have to go home at once. She told Polly she'd be on the next train and put the phone down. Then she went to find Phil to tell him what had happened.

He wasn't pleased but he agreed to let her go. "What shall I tell Sarah?" he asked. "She'll wonder why you aren't at the party."

"Just say I don't feel well and I've gone back to our digs. I'll leave her a note there and try to get back tomorrow."

Andrew Tate was exhausted. He'd been on duty for eighteen hours and was longing for his bed in his comfortable lodgings. As he left the hospital he picked up a copy of the *Evening Standard*, hailed a taxi and settled back to read his paper. The name leapt out at him from the headline: SARAH CHARLTON TO STAR ON BROADWAY.

So little Sarah was now a big star, he thought, smiling as he read the whole article. Of course he had heard about her success in *Little Women* and had been meaning to go and see the show but he just hadn't found the time. Now it was the final performance before they all shipped out on the *Queen Mary* and he'd missed it. He glanced at his watch. The paper said tickets were all sold out but if he went straight to the theatre he might be lucky and find that someone had cancelled at the last minute. He leaned forward and gave the taxi driver his change of destination.

As they drew up outside the theatre he hesitated. What was he thinking of? Musical shows weren't really his sort of thing. He grinned wryly, acknowledging that he wanted to see Sarah — but not for her performance. He was hoping he'd have the chance to speak to her and get news of her sister.

In spite of his best efforts he hadn't been able to get Louise out of his mind, despite trying to lose himself in his work among the East End's poor. He hadn't been down to Holton Regis for months and there had been no mention of the Charltons in Uncle George's infrequent letters.

He paid the taxi driver and crossed the road to the theatre, pleased to find that there was a ticket available. Despite it not being his usual sort of fare, he enjoyed the show and Sarah's performance was outstanding. He

**132**

could understand why she'd had such good reviews. And now she was off to America to enslave new audiences over there.

When the last bow had been taken and the final curtain fell, Andrew got up and made his way to the foyer. He was determined to see Sarah and seek news of her sister, to reassure himself that she was well and happy. But he had reckoned without Sarah's popularity and the hordes of autograph hunters and fans swarming around the stage door, not to mention the burly doorman who refused admittance to anyone not known to him.

Andrew tore a page out of his diary and scribbled a note, pressing some coins into the man's hand. "Please make sure Miss Charlton gets this. It's very important," he said. "I'm a friend of the family."

The man looked sceptical. "You and everyone else," he said.

Andrew turned away, disappointed. At the theatre entrance he looked for a taxi but, finding none, he started to walk. Perhaps it was just as well, he thought. The Charlton sisters were not part of his life now, if they ever had been. He might hear news of them through his uncle from time to time but it was best to try and forget them, especially Louise with her dimpled smile and sparkling eyes.

# CHAPTER
# TEN

When Louise got off the train, she was still simmering with fury. How could Sarah behave like this? She might have known her lie would be discovered and that her mother would collapse in hysterics. And, as usual, it would be left to Louise to smooth things over and make everything all right again.

It had happened so often in the past. Try as she might to convince herself that Sarah was not the self-centred person she appeared to be, that it wasn't her fault she'd always been allowed her own way, Louise couldn't stop the resentment rising to the surface.

Just as she reached Steyne House the door was thrown open and Polly, her face stained with tears, greeted her. "Oh, Miss, I'm so glad you're here. I hope it was all right to phone but I couldn't think what else to do."

"You did the right thing, Polly," Louise assured her. "How is Mother now? And is my father home yet?"

"The mistress is in bed. I managed to calm her down with some camomile tea. The master's not back from his meeting yet."

Louise glanced at her watch. "He shouldn't be long. Perhaps you'd make some tea and sandwiches for both of us." She hung her coat up and put down her overnight bag. "I'll go up and see Mother."

She opened the bedroom door quietly, hoping that Dora was asleep. But as she was about to withdraw, her stepmother sat up in bed.

"Oh, it's you. I suppose you've come to make excuses for that little minx." Dora covered her face with her hands and began to wail. "How could she do this to me? And why didn't you stop her?"

As usual, Dora was thrusting the blame on to her.

"I did try," Louise said. "But she said you'd given permission for her to go."

"She's too young to go all that way. Anything could happen to her." Dora wiped her eyes on a scrap of lace handkerchief, her tears replaced by a grim smile. "Well, she can't go. Stanley will refuse to sign. I'll make sure of that."

It hadn't occurred to Louise that Sarah didn't have her own passport and that, as she was under twenty-one, her parents' signature would be necessary. She'd managed to convince Steve and Maurice, her agent, that all was in order. How had she hoped to get over that hurdle? Louise wondered. Charm and a sweet smile wouldn't convince the hardened officials of the Customs Department.

Although she was still angry at Sarah's deception, Dora's words made Louise want to defend her sister. She knew how much the chance of starring on Broadway meant to her and she had thought Dora would be pleased too — another opportunity to boast to her friends about her talented daughter. But of course, Louise realized, with Sarah so far away, her mother would lose the last remnants of control over her.

Dora continued to try and blame Louise for "encouraging the little minx" and Louise tried to change the subject by asking about her father.

"He's perfectly all right. I don't know why you worry about him. He's well enough to go off to these everlasting meetings of his every night."

"Is it council business?"

Dora flapped a hand. "I don't know — it's all war, war, war. They're getting all steamed up about nothing. Besides, what good are all these preparations? If it does come to anything it will all happen over there, just like last time."

Louise didn't agree but she knew it was no use arguing. Dora had a knack for ignoring anything unpleasant. But she had to try. "Mother, surely you've read the newspapers. And Father wouldn't be getting involved if he didn't think it was going to happen."

"Well, I must admit he does seem worried about it." Dora's eyes welled with tears once more. "That's another reason I don't want Sarah to go. I need her here with me."

"Mother, don't get upset again. Sarah will be all right. Besides, if there is a war, she'll be safer in a far away country." She adjusted Dora's pillows and smoothed the eiderdown. "I'll get you some more camomile tea. Try to rest."

Downstairs, Polly had prepared a tray of tea and sandwiches. "Shall I take it into the dining room, Miss?" she asked.

"No, I'll have it here. Can you take some more tea up to Mother? She might be sleeping by now so don't disturb her. Just leave it by the bed."

Louise sat at the kitchen table and rested her forehead on her hand. Dealing with Dora always gave her a headache. She was starting to doze when her father came in and startled her. She leapt up and embraced him. "I'm so glad you're home."

"What are you doing here? Is anything wrong? Sarah . . .?" He gently disengaged himself. "What's happened?"

"Nothing really. Sarah's fine. Singing her heart out at this very moment I expect."

"So why are you here? I thought you were going to stay for her last performance and then come home with her tomorrow."

"You haven't heard then?"

Stanley shook his head. "What's all the mystery?"

"It's Sarah — she won't be coming home just yet."

"Have they decided to extend the run then?"

"Not exactly." Louise made her father sit down and poured him some tea. Then she told him of Sarah's big chance, her determination to go to America and Dora's equal determination that she would not.

Stanley shook his head. "I don't understand. Dora is so proud of Sarah. Why would she want to stop her going?"

"She's too young — so Mother says."

137

"But it's a wonderful opportunity for her. And of course, you'll be there to look after her."

"No, Father. I don't want to go." She laid a hand on his arm, noting his pallor, the shadows under his eyes. However much he denied it, she could see he was far from well. She decided to try and see Dr Tate on her way to the station the following day. If he reassured her that Stanley's health wasn't in danger she might reconsider. But she wasn't hopeful.

During the train journey to London Louise couldn't stop worrying about her father. She hadn't been reassured by his attempts to laugh off his shortness of breath. He'd just laughed and said, "Getting old, my dear."

When she asked if he had to work such long hours he explained that the business was only now beginning to recover from the disastrous fire and his partner's untimely death. "Things are looking up, though. And I've started to hand over more of the day to day running to young James," he said.

From what she'd seen of his late partner's son, she wasn't so sure. "Didn't you say he wasn't ready for too much responsibility?" she asked.

Stanley reassured her. "He's spending more time in the office now. You worry too much, my dear. I'm fine," he said.

She wanted to take him at his word but she'd still visited the doctor's surgery, without letting her parents know. He had declined to be specific, telling her she should discuss things with her father, but when he realized how anxious she was, he relented.

"I warned him not to work so hard after that first attack," he said.

"What do you mean? What attack? He said he'd had a summer cold. My stepmother said nothing to me either."

"Stanley was trying to shield her — and you — from the truth. You know how easily upset she is. But it was a very mild heart attack. He has his pills now and, with rest, he should go on for many years yet."

Louise choked back a sob. "Are you sure it's nothing more serious? Why didn't he tell me? I would have come home to look after him."

Dr Tate smiled. "I suspect that is precisely why he didn't tell you. You and your sister have been enjoying your time in London, haven't you? He didn't want to spoil that, especially as he knew you'd soon be returning to Holton."

She hadn't told him about the show's transfer to New York and her own offer of a job at the London theatre. But the conversation had made her decision easier.

Earlier, her father had managed to calm Dora's hysterics by saying that, as he was certain the country would soon be at war, he'd feel happier if the girls were far away when the inevitable happened. Eventually, Dora had accepted that she couldn't stand in the way of her daughter's success. They both seemed to think that if Sarah went, Louise would too.

But, as the train drew into Victoria Station, her mind was made up. She would not be going with Sarah, nor would she be taking the theatre job. She was sure now that her place was back in Holton Regis. Her brief flight to freedom was over.

Sarah woke with a blinding headache. The party the night before had been fun but she'd drunk far too much champagne. She turned away from the bar of sunlight which pierced a gap in the curtains and burrowed under the sheets, hoping to doze off again. Then she remembered arriving home and finding Louise's note and she sat up, groaning, wondering how she was going to face her sister.

She knew she shouldn't have lied, but she'd said the first thing that came into her head. She had honestly meant to confess, but as time passed it became harder to speak up. It had simply not occurred to her that her mother would find out before she or Louise had a chance to soften the blow.

Last night, when Phil told her Louise had gone home with a bad headache she'd been furious, once more accusing her of jealousy, although deep down, she knew she was being unjust. But she'd been upset that Louise had left the theatre before the show even began. Hadn't she promised she would be there for her final triumph, the photographs, the bouquets, the applause and the party afterwards?

Back at their digs, when she found the note saying why Louise had returned to Holton she'd immediately felt ashamed. Once more, her sister was bailing her out of trouble, facing up to an angry Dora and smoothing things over as usual.

She threw herself back on the pillows, wondering why her life had to be so complicated. But then her natural optimism reasserted itself and she sat up and swung her legs out of bed. She was going to star on Broadway and nothing was going to stop her.

Humming a tune from the show, she pirouetted over to the window. As she drew back the curtains, she saw Louise striding up the road. Her sister did not look happy. Did that mean she hadn't been successful in talking Mother round? "I don't care. I *am* going, even if I have to stow away," she muttered, turning away from the window.

She threw on some clothes and was waiting anxiously by the time Louise came upstairs. Before her sister could speak she said, "I suppose you're going to tell me I must go home and be a dutiful daughter." She stamped her foot and without waiting for a reply, spoke again. "Well, I won't."

Louise shrugged off her jacket and sat down. "Aren't you even going to ask how your mother is? She was dreadfully upset you know, in a terrible state. And you know Father's not well either."

Sarah tossed her hair back. "Oh, you know Mother. She gets in a state over the slightest little thing." She sat down opposite her sister. "You said she'd found out about America — how?"

"She read it in the paper. You shouldn't have lied to me, Sarah."

Sarah hung her head. "I know — I'm sorry. I do feel bad about it." She straightened up. "Anyway she knows now — the point is, what's she going to do about it?"

"Father and I talked her round. She's not happy, mind. And she'd feel better if I agreed to go with you."

"So will you?"

Louise shook her head. "No, Sarah. I really don't want to go so far away, especially now they say there's definitely going to be a war."

"Oh, war. That's all anyone talks about these days. Besides, if it does happen, surely we'd be better off out of it."

"Maybe — that's what convinced Mother. Father said at least you'd be out of danger. That's why she agreed you could go. But it's not just that, Sarah. I'm really worried about him — he tries to shrug it off but I'm sure he's ill. I just feel I should be at home now."

Sarah felt a brief flash of guilt but she brushed it aside. Louise was such a worrier. She leaned over and took her sister's hand. "I truly am sorry for lying to you and leaving you to pick up the pieces. Thank you. What will I do without you to watch out for me when I get over there?"

"I'm sure you'll be all right. Now, tell me about the party last night."

Sarah needed no encouragement and launched into a lively description of the people who'd been there and the fun she'd had. "And just look at all the bouquets," she said, waving her hand round the room.

Louise had scarcely noticed the masses of flowers which covered every surface of their small sitting room.

142

Now, she looked round and it began to sink in how popular her sister was — a real star. Who knew where she'd end up — Hollywood perhaps, starring in films with the likes of Clark Gable and Errol Flynn? The thought frightened her a little. What effect would it have on her flighty, carefree sister? Should she change her mind and agree to be her chaperon?

No, she thought, as Sarah chattered on, her eyes alight with excitement. Her sister was grown up now. She'd have to take care of herself.

Lost in thought, she hardly registered the name until Sarah shook her arm. "Andrew Tate — old Dr Tate's nephew. He came to the theatre last night."

Louise's eyes widened. "He did? What did he say?"

"Oh, I didn't see him, but he left a note." Sarah began to scrabble in her bag. "I've got it here somewhere. I wonder why he sent it to me and not you?" She looked up, a mischievous twinkle in her eyes. "I mean, it's obvious it's you he fancies."

Louise felt herself beginning to blush. She wanted to believe it but what man could possibly prefer her to her beautiful, lively sister? Sarah handed her the screwed up piece of paper and she smoothed it out. The hastily scrawled note congratulated Sarah on her performance and wished her success in New York. But it was the final sentence which set Louise's heart thumping. "I do hope you will convey my best wishes to your sister when you next write."

Sarah laughed and nudged Louise. "You're blushing. I believe you still carry a torch for him." She took the paper back. "I wonder why he thinks I'll be writing to you?"

"Obviously he doesn't know I've been in London too." And why should he? Louise thought. It was more than a year since that brief encounter on the seafront at Holton. But, she had to admit, he'd seldom been out of her thoughts, try as she would to convince herself that he meant nothing to her.

The next few days were a bustle of preparations for the departure of the cast of *Little Women* but the girls found time to return to Holton for a brief visit. Dora had completely changed her tune and insisted on Sarah accompanying her to church so that she could show off her talented daughter. Sarah basked in the adulation and Louise looked on with amusement. She would never fathom her stepmother out.

Stanley was proud of his daughter too and, as they walked home from church along the promenade, he confided in Louise that he'd always known she would "go places".

"But what about you, my dear? Do you wish you were going with her? It's not too late to change your mind," he said.

"Sarah doesn't really need me any more and I have my own life to live."

"What will you do with yourself now? I know Dora thinks you've no need to work but you're not one to remain idle. Would you like to carry on working in the theatre?"

"I was offered a job but I turned it down. I'd like to stay home for a while, perhaps help you in the office, or help Mother with her church work."

"You mustn't spend your life looking after us, you know. Besides, you'll meet a nice young man, get married . . ."

Louise smiled. "Maybe, one day." How could she tell him that the only young man she was interested in hardly knew she existed? Thoughts of Andrew fled as she realized that even this short stroll along the seafront had brought a blue tinge to her father's lips.

Sarah and her mother had reached home and were waiting impatiently for them to catch up. Indoors, Louise took her father's coat and urged him to sit down while she fetched a glass of water and the phial of pills.

Dora had already gone into the dining room where Polly was waiting to serve their lunch. She called out impatiently and Louise was about to say that Stanley was unwell when he laid a hand on her arm. "It's all right, my dear. I feel better now. Don't let's worry your mother."

Sarah, still bursting with excitement, didn't seem to notice anything amiss and Louise saw no point in worrying her either. The *Queen Mary* was due in at Southampton in a few days and would set sail for New York on 1 September. Sarah and the cast of *Little Women* would be on board.

As they sat down to eat Louise decided not to go back to London. Sarah could do her own packing and travel down to Southampton with her friends. She and her parents would meet her there to see her off.

With Sarah's departure, the house seemed very quiet. Stanley insisted on going to the office and Dora busied herself with her church activities.

Louise, at a loose end, decided to walk along the seafront and then call in at her father's office. It was fine breezy day and she strode along confidently, enjoying the fresh sea air after the smoke and grime of London.

Despite the sandbags piled along the sea wall, it was too nice a day to think about the possibility of war. She concentrated on the sparkle of sun on the waves, the fishing boats bobbing at anchor and the children at play on the sands — until she reached the sand dunes at the end of the promenade and heard shouts. She gasped, her hand at her throat as a group of men in khaki swarmed over the dunes, rifles at the ready. One of the soldiers grinned at her. "Don't worry, miss, just practising."

Her heartbeat returned to normal and she turned away, walking back towards the town. It was real then — the war was really going to happen.

Louise got up on that bright September morning with mixed feelings. Sarah was setting sail for her new life in New York. Although she was excited and pleased for her, she knew her going would leave a huge gap in her own life. She would miss her sister, despite the tears and tantrums.

She went downstairs warily, expecting Dora to be in floods of tears. But she seemed more excited at the prospect of meeting Lucia Lane on board the *Queen*

*Mary*, than by the thought of not seeing her daughter for months or possibly years.

Stanley was already at the breakfast table listening to the wireless. He looked up when Louise came in and she was pleased to see that he looked a lot better.

"They're evacuating the children from the big cities today. I've just heard that a large group is being sent here."

Louise gasped. "So it's really happening."

"I'm afraid so." He stood up. "I'll go and get the car out."

"I thought we were going by train."

"Impossible, today of all days. The trains will be crowded with children. And they're recalling the reservists so there'll be soldiers and sailors as well. It'll be chaos. Best to take the car."

Louise was unhappy about her father driving and wished she'd taken the opportunity to learn. However, she didn't want to worry him by expressing her concern.

She sat at the table and started on her breakfast. "Mother's so excited about seeing Miss Lane," she said.

"Anything to take her mind off saying goodbye to Sarah. I don't think it's fully sunk in yet that we may not see her for a very long time." He patted Louise's shoulder and left the room.

When Dora came in, her face was flushed with excitement. "I don't think I can eat a thing," she said, sitting opposite Louise and proceeding to butter several slices of toast.

Louise smiled. How much easier her stepmother would be to live with if she were always like this. But inevitably, once the ship sailed, her mood would change and she would sink into self pity, wondering how her daughter could leave her, or she would start to blame Stanley and Louise for encouraging her.

On the way to Southampton, the signs of impending war were everywhere — in the towns, sandbags piled against public buildings; in the villages, groups of lost looking children with gas masks round their necks and labels tied to their coats; and as they drove past Portsmouth, the mass of battleship grey vessels moored in the Solent.

Louise had a hollow feeling in the pit of her stomach and she glanced at her father. He gripped the wheel silently, staring at the road ahead. Beside him, Dora didn't seem to feel the tension, chattering brightly as if on a day out.

Her excitement lasted until the last goodbyes were said and the visitors were ushered off the great ocean liner. As they stood on the quayside waving it finally sank in that Sarah was really going. A tear slid down her cheek and she clutched Stanley's hand. "Our little girl," she sobbed. "What will become of her?"

Stanley patted her shoulder and raised his eyebrows at Louise. "Nothing's going to happen to her. She's going to have a wonderful time. And she'll be safer away from here."

Dora wouldn't be comforted and she continued to snuffle into her hankie as they returned to the car.

148

Stanley tried to reassure her but Louise lost patience and got into the back seat, ignoring her stepmother and staring out of the car window. She began to wonder how the coming war would affect the people of Holton Regis. She didn't really remember much of the last war but surely that had all taken place across the Channel. Did the authorities really fear mass bombing or an invasion? She thought of the groups of frightened children they'd passed, torn from their homes and families. Perhaps she could do something to help, possibly join one of her mother's church groups. They were sure to get involved in some sort of war work.

They were almost home when the car came to an abrupt halt. Louise leaned forward, wondering why they'd stopped. Her father was hunched over the steering wheel, while her stepmother gave frantic little cries. "Stanley, what is it? Speak to me."

Louise jumped out, pulled open the driver's door and leaned in. She grasped Stanley's shoulder, easing him gently back against the seat. His face was grey and his breathing erratic. He clasped his chest and his face contorted with pain.

"Father, please, don't die," she whispered, wiping the beads of sweat from his forehead with her handkerchief. "Where are your pills?"

"Top pocket," he gasped.

She tipped one out and placed it under his tongue, holding his hand and murmuring words of comfort. Beside him, Dora was still weeping but Louise ignored her.

After a few moments the colour began to return to Stanley's cheeks and he turned his head, attempting a smile. "Just give me a minute — I'll be all right."

"You can't drive like this. I'll go and get help," Louise said.

"Don't worry about me," Stanley said. He gasped and clutched his chest. "Promise me, you'll look after your mother." Sweat beaded his brow and he tried to speak again.

"Ssh, save your strength," Louise whispered. She turned to Dora. "Take care of him. I won't be long."

Dora looked up, crumpling her hankie in her hand. "Don't leave me. I don't know what to do."

"I must get help." Without waiting for a reply, Louise ran to the end of the road. It wasn't far to Dr Tate's house. She just prayed he would be at home.

He came to the door still chewing and she apologized for interrupting his meal, gasping out what had happened. He grabbed his hat and bag and called out to someone that he would try not to be too long. His car was parked outside the house and Louise climbed in, giving directions to where she'd left her father.

The doctor stopped behind Stanley's car and, as they got out, Dora came towards them.

"Hurry, please," she said.

Louise leaned into the car and took her father's hand. His breathing was more ragged than before and he gasped as he tried to get words out. "Promise me, Lou — promise." He gripped her hand with surprising

**150**

strength. "You will look after Dora, won't you? She's not strong."

"I promise," Louise sobbed, as tears rolled down her face. "Just till you're better . . ."

Dr Tate put his hand on her shoulder. "Let me . . ." he said, moving her gently aside. He loosened Stanley's shirt and placed the stethoscope on his chest.

After a few moments he looked up and shook his head. "I'm so sorry," he said.

Dora began to sob, her wails reaching a crescendo as Louise put her arms round her and tried to comfort her. But who will comfort me, she wondered?

# CHAPTER
# ELEVEN

The announcement that the country was now officially at war with Germany came two days after Stanley's death but it made little impact on the Charlton household.

Louise, numbed by grief, hadn't been able to cry for her father, going through the myriad things that had to be arranged in a state of shock.

George Tate had been a tower of strength, contacting the undertakers on her behalf and helping her with the wording of the telegram to Sarah on board the *Queen Mary*, although so far there'd been no reply.

Dora's friends from church had gathered round and there were constant comings and goings at Steyne House. Louise was glad of the distraction, not only for herself but for Polly, who seemed much calmer when she was kept busy making tea and refreshments for the visitors.

As expected, St Mark's was packed for the funeral. Stanley had been much loved and respected in the small town. His closest friends, fellow church wardens and business associates had been invited back to the house where Louise and Polly had prepared a buffet of sandwiches and cakes before leaving for the church.

After speaking to as many of their guests as possible, Louise was tired and irritable. If only they'd all just go, she thought, leaning against the newel post at the foot of the stairs. From the packed drawing room came the buzz of conversation punctuated by an occasional laugh. The laughter jarred and she wanted to shout at them to stop.

She should rejoin their guests but she couldn't face anyone at that moment. Taking a deep breath she decided to give Polly a hand in the kitchen. As she started down the passage, a voice spoke in her ear. "Are you feeling all right, Miss Charlton? These occasions can be very draining, as I know too well."

"Oh, James. You startled me." She put a hand to her face. "I'm perfectly all right. I just needed a moment to myself that's all." She tried to walk away but James Spencer laid a hand on her arm.

"I know how you feel." He sighed and his mouth turned down at the corners. "It was the same when I lost my father. I just kept expecting him to walk in the room any moment."

Louise understood and she nodded. "I don't know what I'm going to do now. There's so much to think about — my stepmother, the business . . ."

He took her hand and spoke softly. "Don't worry about all that now. The business can get along by itself for a while. And remember, if there's anything you need, I'm there. You only have to telephone or call in at the office."

Louise tried not to show her surprise. She hadn't thought James Spencer so sensitive. She remembered her father's earlier misgivings about him taking William's place in the firm. Perhaps she'd misjudged him. He was still holding on to her hand and, as she tried to pull away, he gripped it more firmly. "Don't forget — any time," he said.

She forced a smile and said, "Thank you, James, that's very sweet of you. Now, I must go and see about that tea."

After she'd spoken to Polly, she returned to the hall where several guests were getting ready to leave. She steeled herself to smile and thank them for coming and was about to close the front door when the doctor came out of the drawing room. "I must go too, my dear. Patients to see," he said, as she handed him his hat. He turned to someone behind him. "You remember my nephew, Andrew, don't you?"

Louise felt the colour rise in her cheeks. "Of course I do. Thank you for coming, Doctor." She hadn't noticed him at the funeral. But then, she'd been too wrapped in grief to really take note of who was there.

"It was good of you to come," she said. "I didn't know you were in Holton."

"I've been here a week and I should have called before," he said. "But I've been busy organizing things for these poor children from London."

Louise knew that hundreds of evacuated children had descended on Holton in the past week but she couldn't imagine what it had to do with Andrew.

Dr Tate beamed. "My nephew has arranged for the patients from his clinic to come to Holton. He's

154

persuaded the authorities to take over the old dance hall as a hospital."

The remains of the former Winter Gardens theatre and dance hall had remained empty since the fire but Louise remembered her father mentioning the scheme at dinner the night before they'd gone down to Southampton. She'd thought then that it was hardly a fit place to house sick children.

Andrew seemed to read her thoughts. "It's not ideal but they'll be safe from the bombing. The dance hall was hardly damaged in the fire and I've had an army of volunteers scrubbing and cleaning. We've also had some of the equipment brought down from London."

"Does that mean you'll be staying in Holton?" Louise asked.

Andrew shook his head. "I'm afraid not — much as I'd like to. I have other patients who can't be moved. And if there is any bombing I'll be needed there."

Louise swallowed her disappointment and managed a smile. "I expect you'll need volunteers. I'd be happy to help."

"Thank you. But I'm sure you have plenty to occupy you at present. Maybe later you can have a word with my uncle. He's going to oversee the project for the time being." He shook her hand and followed his uncle out to the car.

When they'd gone Louise took a few moments to compose herself. She wasn't sure how she felt. Delight at seeing Andrew once more warred with the feeling that she was wasting her time mooning over him. What was it about this man who popped in and out of her life

155

so fleetingly? And why did he continue to haunt her thoughts, especially as he always seemed so anxious to return to London after speaking with her? Once more, Louise wished she was more like her half-sister and could laugh and flirt and pretend she didn't care.

Reluctantly, she returned to the drawing room where the solicitor was waiting to read her father's will and Dora was still playing the grieving widow.

Her stepmother looked up as she entered the room. "Oh there you are," she said. "I was just saying to Mrs Howard that I don't know what I'd do without you." She raised her handkerchief and sniffed delicately. "Now that my dear Stanley's gone and Sarah is so far away . . ." She allowed a tear to roll down her cheek and Mrs Howard patted her hand.

"You are so fortunate in having a devoted daughter to care for you," Dora's friend said.

"Stepdaughter," Dora muttered and Louise's cheeks began to burn.

When the church ladies had left, Louise sat beside Dora to hear what David Webster, the solicitor, had to say. But the legal words washed over her and her thoughts kept straying back to Andrew Tate and the turmoil of emotions he always aroused in her.

After the solicitor had gone, she began helping Polly to clear away the used cups and plates. As far as she could tell from the little she'd absorbed of the will, Dora had been well provided for and James would run the business. If she'd been a son she might have been given a share. She tried not to feel bitter as a vision of the future rose in front of her and she wondered if it was too late to take up Phil's offer of a job at the theatre. After all, with Father and Sarah gone, there was nothing to keep her here. But then she remembered her promise to her father — a promise she felt duty-bound to keep.

The last cup had been washed and put away, the remains of the food disposed of and Polly sent up to bed. Louise, exhausted emotionally and physically, was ready for her own bed but she decided to look in on her stepmother. Dora had retired to her room as soon as everyone had gone, demanding her smelling salts, her pills and cocoa and biscuits.

Hoping she was already asleep, Louise opened the door quietly. Dora sat up and beckoned her inside. "Sit down, dear. We need to have a little chat."

Louise sighed inwardly. "Can't it wait till morning?" She was already beginning to wish she hadn't made that promise.

"I just wanted to thank you for all you've done these past few days, dear. I don't know how I would have got through it without you." She held out a hand and patted the bed beside her.

It was so unlike Dora to give praise that Louise gave an involuntary smile and sat down, taking her stepmother's hand. "I only did what any daughter would do," she said, pushing aside the memory of that barbed reminder that she was only a stepdaughter. Besides, she'd done it for her father, not Dora.

"Nevertheless, dear, I'm grateful." The older woman leaned back against the pillows and closed her eyes, a little sigh escaping her lips. "I suppose you'll be going back to London now," she said. "Sarah told me you'd been offered a permanent job at the theatre." She sighed again. "I'll be all alone then — Sarah off to America, you in London . . . Well, you young people have your own lives to live I suppose."

Guilt smote Louise and for the first time she noticed the threads of grey in the blonde hair, the lines around her mouth, the veins standing out on her hands. Dora had always seemed young for her age, and had worked hard at keeping the years at bay. Now, faced with the threat of a lonely future, she seemed to have aged overnight. I'm not the only one grieving, Louise realized.

She patted Dora's hand. "I'll stay as long as you need me," she said. "Go to sleep now; we'll talk in the morning."

As she went along the passage to her room, Louise wondered what she'd let herself in for. She undressed and got into bed, firmly telling herself that the theatre job had probably already gone to someone else. Besides, if she stayed in Holton, there'd be plenty to keep her busy now that the country was at war. She would volunteer to help at the children's hospital she decided, thrusting aside the thought that it might be an opportunity to see more of Andrew Tate. He was sure to come down from London now and then to oversee his project.

But, as she fell asleep, it was James Spencer who crept into her thoughts. Why had he been so nice to her? Had he really changed that much?

★　★　★

When Andrew had said goodbye to his uncle, who was anxious to get back for evening surgery, he'd walked slowly down towards the seafront. He knew he ought to get back to the hospital but he needed time to think.

He walked along the esplanade, remembering earlier visits to Holton — in particular that windy day when he'd bumped into the Charlton sisters. Most men would have gone for the lively, pretty Sarah, but from the moment he'd first seen her it was Louise who had captured his heart. He'd been so relieved when he heard that she had turned down the chance to go to Africa. Now, it seemed someone else was courting her and he cursed his reserve and the fear of rejection that had stopped him making his feelings known. He'd been determined to speak to her the next time he came to Holton but her father's funeral was hardly the place to suggest a date.

Supervising the removal of the children from the East End clinic had been his first visit to Holton in over a year. He'd read in the newspaper that Sarah had sailed on the *Queen Mary* the day before and when his uncle greeted him with the news of Stanley Charlton's death, his first thought had been one of sadness that someone he liked and respected had died with his daughters both out of reach. But Uncle George had said Louise was with him when he was taken ill.

"You told me she was working in the theatre," Andrew had said, remembering how he'd felt when he'd heard. If only he'd known when he'd gone to the show a few weeks ago. Now Uncle George was telling him she was back in Holton.

**159**

"She'll be going back to London after the funeral I suppose?" he asked.

"Dora Charlton wants her to stay here. Now she hasn't got Stanley to run around after her . . ."

"I hope she doesn't let herself be talked into staying."

George Tate's next words hit him like a physical blow. "She only went to London to be near her sister. I think she might stay — at least I'm sure young James Spencer is hoping she will."

"How does she feel about that?"

"How would I know?" George asked with a grin. "You'd better ask her yourself."

But Andrew hadn't been able to overcome his natural reserve and had put off calling at Steyne House. His uncle had gone on to say that Dora would be pleased if a match between James and Louise meant keeping Charlton and Spencer in the family.

He hadn't seen Louise until today. Now, as he went down the steps onto the beach, he re-played in his mind the scene he'd witnessed in the hall at Steyne House. James and Louise had seemed more than friendly.

He picked up a pebble, throwing it violently into the heaving surf. Another followed it with equal force. With an angry exclamation, he kicked at a tangle of seaweed and a short laugh escaped his lips. How was it that where his work was concerned he exuded confidence, but when it came to falling in love . . . ?

When Louise woke early the next morning she regretted her hasty promise to stay in Holton. She and her stepmother had never really got on and, without her father there to keep the peace, she knew she'd find it hard to bite her tongue. But Father had made her promise to take care of Dora and she couldn't go back on her word.

Besides, she'd turned down the theatre job and given up the lodgings she'd shared with Sarah. And could she really abandon Dora so soon after her loss? Despite her selfishness, she'd been really fond of Stanley as well as depending on him for everything. She wasn't the sort of woman who would manage on her own.

With a sigh, Louise got dressed and went downstairs to find that Polly had already prepared Dora's breakfast tray. "I'll take it up," she offered. Poor Polly had enough to do. Louise hadn't realized quite how hard the girl worked and she wondered if perhaps she should engage someone to help her.

Upstairs, Dora was sitting up in bed, her face gleaming with cold cream, a lacy bed jacket round her shoulders. Louise set the tray down and drew the curtains, letting in a burst of sunshine. She looked out of the window towards the beach and the sparkling sea. "It's a lovely morning, Mother. Perhaps we'll go out for a little walk later on."

Dora put her hand to her chest. "I couldn't possibly go out. I feel much too weak. I've been awake all night with dreadful palpitations."

"I'm sorry to hear that. I had a restless night, too. It's understandable after what we've been through lately." Louise poured the tea and set the tray across Dora's knees. "Here's your breakfast. You'll feel better for something to eat."

"I don't think I can . . ."

"You must keep your strength up." Louise hated speaking in platitudes when what she really wanted to do was give her stepmother a good shaking. Dora wasn't the only one grieving. She hadn't once expressed any sympathy for Louise or for her own daughter and how she must be feeling after getting the telegram on board the *Queen Mary*.

Poor Sarah, she thought. What a shock for her. And how hard it must be, knowing she couldn't get back to England for the funeral. But what would be the point of her coming back now?

Steeling herself to hide her impatience with Dora, she said, "Try to eat a little, Mother."

As she left the room Dora picked up a piece of toast and began to nibble at it. But when Polly brought the tray down later, hardly anything had been touched.

Louise was sitting at the kitchen table making a shopping list and she looked up to ask, "Do you always take Mother a breakfast tray?"

Polly looked surprised. "Yes, the master always said he liked a bit of quiet in the mornings to read his paper." She gave a little sob. "I used to serve him in the dining room. The mistress never came down till after he'd left for the office."

Louise remembered that they'd always sat down to breakfast as a family before she and Sarah had gone to live in London. There had been a lot of changes since then. She resolved that if she were going to stay, things

**162**

would have to change even more. When she was a child they'd had Cookie and a daily woman as well as Polly. It was too much to expect one person to look after this big house and run about after its inhabitants as well. Well, for a start there'll be no more running up and down stairs with trays, she resolved.

As she finished her breakfast, Louise began to make plans. Before she could do anything about engaging extra help in the house she would have to investigate their financial situation. Her father had been adamant that they could not replace Cookie after her accident and they had let the gardener go as well, but that had been during the slump. There'd also been a few problems after the fire but Louise was sure that business had improved recently. She wished now she'd listened more carefully when David Webster was explaining the ramifications of her father's will. She would have to make an appointment to see him. But first she'd go to the office and speak to Miss Baines or James Spencer.

She walked briskly through the town to the offices of Charlton and Spencer, barely acknowledging the greetings and condolences of the many people who had known her father. She walked up the steps and pushed open the door to the foyer, expecting see Miss Baines at her usual post. Instead, it was James who looked up from opening the mail that was piled on the secretary's desk.

"Miss Charlton — Louise — I didn't expect to see you today." He stood up and came towards her, taking her hands and leading her to one of the comfortable

**163**

chairs set in the bay window. "What can I do for you?" His tone was solicitous and he patted her hand.

The gesture was too much for Louise and the tensions of the past few days erupted in a storm of tears. She snatched the handkerchief James offered her and tried to apologize, sniffing and shaking her head. "It was just — being here. I suddenly realized I'd never see Father again." She burst into tears again.

Gently, James put his arm round her, easing her out of the chair and leading her into her father's old office. "Sit here for a minute. I'll get you a drink of water."

He left her alone and she tried to compose herself, taking a few shaky breaths and wiping her eyes. She straightened her shoulders and stood up, taking a few paces around the room, looking at the framed photographs on the walls — buildings her father had designed, a picture of him with William Spencer and the mayor. Seeing his beloved face smiling down at her almost brought tears once more. But she was distracted by the sound of raised voices from the outer office.

When James returned, his face was red and his voice tight. "That woman's getting too big for her boots. I kept telling your father he was giving her too much responsibility. She's just a secretary, here to take orders."

Louise wondered what the inoffensive Miss Baines could have done to make James so angry. "My father relied on her a great deal, especially after your father died," she said.

"But he didn't need to when I took on my father's share of the work." He paced the room, muttering. "I

**164**

can't have her poking her nose into private papers." He stopped abruptly and caught Louise's eye. "Client confidentiality, you know," he said.

"I'm sure Miss Baines is very discreet."

"You're right." He gave an embarrassed laugh. "I probably overreacted. Things have been getting on top of me since your father . . ."

Louise put her hand on his arm. "I understand. That's why I'm here."

"What do you mean? I thought you'd come in to find out where you stand — with money and so." He gave a little cough. "I know from what the solicitor said yesterday that there are a few legal things to sort out as your father hadn't made a new will after the fire."

Louise vaguely remembered something being said but she brushed it aside. "I meant that I can help with the business. There must be something I can do. Before I went to London, Father used to talk to me about his projects. He wanted me to work with him but Mother was against it. I'm old enough to make my own decisions now."

James shook his head. "I think Mrs Charlton was right. Besides, you don't have any secretarial qualifications do you?"

"I wasn't thinking of being a secretary." Louise was indignant. She might not be a qualified architect or surveyor but she felt she knew just as much about property and estate agency as James did.

"I'm sorry. I didn't mean . . . It's just that it's a bit soon to be making decisions like that. Besides, your stepmother probably needs you more than the business does right now, especially with your sister being so far away."

"Perhaps." Louise nodded slowly.

James smiled. "Let's not think about work right now. I'll take you out to lunch. They do a good roast at the Esplanade Hotel."

# CHAPTER
# TWELVE

When Louise returned to Steyne House, she found Polly in tears once more.

"Oh, Miss Louise, I didn't know what to do. The mistress was in such a state. I didn't know when you'd be back so I phoned Dr Tate." She sniffed. "He's still here."

Louise patted Polly's arm. "You did the right thing," she said, before running up the stairs two at a time.

On the landing she was brought up short as Andrew Tate came out of her stepmother's bedroom. "Oh, it's you," she said, feeling the familiar flush creeping over her face.

"Uncle George was out on a call so . . ."

"I thought you'd gone back to London." Louise tried to calm her racing heart. She hadn't expected to run into Andrew again so soon. "Is my stepmother all right?" she asked.

"She just got herself in a bit of a state. She's finding it hard to cope with your father's death," he said.

So am I, thought Louise, but I don't carry on like that. She bit her lip, ashamed of her uncharitable thoughts. "Are you sure that's all it is?"

Andrew smiled reassuringly. "Positive. She mentioned palpitations and she's sure there's something wrong with her heart. But, really, it's just the stress of the past week. She'll be all right."

"I should go and see her," Louise said.

"Leave her — I've given her a sedative. A good sleep will do her good."

"I shouldn't have left her. I knew she wasn't feeling herself."

"Nonsense, you have to go out some time."

"I didn't mean to be gone so long. But James took me to lunch and we lingered over our coffee. There was so much to talk about."

"I understand. You mustn't feel guilty for enjoying yourself."

Louise wanted to tell him it had been more of a business meeting than enjoyment. But before she could speak he had hurried downstairs and grabbed his hat from the hallstand.

"I have to go back to London tomorrow but if you're worried, my uncle will call round any time," he said.

Louise thanked him and let him out of the front door. He stood on the step for a moment looking towards the sea. "It's hard to believe we're really at war on such a lovely day. I fear this is just the lull before the storm, though. It's a good job we managed to get those children out of London."

"You really think it will be bad then?"

Andrew shrugged. "Let's hope we're being pessimistic. And if nothing else happens, at least this sea air will do wonders for those poor children."

"That's true. I love being by the sea."

"You're going to stay then?"

Louise nodded.

He walked away and, as she watched him go, she wished she were returning to London too. There was nothing here for her. James had made it quite clear that he didn't want her interfering in the business. If she'd accepted Phil's offer of a job in the theatre, she could have returned for her father's funeral and then gone straight back — away from her stepmother's selfish demands and the worry of running the house.

Much as she loved the little seaside town where she'd been born, she realized that, in coming back for good, she was giving up any chance she might have had of the freedom to live her own life.

Polly had calmed down by the time Louise joined her in the kitchen. She sat the maid down at the scrubbed table and spoke firmly. "I know you get upset when Mother's in one of her states, but you must be strong and not let her bully you."

"But she's the mistress. I have to do what she says."

"No, Polly, you don't have to run up and down with trays and cater to her every whim. Dr Tate says she's not really ill and it will do her good to get up and come downstairs. She can't expect you to run around after her. You have enough to do."

"If you're sure, Miss."

"I am. From now on, you take your orders from me." Louise gave a little laugh. "Don't worry, I won't be giving orders as such. We'll share the work."

Polly nodded and managed a tentative smile. "It'll be like when you were a little girl, helping me and Cookie in the kitchen, making cakes and biscuits."

Louise nodded. "Those were happy days, weren't they?" Before Dora came into our lives she added silently. She felt a lump in her throat and got up to fill the kettle.

She turned to Polly. "What brought it on?" she asked, referring to her stepmother's attack of hysteria. "She was perfectly all right when I went out."

"Well, she wasn't best pleased when I told her you'd gone to your father's office. She said it was nothing to do with you and Mr James could manage perfectly well."

"Was that all?"

Polly shook her head. "She'd just got dressed and come down when that Mrs Bennett turned up. She had one of those clipboard things and a list as long as your arm and said she needed to see Mrs Charlton about war work. So I showed her in and went to get some tea."

"I would have thought Mother would be pleased to help." Louise knew Dora loved to be involved in church committees and charities.

"Well, of course, I didn't hear everything but when I came back with the tea Mrs Bennett said something about it being Mrs Charlton's duty to do everything she could for the war effort and she hadn't asked before because of her recent bereavement."

"What did she want Mother to do?"

"Take in some of those poor little kiddies from London. Mrs Bennett is what they call a billeting officer. She has to find places for them to stay."

"And Mother refused?"

Polly nodded. "That's when she got all hysterical. Mrs Bennett left and told me to call the doctor."

Louise couldn't help agreeing with Dora — but for different reasons. Steyne House was no place for a lively child she thought, recalling her own and Sarah's childhood when they weren't allowed to run and play or sing because Mother had "one of her heads".

Still, she wouldn't mind having a child to stay. After all, they had plenty of room. With a short laugh, Louise knew that it would never work. But she resolved to try and persuade her stepmother.

And, if they couldn't have a child to stay, there were plenty of other jobs she could do. She'd offered to help with the children's hospital but now she wasn't so sure. It was obvious from Andrew Tate's cool manner and his eagerness to return to London, that he had no interest in her and it would be embarrassing to keep running into him.

She'd go and see Mrs Bennett to see what she could do to help but first she'd speak to Dora and try to persuade her take in one child at least.

She was sitting in the kitchen having a cup of tea with Polly when Dora appeared in the doorway. She was still in her dressing gown and her hair was unkempt. Her cheeks were flushed and her eyes glittered with a kind of fever. She really did look ill, Louise thought, jumping up in alarm.

**171**

"Mother, come and sit down. Let me get you some tea," she said.

Dora's eyes flashed. "We do not drink tea in the kitchen with servants," she said. "Polly, I've been calling and calling. Bring a tray into the drawing room — now. Louise, come with me."

Before Louise could reply, she had turned away.

Polly jumped up and grabbed a tray but Louise stopped her. "I'll do it. Finish your own tea."

She was furious as she realized it was not illness but temper that had caused Dora's flushed cheeks and glittering eyes. Surely she could see that poor Polly was worn out. It wouldn't hurt her to get her own tea for once. She took the tray into the drawing room and set it on a low table beside her stepmother's armchair.

"Mother, you shouldn't speak to Polly like that. She may be a servant but she has feelings."

"Oh, the girl's impossible. Can't do the simplest things and she's getting so surly." Dora took the cup and saucer that Louise offered her. "And you make things worse, treating her like a member of the family. We pay her wages and she must do as she's told."

Louise wanted to say that she thought of Polly as family, remembering how she'd looked after her when she was a child. She had been with them for over twenty years and, until Dora had come on the scene, had been, if not like a mother, at least a big sister to the lonely child Louise had been. It was no use, though. Her stepmother had got used to having someone to order about and was anxious to maintain her perceived status as wife of one of the town's prominent businessmen.

So far, the war hadn't made much difference to the lives of the people of Holton Regis. After the flurry of activity in the first couple of months, the gas drills, the sandbags stacked against the main buildings in the town and the threat of rationing, people had started to call it the phony war.

For Louise, life at Steyne House began to revolve round Dora's demands and it was almost as if those months in London had been a dream. She had now begun to realize just how much work was involved in running the big house and she wondered how Polly had managed for so long without any help.

Despite her promise to engage someone else, it had proved impossible. Young girls didn't want to go into service any more. There were far more exciting prospects in the women's services and more money to be earned in the burgeoning wartime factories. How Louise envied them the freedom to choose. She could have left, of course, joined the ATS or the WAAFs, but she couldn't bring herself to abandon Dora.

The letter from her half-sister had arrived two weeks after the funeral, written after her arrival in New York — three tear-stained pages of grief for her father and guilt that she hadn't been with him. "If only I had realized how ill he was, I would have stayed," she had written. She had ended with a plea to Louise to "look after Mother. I couldn't bear to lose her too."

She had written back to say that she would stay as long as she was needed. Now, it looked as if that would be for a very long time. Dora had taken to her bed almost permanently, only coming downstairs to berate Louise or Polly for some imagined neglect of their duties. That was the word Dora used — "duty" — and Louise was beginning to hate the sound of it.

She was doing her best and was grateful for Polly's willingness to work hard. Life would have been easier if Dora would agree to shutting up some of the rooms, to eat in the kitchen and to dispense with fires in the bedrooms. But everything had to be done "properly".

One bitterly cold morning, Polly was filling the coal scuttle to take up to Dora's bedroom. "She says she's not feeling well again," she said, when Louise questioned her.

"Doesn't she understand that the coal has to last?" Louise sighed. "If she has a fire up there it means we have to go cold."

"That don't worry her," Polly said.

Once, Louise would have chided her for her outspokenness, but now she could only agree. Dora's selfishness was becoming more marked and she seemed unable to grasp the inevitable changes that war was bringing to their lives. It was turning out to be the coldest winter for years and already there was a shortage of coal. And now that bacon, butter and sugar were rationed Louise was finding it harder to manage the housekeeping.

She decided it was time to take a firm stand. "There's a fire in the morning room," she said. "If

174

Mother feels cold, she must come downstairs. Fires in the bedroom are a luxury we cannot afford at present."

It was true. Since her father's death Louise had begun to realize just how privileged she had been. Despite the problems caused by the nationwide slump as well as the fire, she'd never really had to worry about money. Since her talk with James Spencer a few days ago she'd had to face up to the fact that the business wasn't doing so well. "The war is bound to make a difference," he'd said. "Who wants to build new houses when they might be bombed?"

"You really think that'll happen?"

"It's the lull before the storm," James said. "Everyone says so."

"But we have the rents from the properties," she said.

"That's only a small part of the business." James had placed a hand over hers. "I don't want you to worry."

Louise was worried, though. And Dora had no idea of the situation, or if she had, she was refusing to face up to it.

# CHAPTER
# THIRTEEN

Sarah sat in front of the dressing room mirror, powder puff in hand. She leaned forward, peering into the glass, wondering where the naïve young girl she had once been had gone. Life here in New York was so different — noisier, brasher, faster — and she loved it.

"My destiny," she whispered.

Since disembarking from the *Queen Mary* all those months ago she'd hardly spared a thought for those she had left behind. Of course, she had wept when she said goodbye to her family on the quayside at Southampton but she'd soon recovered in the excitement of her new adventure. Then the telegram about her father had come and she had cried again. The tears hadn't lasted long. She sternly told herself that there was nothing she could do. She could have gone back — the voyage only took four or five days and she could have telegraphed asking Louise to delay the funeral. But what would be the point? she asked herself. Besides, she had signed a contract and she couldn't let the others down. At least, that was what she told herself.

The show was a success, enjoying rave reviews, especially for the young unknown singer playing the part of Amy. Offers were already flooding in, including one from a top Hollywood producer. She sighed, wondering if the price had been too high. Was starring in films worth what she'd had to do to hold Ralph Beauchamp's interest? She looked at her reflection and pulled a face. She'd learned a lot since that first experience with Steve Forbes and the main lesson had been that, with her looks, men were easily manipulated.

The show had another week to run and then she'd be off, across that vast continent to embark on yet another adventure — that's how she must think of it, an adventure.

A tap on the dressing-room door warned her that she was due on stage.

"Coming," she called and stood up, throwing down the powder puff in a cloud of perfumed dust which settled on the letter lying among the tubes and jars of make-up.

As usual the show finished to tumultuous applause and many curtain calls. Sarah took her final bow, then rushed off stage. She was exhausted and, despite the exhilaration she always felt at the end of a successful performance, she wasn't sorry that the end of the run was in sight. It was time to spread her wings, to tackle something more demanding than the part of the youngest March sister.

As she began to remove her make-up, her hand brushed against the letter. When it had arrived, she'd only glanced at it briefly, unwilling to be reminded that, while everything was going so well for her, the sister she loved seemed to be trapped in a life of boring domesticity. Not that Louise complained of course. But

177

Sarah could read between the lines. Rather her than me, she thought, at the same time chiding herself for her selfish thought.

"I'll write later," she promised herself. "Tomorrow, when I'm not so tired."

But she wasn't too tired to join her friends for a late supper and drink. And in the small hours of the morning, as she tried to sleep, her thoughts reluctantly returned to Holton Regis and the family she'd left behind. It was hard to imagine Steyne House without her father. How were they coping without him? And was her mother really ill? Sarah had long suspected that Dora's famous "heads" were a bid for attention and that Stanley had always indulged her.

Louise had told her she was volunteering at the children's hospital and Sarah was glad she was able to get away from Dora's demands for a little while. She seemed very happy with her "war work", although as far as Sarah could tell nothing much had happened after the first panics about bombs and gas attacks. It all seemed very far away to her.

I'm glad I got away in time, she thought, as she drifted off to sleep. Poor Louise, stupid Louise. Why didn't she stand up for herself, make a life for herself? She could have been married with her own family by now or if, like Sarah herself, she wanted a career, she should have stayed on in the theatre. Now, she was stuck in Holton Regis, an old maid, doing good works and running around after Mother.

★   ★   ★

178

Sarah woke late the next morning, a sour taste in her mouth from the cocktails she'd drunk the night before. Thank God there was no matinee today, she thought, pulling the satin quilt up over her head. But she couldn't get back to sleep.

Rubbing her eyes, she sat up, blinking in the bright sunshine that streamed through the uncurtained window. "Coffee," she muttered, and staggered across to the corner of the room where a sink and a gas ring served as a kitchen.

While she waited for the coffee to percolate, she tipped everything out of her handbag, hoping there was a cigarette left in the packet. As she snatched at it, she caught sight of Louise's letter. As she re-read it, she could tell her sister wasn't really happy despite her efforts to sound cheerful. It couldn't be much fun, looking after Mother with only Polly to help in that great big house, and now there was rationing to put up with as well. At least there'd been no bombs so far, Louise wrote, although being so far from any big city, that wasn't really a worry.

She should have come out here with me, Sarah thought, as she lit her cigarette and took a deep drag. She poured the coffee, adding a generous helping of sugar and sat down at the little table by the window, looking down on the busy streetscape below. So many people, so much noise, so much *life*. If only Louise could see it, she'd realize what she was missing. She stubbed out the cigarette and went to the dresser, scrabbling in the drawers for pen and paper. She'd invite her for a visit. They could travel out to California together. Surely she could leave Mother for a week or two.

But, as she sat down to write, chewing the end of her pen, she realized it would be impossible. The Atlantic liners had all been requisitioned as troop ships and besides, ships were being sunk by U-boats every day. Louise's visit would have to wait till the end of the war, and who knew how long that would be? Perhaps it was just as well, Sarah thought. Much as she loved her half-sister, she knew Louise would not approve of the way she was living now — the drinks, the parties, her relationship with Ralph. In the end she wrote very briefly saying she hoped Mother would be better soon and reassuring her family that everything was going well for her.

She didn't mention that the Hollywood producer wanted her to change her name, or what she'd had to do to ensure a starring part in his next film.

The letter took a long time to reach Holton. When it came through the letterbox, Louise snatched it up eagerly; it was months since they'd heard from Sarah. Standing in the hall, she scanned the single sheet, relieved that everything was going well for her half-sister but disappointed that it didn't contain more detailed news.

A querulous voice came from upstairs. "Was that the post, Louise?"

Louise sighed. "Yes, Mother. I'll bring it up in a minute." She went into the kitchen, lit the gas under the kettle and began to prepare Dora's breakfast tray.

Despite her determination not to dance to her stepmother's tune, she had begun to realize it was easier to give in than to make a stand. Since Polly had left them to work in the Vickers factory in Southampton, she'd had to manage alone.

In a way, it was a relief that nowadays Dora rarely left her room, spending most of the day in bed and only getting up for a short while in the mornings. She didn't come downstairs but sat at the window, watching and commenting on everything, from the amount of time the ARP warden spent in his hut at the end of the road to the shabby look of the Local Defence Volunteers as they drilled along the promenade.

When Louise came up to remove her tray or to help her to the bathroom, she would try to detain her, going on at length about the shortcomings of those who were mismanaging the war in general and Holton Regis in particular. "I'm going to write to the council about it," was her frequent threat and Louise would fetch her notepaper and fountain pen, pleased that she had something to occupy her.

Thank goodness she doesn't come downstairs these days, she thought, glancing round the shabby kitchen where she spent most of her time now. She'd have plenty to criticize here. She finished setting the tray and put Sarah's letter on it.

She settled Dora in her chair, making sure she had her spectacles, pen and paper, and edged towards the door.

"Sarah doesn't have much to say for herself, hardly worth writing at all," Dora said.

"I expect she's busy."

"Too busy to write to her mother?" Dora's voice was sharp. "And why did she address it to you?"

"It's to both of us, Mother. It would be silly to write separate letters."

"I suppose so." Dora sighed. "I'll have to write back, though I don't know what I'll say. You shouldn't have told her I was ill. I don't want her worrying."

"Why not tell her about the Red Cross parcels? She'll be reassured if she knows you're well enough to do war work."

In an effort to keep Dora occupied and to stop her from dwelling on her imagined ill health, Louise had enlisted the help of Mrs Howard, who was in the WVS. Since Dora refused to get actively involved, Mrs Howard had provided wool and needles and persuaded her to knit socks and scarves for the troops. It hadn't really worked; often Louise came into the room to see her stepmother gazing out of the window, her knitting idle in her lap.

"I don't really feel up to doing anything today." Dora crumbled her toast and pushed the plate away. "I can't eat this. Isn't there any bacon?"

"Mother, you know it's rationed now. We've had our share for the week." Louise didn't tell Dora that she'd eaten her ration as well.

"I don't understand it. Surely we produce bacon in this country. I can understand rationing stuff that comes from abroad but —"

"It's to make things fair and to stop people profiteering from the war, Mother," Louise said. "Now,

**182**

are you sure you have everything you need. I have to go out in a minute."

"Do you have to? I hate being alone."

"Yes, I do. It's war work, Mother. We all have to do our bit." She closed the door and ran downstairs with a sense of freedom. Three hours away from the house, away from Dora's whining, three hours doing the work she had come to love.

She walked out into the fresh spring morning with a smile on her face, her shoulders back, her step light, as if a burden had fallen from her shoulders. She loved her work at the children's hospital and was pleased that she'd dismissed her earlier misgivings.

Her good mood almost evaporated as she recalled the contents of Sarah's letter. Surely she could have said more about the Hollywood offer and when she would be leaving New York? Still, she knew from experience that the hours at the theatre were long and tiring and she supposed they were lucky to have received a letter at all.

She'd write back tonight, tell Sarah about Alfie and her voluntary work. She wasn't sure if she'd mention her growing friendship with James, though. She didn't want Sarah reading too much into it. She wasn't even sure herself if friendship was the right word.

She crossed the road and entered the former dance hall that had escaped the worst of the fire. It had remained boarded up for years while the council tried to decide whether they should find a use for it or have it demolished. For some time it had been used as a furniture warehouse and when Dr Tate had suggested using it as temporary hospital for the children from London, there had been some opposition. But his nephew had gathered a band of volunteers who had put up partitions, installed plumbing and painted the building inside and out.

The wall that faced the sea across the stretch of grass was now almost entirely glass and the children's beds faced the windows. It was the first time some of them had been exposed to so much light and sunshine and they thrived on it.

Louise smiled and waved, getting waves in return. She entered by the side door, leaving her coat in the cloakroom.

"Good morning, Miss Charlton. Lovely morning, isn't it?" Matron said, getting up from her desk.

"What would you like me to do today?" The real nursing was done by the staff who'd come down from London with the children. But Louise had shown herself willing to do anything to help, whether it was feeding a child too sick to hold a spoon, cleaning up after them or simply comforting a child crying for its mother.

Most of the patients weren't really ill. They'd been brought to Andrew's East End clinic suffering from a variety of ailments, many of them the result of poverty and malnutrition. In the past the parents had often been reluctant to send their children away to convalesce. With the coming of war Andrew, with the backing of the government's mass evacuation plans, had persuaded them that the seaside was the best place for them.

Now, after several months of good food and sea air, Louise was delighted to see the pale under-nourished children beginning to bloom.

"I wondered if you'd like to take little Alfie Briggs out in his wheelchair as it's such a nice day. He's a bit down this morning," Matron said.

"Any particular reason?" Louise had grown fond of Alfie, although she told herself sternly that she didn't have favourites.

"His friend Susie went back to London yesterday."

"Back? Is she well enough?"

"She's much improved. When her mother turned up saying there's not going to be any bombing and that she's needed at home we couldn't refuse." Matron sighed, "I wish the doctor had been here. He might have been able to persuade her to let Susie stay."

"Why is she needed at home?" Susie was eleven and Louise knew that often older children were needed to look after their smaller brothers and sisters. But Susie's two brothers had been evacuated to Somerset.

Matron coughed. "Well, Mrs Tyler's in a certain condition and she'll need Susie when the baby comes."

Louise nodded. What a burden for the poor child. Her own discontent with her lot seemed trivial when she considered what hard lives some of these children had. "I expect Alfie will miss her. A walk along the prom might cheer him up. I'll be back in time to help with the lunches," she said.

Alfie's pale narrow face lit up when he saw Louise pushing the wheelchair towards him. "We goin' aht then?" he asked.

She bundled him up in his outdoor clothes and tucked a blanket around him. "It's sunny, but the wind's cold," she said. "Right, off we go."

She pushed the chair along the promenade, enjoying the wind in her hair and the taste of salt on her lips. Two Royal Navy destroyers were a grey smudge on the horizon but even that reminder of the war couldn't dampen her spirits on such a beautiful spring day.

She started to sing. "Oh, I do like to be beside the seaside," and Alfie joined in. When they got to the words, "the brass band plays . . ." Alfie stopped. "But there ain't no brass band is there, Miss?"

"There will be, one day. When the war's over, they'll put the flags out and there'll be bands playing and everything."

Alfie was silent and Louise stooped down to look into Alfie's pinched face. His eyes were bright with unshed tears. "Will it really be over one day," he asked. "Will my dad come back?"

"I'm sure he will. And you'll go back home and be with your family again."

Alfie sniffed. "I want to be with my family, but I don't wanna go back to London. I like it 'ere — beside the seaside." He grinned suddenly. "P'raps me dad can get a job 'ere, when he gets out of the army."

"That would be nice," Louise said, smiling. She continued along the promenade daydreaming as she often did of a future in which she saw herself as a married woman, and it wasn't a wheelchair she was pushing but a pram with her own child in it. She knew it was the life she wanted. She wasn't like Sarah with her longing for fame and fortune. Not that it was likely to happen unless she gave in to James and accepted his proposal. He loved her, he'd said so many times and couldn't understand her reluctance to commit herself. How could she tell him that in her daydreams it wasn't his face that filled her thoughts but that of Andrew Tate?

She shook her head at her foolish thoughts. Andrew was out of reach. But she would never marry James. Better to be a spinster than to marry for the wrong reasons.

Alfie's reedy voice interrupted her thoughts. "'Ere, is that a real gun, Mister?"

Louise came back to the present, smiling as the man bent down to answer the little boy and show him the rifle.

As he started to explain how it worked, Alfie's face grew animated and he turned to Louise. "When I'm better, I'm gonna join the LDV. I'm gonna have a gun too."

"'Course you will, son," the man said, smiling sympathetically over the boy's shoulder at Louise as she tucked the blanket round him.

"Better get back," she said. "Matron will kill me if we're late for lunch." She thanked the man for his kindness and walked away, swallowing a lump in her throat. Despite his brave words, she thought Alfie would probably never be strong enough to fulfil his ambition.

As they neared the hospital, she caught a glimpse of James turning a corner. She was glad that he hadn't seen her. He'd recently expressed concern that she was getting too fond of the children in her care, especially young Alfie.

"I'm only thinking of you," he'd said. "They'll all have to go home eventually. I just don't want you being upset."

Louise sighed. He was right. Already, it was hard to imagine her life without Alfie and the other children. Matron had said something similar only the other day. But she loved volunteering at the hospital and, besides, what other war work could she do, tied as she was to her stepmother? She couldn't join the forces or go to work on the land as so many of her old school friends had done. Even Peggy, who'd married her naval lieutenant, had joined the WRNS and was now stationed in Portsmouth.

# CHAPTER
# FOURTEEN

When she had finished her shift at the hospital, Louise reluctantly returned to Steyne House, steeling herself for the usual barrage of complaints she knew would await her. As the querulous voice floated down the stairs, she wondered whether James was right in thinking that she indulged Dora's whims too much. "If you weren't there, she'd have to get her own meals ready," he'd said.

But Louise couldn't bring herself to abandon her stepmother. She'd promised her father that she would look after her and she meant to keep that promise.

Ignoring Dora for the moment, she went into the kitchen and tried to decide what to cook to tempt her stepmother's appetite. She'd left some sandwiches for her before she went out, but she would want a proper meal later on.

Louise wasn't hungry herself, having already joined the children for a substantial meal of steak and kidney pie before settling them for their afternoon nap. She counted herself lucky that since meat had been rationed earlier in the month she was able to take some of her meals at the hospital.

Feeding Dora, who was so fussy, had become a nightmare. She seemed incapable of understanding that the foods she loved were simply not available. Since her marriage to Stanley she'd never wanted for anything and had become used to having her demands met.

Louise had become tired of explaining and often now she would just take the tray in and put it in front of Dora without a word, leaving the room with the excuse that she had heard the telephone ringing or had left something on the stove.

This time she didn't need an excuse. As she opened the larder door and inspected the contents, there was a ring at the door. She opened it, expecting to see Mrs Howard or the vicar, who often called to see how Dora was.

She was startled to be confronted by James. "Why aren't you at the office?" she asked.

"I had to call on a client near here," he said with a smile. "Besides, do I need an excuse to call on my best girl?"

When she hesitated, he smiled and said, "If you're busy I'll come back later."

"No — it's all right, I've just got back from the hospital. Come in, James. I was just about to go up to Mother, but she can wait."

"Ah, taking my advice then?"

"What do you mean?"

"Not running up and downstairs after her."

"That's not very nice. You know she's not well." But despite her protests, she knew James was right. Hadn't Dr Tate often told her that her mother wasn't really ill?

But she couldn't take the risk. She already felt guilty enough for not taking sufficient notice of her father's ill health.

James didn't reply and she showed him into the drawing room. There was no fire in the grate and it was chilly despite the spring sunshine filtering through the net curtains. "Do sit down," she said. "I'll bring some tea in a moment."

"Can't Polly do it?"

"She's left us — gone to work at Vickers. Didn't I tell you?"

"I remember now. Can't you get someone else? You can't manage alone, surely." He paced the room, rubbing his hands together.

"There's a war on, James — or had you forgotten? All the young women are off in the forces or the factories. Besides, I'm managing very well, thank you."

He took her hand, running his fingers over the rough skin. "I'm sure you're very capable. But I worry about you. I don't like to see you ruining your hands with housework and looking so tired all the time."

"It's nice of you to be concerned, but I'm all right."

"Of course I'm concerned. I want to take care of you — if only you'd let me." He pulled her towards him and kissed her — a soft gentle kiss.

She leaned in to him and laid her head against his chest. Just for a moment she felt it would be nice to be taken care of, to have someone help her shoulder the burdens of running the house and looking after her stepmother. But was James really the one to do it? She resolutely thrust the thought of Andrew away and smiled up at him.

"Do you really mean it, James?" she asked.

"You know I do. Marry me and your troubles will be over." He grinned down at her, that cheeky, little boy grin which had always disarmed her.

"I'll think about it," she said.

He laughed aloud and picked her up, swinging her round and almost knocking over a small table.

"Put me down, James," she squealed, and laughed too, her face flushed.

A loud banging from upstairs silenced them. "Mother," Louise gasped. "I'd better go up and see what she wants."

James's lips tightened but he let her go without saying anything.

Outside Dora's bedroom door, Louise paused for a moment, smoothing her hair and taking a deep breath.

"What's all that noise?" her stepmother asked. "I thought the bombing had started."

"It's all right, Mother. I just bumped into the table."

"I heard voices. Is James here? Why don't you bring him up?"

"He only popped in for a minute." Louse felt herself blushing. "Let me tidy you first and then I'll send him up. Do you want something to eat?"

"Is there any cake?"

"I'll see." Louise helped her stepmother to sit up and propped the pillows behind her. She tidied her hair and handed her the small mirror.

Dora regarded herself critically. "Some lipstick I think. Must look my best when a young man comes visiting." She gave a girlish giggle. "Not that he's here to visit an old woman. We know what he's here for."

Louise's blush deepened and Dora smiled knowingly. "Fetch him up then," she said.

James was not in the drawing room when she went downstairs and she wondered if he'd got impatient and left. Part of her wished he had. She was already regretting her impulsive reply to his mention of marriage. Would he infer that "thinking about it" meant she was taking him seriously? She should have said an emphatic "no" and she would do just that next time she saw him.

She crossed the hall to the kitchen, jumping back in alarm as the door to the cellar opened and James appeared carrying a bucket of coal. "I thought I'd light the fire for you. It's still very cold for the time of year," he said.

"That's kind of you. But we don't have a fire in there unless we have company."

"What am I then?" His sharp voice belied the grin.

"You know what I mean. It may not be rationed like so many things but it is in short supply. We have to ration ourselves. I need to keep the range going in the kitchen as well as the fire in Mother's room. She doesn't come down these days. I spend most of my time in the kitchen anyway."

James put the coal scuttle down and put his arms round her. "My poor darling. I didn't realize things were so difficult for you." He looked into her eyes. "Never mind, that will all change once we're married."

Louise's stomach lurched but she managed a smile. So he'd been serious then. She must speak up before it was too late. "James . . ." She struggled to find the right words, but before she could speak, her stepmother's voice floated downstairs.

"James, where are you?"

Louise sighed and said, "You'd better go up. She loves having visitors." She gave him a gentle push. "Go on. I'll make some tea."

"I'd rather stay down here with you — even if we do have to drink tea in the kitchen," he said.

"Mother will get upset if you don't go and say hello," she said.

He turned away reluctantly and mounted the stairs.

Louise leaned against the kitchen counter as she waited for the kettle to boil, wishing she'd spoken up. As she laid the tray and took the cake out of the tin, she wondered what it would be like to be married to James. She pictured a neat villa — not too big — on the outskirts of Holton. Far easier to manage than this warren of a house with its high ceilings and cold, unused rooms. They couldn't sell it of course. It had been left to Dora for her lifetime.

Surely they could afford one of those nice houses out on the Chichester road though. Business might be slow but James still had the money from the sale of his parents' house. After his father's death he'd moved into a small bachelor flat. Well, they certainly couldn't live there. Perhaps they ought to wait till the war ended.

**194**

Business would pick up then and they'd be able to afford a nurse or companion for Dora.

The relief at the thought of handing over the responsibility to someone else, of not having to listen to that shrill voice every day, made Louise think more warmly of James than she had up till now. It might not be the life she had dreamed of but it could be a good life, she thought. Perhaps she would accept him after all.

The whistle of the kettle brought an end to her daydreams and she filled the teapot and picked up the tray. As she carried the heavy load upstairs she heard laughter from her stepmother's room and the deep rumble of James's voice. She stopped abruptly, her foot on the top step. What had she been thinking of? She couldn't marry James. She was fond of him, but she didn't love him. How could she marry one man when another still held a place in her heart?

If she couldn't have Andrew she would never marry. She would stay in this gloomy old house and look after her stepmother as she'd promised her father she would. And she would fill her empty life with caring for those poor neglected children in the hospital up the road.

She put the tray down on a small table on the landing and opened the bedroom door.

James was sitting on the bed holding Dora's hand and smiling. He jumped up as Louise came in and took the tray from her, setting it down beside the bed. Before she could pour the tea, Dora spoke.

"James tells me congratulations are in order, my dear. I'm so pleased for you both. Your father would have been so happy."

"Charlton and Spencer — a real family firm," James said, taking Louise's hand.

Louise went cold and pulled her hand away. "But, Mother . . ." How could he?

Dora flapped her hand. "I know, I know. You wanted to tell me yourself. But James is so happy, he couldn't wait to break the news."

It was so rare to see Dora animated and flushed with pleasure that Louise couldn't bear to spoil her mood. She would speak to her later — after she had told James her decision. She didn't think Dora would be quite so happy once she realized that Louise would be moving out of Steyne House and leaving her with a paid companion to pander to her whims.

James had long gone and Dora was asleep having taken a pill to calm her palpitations after all the excitement. But Louise could not sleep.

Despite several tentative efforts on her part, she hadn't been able to voice her doubts. Dora had been so excited at the thought of a wedding she'd quite forgotten her aches and pains and had begun to make plans at once. James had joined in with enthusiasm and Louise had sat by, unable to say a word.

The final straw was Dora's triumphant announcement. "And you won't have to worry about finding somewhere to live," she said.

"But James's flat —"

"Don't be silly. You can't live there. James will move in here, of course." Dora waved a hand round the room. "We'll have to make some changes but you can have this room and James can have your father's old room as a dressing room. I'll move into the large guest room. We never have guests so . . ."

James had taken her hand, smiling into her eyes. "Don't you think that's the perfect solution, darling?" he said. "I wouldn't dream of taking you away from your home and family."

Perfect for him, maybe. Perfect for Dora, Louise thought, as she turned over in bed and gazed at the ceiling. They had both looked so pleased with themselves, almost as if they'd planned it all between them while she was still downstairs.

But what about me? What about what I want? The headache that had been building all evening tightened its steel band round her forehead and she closed her eyes as a slow tear slid down her cheek. She thought of Sarah, wishing she were here to talk it over with. There was no one else; her old school friends were either married with their own families or had left to join the forces.

She'd write to her sister tomorrow, she thought. It would help if she put her thoughts down on paper. Whether she would send the letter was another matter. She knew what Sarah would say — that she was lucky to be getting a chance at marriage instead of being doomed to spinsterhood; as if marriage was the only option for women these days. Look at Sarah with her glamorous life in Hollywood. Louise had never really been jealous of her sister, but as she drifted off to sleep, she wished she'd taken the opportunity to go with her and start a new life.

When Louise woke the next morning she still had a splitting headache. Her throat was dry and all her limbs ached. She tried to sit up, telling herself it was the result of her sleepless night. The sun streaming through the partly opened curtains hurt her eyes and she fell back on the pillow with a groan.

She made another attempt to rise but as she swung her legs out of bed a bout of nausea overcame her and she just made it to the bathroom in time. As she staggered back to her own room, she heard Dora calling. Ignoring her, she flopped onto the bed and closed her eyes.

It seemed only a moment before she was forced to open them, to see Dora standing over her, face white with fury.

"Didn't you hear me calling?" she demanded.

Louise answered with a groan and closed her eyes against the glare from the window.

"Are you ill?" Dora's voice changed as she put a hand on Louise's forehead, only to snatch it away immediately. "You're burning up. I'll have to call the doctor."

Louise winced as Dora's shrill voice demanded that Dr Tate come at once. She kept her eyes closed as her stepmother came back into the room, trying to shut out the noise of her bustling around, tidying up and muttering as she did so. "I knew no good would come of it — working in that hospital. Who knows what nasty germs and diseases those children brought with them."

Louise felt the bile rising in her throat and frantically tried to get up. Dora was there with the china bowl from the washstand and Louise tried to smile her gratitude. Dora shook her head, an expression of distaste on her face. "If you're going to be ill, we'll have to get a nurse in," she said. "I can't cope with this in my delicate state of health."

Not as delicate as mine, Louise thought with grim humour. And that was her last conscious thought before she descended into a black hole of pain, nausea and delirium.

# CHAPTER
# FIFTEEN

Louise wasn't sure what was real and what was hallucination brought on by the fever.

James was there, and a pretty woman she half-recognized. Old Dr Tate and his nephew featured in her waking dreams. Dora never came near but Louise thought she heard her voice — complaining or, more often, demanding.

As the fever abated and she began to take notice of her surroundings, she was able to sit up for short periods and to hold a glass of water to her lips without spilling it. She still slept for long periods and when she tried to get up her legs felt weak.

One morning she opened her eyes to see a young woman in a nurse's uniform sitting beside the bed, cool fingers on her wrist as she took her pulse. As she struggled to sit up, the nurse gently pushed her back on the pillow and held out a thermometer.

"I think you're back to normal now but we'd better just check," she said with a warm smile.

Louise lay back and studied the young woman, the one who'd appeared alongside Andrew Tate in her delirious dreams. She recognized her now — Nurse Faversham from the children's hospital — the one whose eyes followed Andrew with the devotion of a puppy. Just as mine do, she thought ruefully. But is he as unaware of her as he seems to be of me? she wondered.

She swallowed painfully as she tried to speak and Nurse Faversham held a glass to her lips. She took a sip and moistened her cracked lips. "What are you doing here? I don't need a nurse. It's just a touch of flu. Surely you're needed at the hospital."

The nurse smiled. "You've had more than a touch of flu, Miss Charlton. You've been very ill. Mrs Charlton couldn't nurse you herself and Matron said I could be spared from the hospital. Besides, the doctor was worried about your mother catching the fever.

"He's a good doctor. He's looked after me since I was a baby."

"Not him. I mean young Dr Tate. He's called in every day to check on you." Nurse Faversham giggled. "Lucky you, having two handsome young men fussing over you."

So Andrew was here, Louise thought, smiling. It wasn't just a dream.

"Your fiancé was so worried about you," the nurse said. "Wish I had a young man who cared for me like that."

"My fiancé?" Louise was confused until it came rushing back to her — James and her mother making plans while she just sat there, dumb, trying to ignore the pounding of her head. She didn't remember actually accepting his proposal. Had she really agreed to marry him? Was it too late to change her mind? She covered her confusion by asking for another drink of water.

"I think you might get up for a while today. You can sit in the chair by the window. It's a lovely day. I don't think you're strong enough for a bath yet so I'll fetch some water for you." Nurse Faversham chattered on while Louise tried to remember exactly what had been said before she had fallen ill.

"I expect Mr Spencer will call in later." The nurse settled Louise into a chair and tucked a blanket round her. "There, I'll just comb your hair for you. And you'd better put this bed jacket on, it's a bit chilly, but your mother said you like the window open and Doctor says fresh air is good for you." She helped her to put on the pretty pink jacket with its silk ribbons and stepped back with a smile. "There, you look so much better — even got some roses in your cheeks. Mr Spencer will be so pleased you're on the mend." She giggled again. "He's so sweet, isn't he? Not many men would take on a mother-in-law as well as a bride. You're so lucky," she said again and gave a little sigh.

Louise gazed out of the window and didn't reply. Sweet wasn't the word she'd apply to James. He was good company and, although he insisted he didn't need her help in the office, he didn't try to put her down when she voiced her opinions. She couldn't deny that she enjoyed being seen on the arm of a good-looking young man and that he was becoming an asset to the family business. But he could be moody and, more worryingly, he had a tendency to be extravagant.

202

The nurse was still fussing around her but Louise ignored her, busy with her own thoughts. She must speak to James as soon as possible. She couldn't let this situation go on.

Gazing out of the window towards the sea she was distracted by shouting from the direction of the pier. "What's going on?" she asked, sitting upright in her chair.

"They're putting another gun in place," said Nurse Faversham.

"Gun?"

"Yes. They've already put one up by the bandstand. It's to be manned night and day — in case of invasion."

"Do they really think . . .?"

"Oh, I forgot. You wouldn't know. So much has happened while you've been ill." The nurse took a deep breath. "It's quite frightening really. Ever since they brought the army back from Dunkirk, we've been expecting it. And being so near the coast . . ."

"Now, now, Nurse. Stop scaring our patient." The door had opened and Andrew came in. "Good to see you sitting out, Miss Charlton. A great improvement. You had us worried for a while there."

Louise's heartbeat quickened but she managed to smile. "I'm feeling much better. A little tired though."

"Only natural of course. Be careful not to overdo it." He beckoned the nurse and they held a conversation in low voices.

Louise tried to ignore the way Nurse Faversham gazed at him adoringly, hanging on his every word. She turned away to look out of the window once more, noticing now the tangles of barbed wire along the beach, the concrete blocks placed at intervals. And what had happened to the pier? She heard the door close and turned round. Andrew came towards her and sat down.

"I've sent her to the chemist for your medicine. Now, you must take it easy for a while, get your strength up. Young Spencer will never forgive me if you're not fit for your wedding."

"Wedding?" Her heart sank. He thought she was getting married. She wanted to tell him it was all a mistake — not that he cared, of course. But she had to speak to James first.

As if in answer to her thought there was a tap at the door and James put his head round. "Can I come in?" Without waiting for a reply he strode across the room, bent and kissed Louise's cheek and thrust a huge bunch of tulips at her.

Andrew stood up. "Good morning, Spencer. Good to see the patient on the mend, isn't it? I must be off." He turned to Louise. "Actually I came to say goodbye. I have to go back to London today but I had to make sure you were really over the worst. My uncle will keep an eye on you. And Nurse Faversham is yours for as long as you need her. She's an excellent nurse, don't know what we would have done without her."

Louise thanked him and he shook hands with James and turned to go. At the door he paused. "I'm sorry I won't be here for the wedding. Look after her, won't you, Spencer?"

★  ★  ★

Andrew paused on the landing to collect his thoughts. What a fool he'd been not to have made his feelings clear before now. The sight of James Spencer hovering over Louise, kissing her, bringing her flowers, brought a bitter taste to his mouth. Of course he wanted her to be happy, should be pleased she'd found someone to love. If only it was some other man; he couldn't stand James Spencer and not solely because he had a place in Louise's affections.

His uncle had no time for the young man either and had confided only the other day that it was a good job William had died when he did, before he could find out that his son was a spendthrift and a gambler. Andrew was sure that no such rumours had reached Louise. If they had, he was sure that she would never have been swayed by his charm. She was far too sensible to tie herself to a scoundrel.

But they say love is blind, he thought, as he started downstairs. And there was no denying James was a charming young man, as well as being in charge of the family business.

As he reached the front door, Dora came along the hallway. "Just off, Doctor? Won't you stop for some refreshment?"

"I'm sorry, Mrs Charlton. I have to catch the London train."

"Will you be back for the wedding?"

Andrew shook his head. "I've already given my apologies. I have neglected the London clinic for far too long."

Dora's lips tightened. "I don't know how you can work in such a place. And bringing those children down here with their dirt and germs . . ." She gave a little shudder. "I'm sure that's how poor Louise caught the fever."

"You may be right, Mrs Charlton."

"There, you see. I knew it. I never should have allowed her to work in that hospital."

Andrew kept his temper with difficulty. "Miss Charlton is a grown woman, perfectly capable of deciding for herself." He was tempted to say more but he picked up his hat and opened the front door.

As he left, Dora said, "Well, I'm sure James will put a stop to it once they're married."

Poor Louise, he thought as he hurried towards the station. What sort of a life would she have with those two? Why hadn't she stayed in London when she had the chance?

Well, at least she still had a life, he thought, thanking God that she'd recovered from the fever that had almost killed her. His prayers for a patient had never been as fervent as those he'd said at her bedside every day for the past three weeks.

As the train steamed through the lush green countryside he couldn't stop thinking about Louise, cursing the reserve that had prevented him from making his feelings known when he'd first fallen in love with her. But that one bad experience years ago had left its mark and he had vowed never to be taken in again.

His first encounter with the Charlton family had brought it all back. In Dora Charlton's manipulative character and Sarah's blithe assurance that everything would go her way, he had seen echoes of Celia and he had determined not to get too involved with the family. But he had soon realized that Louise was different. She was quiet and serious, with a keen sense of duty to her undeserving and demanding family. But he'd seen flashes of a dormant sense of fun in her relationship with her sister. How he wished he could have been the one to bring out that light-heartedness — the person he thought of as the real Louise.

He tried to tell himself it was nothing to do with him how she lived her life and he truly hoped she would be happy. If only he could be sure that she'd really fallen for James Spencer and wasn't, as he suspected, being pushed into the marriage by her manipulative stepmother. Dora was delighted at the match and had mentioned more than once how nice it was that, although the founders of the firm were no longer with them, Charlton and Spencer would live on, the two families joined in marriage.

Andrew couldn't believe that Louise would let herself be pushed into something she didn't really want. He'd always admired her devotion to her family, but she wasn't a doormat and he knew she was capable of standing up for herself.

He sighed and stood up as the train crossed the bridge over the Thames and steamed into Victoria Station. He pushed his way through the crowds towards the Underground, noticing the number of men in uniform milling around. It wouldn't be long before the soldiers recently rescued from Dunkirk would be off again to fight on another battlefront. He just hoped that the fight wouldn't be on English soil this time and once more his thoughts were drawn to Louise and the vulnerability of her home on the south coast.

The word "invasion" was on everyone's lips and his heart gave a little lurch at the thought — not just for Louise but for the children and staff of the hospital in Holton. He plunged down the steps, in a hurry now to return to the clinic where he was due to discuss plans for moving the children away from danger. His personal concerns would have to take a back seat for a while: the children were his first priority.

# CHAPTER
# SIXTEEN

What have I let myself in for, Louise asked herself as she was swept along in the preparations for her forthcoming marriage. Still weak from the debilitating fever, she couldn't believe that her stepmother, aided and abetted by James, had gone ahead and booked the church. Hymns had been chosen and flowers ordered without any attempt to discover her preferences.

She was seated in her chair by the open window, still trying to convince herself it had been part of her delirium, when Dora came into her room clutching a swatch of material.

"There's just your dress to be made now," she said excitedly. "I thought this cream satin was nice. What do you think?" Without giving Louise a chance to reply, she continued, "And what about bridesmaids? I thought I'd leave that to you, dear."

Too weak to protest, Louise shook her head and closed her eyes. Pity she didn't leave everything else to me, she thought. How could they have done this to her? And what was the rush? She really needed more time to think about it.

Dora was still talking. "Louise, I know it has to be a quiet affair because of your father . . ." A small sob and a dab at her eyes with a handkerchief. "We're still in mourning after all." Her voice brightened. "But you must have a bridesmaid. What about Peggy?"

"Peggy's joined the WRNS — I don't suppose she can get leave," Louise said. "Anyway, I don't need bridesmaids." With that, she realized that things had gone too far for her to back out. But there would still be no escape from Dora's demands. At least with James moving into Steyne House she would be able to keep her promise to her father and look after her. James seemed genuinely fond of Dora and, Louise hoped, would help her to deal with the older woman.

"You must have at least one, Louise. It would look odd." Dora was still harping on about bridesmaids.

"I'd have Sarah, if she were here. As it is . . ." She closed her eyes again.

Defeated, Dora stood up. "I can see I'm tiring you. I'll leave you to rest and think about it."

When she'd gone, Louise sat up and a slow smile spread over her face. She would have a bridesmaid and Dora would just have to accept it. She would pick one or two little girls from the hospital. Some of them were now convalescent and would have been sent home were it not for the war. They would love to dress up in party clothes.

It was a shame that Sarah couldn't be here though. Louise stood up, still a little unsteady on her feet, and fetched writing paper and a pen. She would write to her sister. Dora had probably already told her about her illness and the forthcoming wedding, but only to Sarah could Louise pour out her true feelings.

**210**

Sarah was on the set having her make-up repaired. She'd been so lucky to get a starring part so early on in her film career and she intended to make the most of it. She stared into the mirror, amazed at the different girl who looked back at her. No longer the demure young Amy from *Little Women*, her dark curls were now a smooth platinum bob. Her figure had filled out over the past year and the low cut gown revealed what her lover, Ralph Beauchamp, called teasingly her greatest assets.

It was thanks to Ralph that Sally Charles, as she was now known, had hit the headlines in her first film. He had introduced her to Hollywood, coached and groomed her for her minor role in a B western, made sure her publicity photos reached the right places. And now, here she was, her name above the title on all the posters — "Sally Charles in *The Sultan's Treasure* — a story of passion and intrigue". Sally was the name chosen by Ralph who had deemed "Sarah" rather dull for a rising star.

Perhaps it wasn't quite how she'd pictured her new life in America but she wouldn't change a minute of it. It was as if her early life in Sussex, her time in the London theatre, had happened to someone else. Only when a letter arrived from her half-sister did she think of Louise, pitying her dull life and lost opportunities.

But the letter she'd received today had her worried. She tossed her head and smoothed her hair, pushing the make-up girl away.

"That'll do," she said, standing up and deliberately erasing thoughts of her far away family. She must concentrate, remember her place on the set, her lines, the gestures to accompany her words. Nothing must interfere with her performance.

It wasn't until the following day that she retrieved Louise's letter from her bag and read it properly. She'd only skimmed through it earlier, relieved that because Louise had written herself she must be fully recovered from the mysterious fever that had kept her bedridden for so many weeks. She hadn't taken in the fact that her half-sister was really getting married — would probably already be a bride by the time the letter arrived. And to James Spencer of all people.

What was she thinking of? Sarah knew that there'd been talk of an engagement. Her mother was all for it. But, knowing how her half-sister felt about Andrew Tate, she'd never dreamed that Louise would settle for second best.

Filming over for the day, Sarah settled back on the velvet daybed in the luxury apartment furnished and paid for by Ralph Beauchamp and began to read her sister's letter.

I should be happy. James was so attentive when I was ill. He was here every day and Mother says he was devastated when they thought I might die. He brings me flowers and chocolate. And he swears on his life that he will do everything he can to make me happy. But I can't really forgive him or Mother for arranging everything when I was still too ill to have any say in the matter.

When I protested, Mother said it gave them something to hang on to while I was ill. By planning for the future James was able to convince himself that we actually had a future. But Sarah, I don't even remember accepting his proposal.

I must have done, mustn't I? What reason could James have for tricking me into marriage? After all, it isn't as if I have any money to speak of. He says he loves me and I must believe him.

My dear sister, I can never tell anyone but you and I know you will respect my confidence. I don't love him. I've never said I did. You know who my heart belongs to. But he has never indicated that he feels the same about me so why should I remain single, waiting and hoping? I want a home and a family of my own.

Poor foolish Louise, thought Sarah, turning the page and ignoring the twinge of conscience as she remembered what she had done to achieve her own dream. She read on.

Which brings me to another thing. James is going to move in to Steyne House so that I can still look after Mother. I had hoped we would have our own home. Still, the consolation is that with James around he will help to brighten up the gloom. He has the knack of making Mother smile and forget her imagined ills. That fact alone is enough to resign me to making the best of things.

Dearest Sarah, how selfish you must think me, to write so much about my troubles. Not a word of congratulation for landing the starring role in your next film, of how proud we all are in Holton Regis of our local girl made good. We are eagerly anticipating the arrival of *Guns at Midday* at the Picturedrome and catching a glimpse of you. It hasn't reached Holton yet. They closed all the places of entertainment at the outbreak of the war but soon realized that people need something to take their minds off the current situation. I won't bore you with all the things we have to put up with now — the blackout and rationing etc. Just be assured we are all quite safe. As the posters say we are "keeping calm and carrying on".

Suffice to say Mother and I will be first in the queue at the Picturedrome when it arrives here.

Sarah reached the end of the letter, then turned back to look at the date, realizing that it had taken so long to reach her that Louise was now Mrs Spencer. It wasn't like her sister to be so open about her feelings and Sarah was sure there was more to it than she had revealed. Remembering James as she'd known him when they were still children, she felt sure that Louise was doing the wrong thing. He could have changed, of course. He was running the business now and everyone seemed to think he had grown up and accepted his responsibilities. Sarah wasn't so sure. She just hoped she was wrong. Anyway, even if she'd had any hope of getting Louise to change her mind, it was too late now.

The door opened and Ralph came in. She put the letter to one side and stood up, her satin housecoat falling open as she moved towards him. The reply to Sarah would have to wait.

Louise's wedding was not the happiest day of her life. Right until the last minute she'd been on the verge of backing out. But the fact that contact with James would be unavoidable in such a small town, never mind the family business connection, steeled her to go through with it. She couldn't bear the thought of the scandal that would ensue, not to mention Dora's hysterics and the inevitable recriminations.

It was easier to go through the motions and tell herself that many people married for convenience. She was sure that some of the couples she knew had never really been in love. Respect and security were just as valid reasons to marry.

There were no bridesmaids after all, much to Dora's chagrin. But Louise was spared a fight over inviting the children from the hospital. Since the evacuation from Dunkirk and the subsequent fear of an imminent invasion, the children's hospital had been closed. Those who were fit enough had gone home, while the more vulnerable, including young Alfie, had moved inland. Andrew had been able to requisition a small country house on the other side of the Downs near Midhurst.

The move was taking place on her wedding day and Louise was sad that Alfie couldn't be there. Andrew had sent a note saying that the boy was still not fully recovered from the illness which had struck many of his patients as well as Louise herself. Dora had been right. The infection had been brought in by a new patient.

Louise hadn't seen Andrew since his short visit after her illness, for which she was thankful. Dora had invited both him and his uncle to the wedding but, to her relief, he'd sent a cool little note of refusal. His wishes for her future happiness had cut her to the heart. Now she was certain he didn't care for her except as a friend, otherwise he would surely sense her reluctance to marry James.

The service at St Mark's passed in a blur. Louise made her responses in a low voice and her hand shook as James placed the ring on her finger. When they turned to make their way down the aisle, her knees trembled and James gripped her arm firmly.

At the hotel she could scarcely eat. Old Dr Tate, who had given her away in lieu of her father, sat beside her. He smiled reassuringly. "You were right to insist on a quiet do," he said. "You're still not fully recovered." He lowered his voice. "I've had a word with young James — told him you're still quite delicate."

Louise felt the blush rise up her neck to her cheeks. She knew what he meant. It was something she'd been trying not to think about.

At last the reception was over and the few guests took their leave. Dr Tate drove Dora and the newlyweds back to the house so that Louise could get changed. Petrol rationing and restrictions on travel meant they couldn't go far afield for a honeymoon and Louise would have preferred to stay home. But she found the idea of spending the first night of her marriage so close to her stepmother embarrassing and she'd agreed to a couple of days away.

James said it was to be a surprise and Louise, although she didn't really care where they went, was

**216**

dismayed when she realized their destination. She had hoped that perhaps he was taking her to a small village with a quaint old inn.

"Why Brighton?" she asked.

"I know you love the seaside, my dear," he replied, turning to smile at her. "There's more to do here. I've booked a room facing the sea. You'll love it."

We might as well have stayed in Holton, Louise thought. She didn't care for Brighton, a bigger, brasher version of her home town. As they drove along the road parallel to the promenade, signs of war were visible. The beautiful Palace Pier, which had been extended only a few years before, now showed huge gaps where it had been partly demolished to deter landing craft. Concrete tank traps and coils of barbed wire littered the beach and there were notices forbidding access. Manned gun emplacements at intervals underlined the very real fear of the threat from across the Channel.

Louise wasn't interested in the brash entertainment the resort had to offer and could see no point in being at the seaside when you couldn't walk along the beach or swim in the sea. Not wanting to disappoint James, though, she tried to hide her dismay.

As the car drew up in front of the hotel he was grinning. "Not like dreary old Holton is it?" he said, leaping out and standing with his hands on his hips. "I love this place."

The commissionaire hurried forward to take their bags and Louise slowly got out of the car. Her stomach churned with apprehension as she followed James into the foyer and her hand shook as she signed the register, faltering as she remembered that her name was no longer Charlton.

In their room, she glanced around indifferently while James prowled around examining their bathroom, opening wardrobes and drawers. Suddenly weary, she sat on the window seat and closed her eyes against the sparkle of sun on sea.

James gave a muttered exclamation and she opened her eyes to see him picking up the house telephone. She was about to say she would like tea when he spoke, loudly and angrily. "The bath hasn't been cleaned properly. It's not good enough."

"James, what's the matter?"

He waved a hand to silence her. "I don't want excuses," he shouted into the phone. "Send someone up immediately." He slammed the receiver down. "Disgraceful. It never used to be like this."

"Have you stayed here before then?"

James hesitated. "I just meant that standards in general are slipping."

"I don't expect they can get the staff now. Everyone's either been called up or volunteered for war work."

"It's easy to blame the war. But —"

A knock came at the door and a timid maid appeared carrying cleaning materials.

"In there," James barked. "And make sure you do a good job this time." He followed her and stood by the door watching as she scrubbed at the bath.

Louise gazed out the window, hot with embarrassment. She'd had no idea that James was so fastidious. She thought about Polly who had been willing if sometimes a bit slapdash. What would James have thought of her housekeeping skills? Thank goodness the poor girl no longer worked for them. She hoped he wouldn't be too critical of her own standards. Cooking and running around after Dora, as well as her voluntary work, left little time to worry about the layers of dust in the seldom used rooms of Steyne House.

With a pang she remembered that the hospital had closed and she no longer had a job. When she was fit again she'd have to find something else to do for the war effort until she was called up. She had avoided being drafted into the forces so far due to having a relative to care for and the fact that she was already working at the hospital. But there were rumours that married women would soon be required to work in factories, on the land or in the forces. Besides, if James was called up and had to go away she'd need something to fill her time.

"That'll do." James's voice roused her from her thoughts and she stood up as the maid scuttled out of the room.

"I think I'll have a bath before dinner. I got so hot and sticky in the car." She took her wash bag out of her suitcase.

"Aren't you going to unpack? I thought you'd have done it by now."

"I want a bath and a change of clothes first. There's plenty of time. We are on holiday after all," Louise protested.

"All right. But I don't like a mess. Hurry up then. You can do it while I'm in the bathroom."

As Louise lay in the scented water she wondered how many other men would have worried about unpacking or cleaning the bath on the first day of their honeymoon. Where was the romantic James who had wooed her with chocolate and flowers?

She sighed and told herself he was probably as tired as she was. After all, he had worked hard while she was convalescing, supervising the removal of his belongings from the bachelor flat, rearranging the rooms at home, as well as going in to the office each day.

They would have a leisurely meal in the dining room, perhaps a quiet stroll long the seafront, then back to the hotel. Her mind shied away from picturing the next scene. She wasn't a naïve young girl. She knew what to expect and she tried to reassure herself that everything would be all right.

A loud knock on the bathroom door startled her and she sat up, splashing water over the edge of the bath. She climbed out and wrapped herself in the towelling bathrobe that hung behind the door. "Just coming," she called.

When she opened the door James pushed past her. "You took your time. And just look at the mess."

"Have your bath, James. I'll clean up afterwards."

"I told you, I don't like mess."

Louise's lips tightened. "I said I'd do it afterwards. I'm going to get dressed now and unpack." She turned her back and he grabbed her arm, swinging her round to face him.

She flinched at the look on his face and he quickly let go, giving a shamefaced smile, like a naughty schoolboy caught out in some mischief. "Sorry, darling. I'm a bit on edge. Tired, I expect."

Louise forced a smile. "Me too. Do you want to go down for dinner, or shall we order room service?"

He pulled her towards him and kissed her cheek. "We'll go down. I'll feel better after freshening up."

He closed the bathroom door and Louise finished drying herself and put on a fresh blouse and skirt. She brushed her hair and, although she didn't usually use much make-up, she decided a little rouge would improve her looks. She was still very pale after her illness and she wanted to look her best.

James must have thought so. Before they went down to dinner he looked her up and down, smiling. "My lovely bride," he said, tucking her hand into his arm.

During dinner he seemed to have recovered his usual happy-go-lucky manner, laughing and teasing her, paying compliments and raising his glass to toast his "lovely bride". As they ate dessert he took her hand, caressing each finger in turn. Too soon, the meal came to an end, but as they stood up to leave the dining room, James said, "That bloke over there's been giving you the eye all evening. I've a good mind to go over and give him a piece of my mind."

Louise clutched his arm. "Oh please don't. I'm sure he doesn't mean any harm."

"Maybe." James pursed his lips and his hand came up to wipe some of the rouge off her cheek. "Perhaps he wouldn't have noticed you if you hadn't plastered your face with this stuff."

Louise was shocked and for a moment she wasn't sure how to respond. She gave a little sob. "I made myself up for you, James. I wanted to look nice for you." She must have said the right thing. His hand fell to his side and he leaned forward to kiss her cheek.

"That's all right then," he said.

"Shall we go up?" Louise's voice was steady although she was trembling inside.

"You go, darling," he said. "I'll just have a nightcap and follow you later."

She smiled and turned away, pleased at the respite. His swift changes of mood had unnerved her. He'd never behaved like this before. Was it just tiredness or nerves? Was he as anxious as she was about the coming night?

She undressed slowly and removed her make-up, listening for James's footsteps. After half an hour she got into bed, eyes straining towards the door. Eventually, tiredness overwhelmed her and she slept.

The room was in darkness when she woke with a start, feeling a weight on her body, hands fumbling at her nightdress. She started to struggle until, fully awake, she realized it was James — her husband.

"James, stop, please . . ." she said.

"You should have waited for me. It's our wedding night. How could you fall asleep?"

"But Dr Tate said . . ." Louise had thought James would give her more time. She had never dreamt that he would leap on her like an animal while she slept.

"Sod that old buffer. What does he know? You're my wife so . . ." He grabbed at her breast, twisting her nipple.

Louise gasped and bit her lip.

"There, you see, I knew you liked it really."

Louise did not like it; she endured it. It was nothing like she'd imagined. Where was the romance, the love? At last he was satisfied and he rolled away, falling into a deep sleep almost immediately. She didn't sleep at all, staring into the darkness and cursing her foolishness for allowing herself to be talked into a marriage without love. She'd convinced herself that liking and respect were enough. Too late she realized that, after his behaviour tonight as well as earlier in the dining room, she did not even like James, much less respect him.

# CHAPTER
# SEVENTEEN

## 1941

Louise leaned on the sink while she waited for the kettle to boil. She was so tired but she dared not go to bed yet. Dora was already asleep and James was still out. She'd been married for almost a year and she'd never been so unhappy. But she only had herself to blame and she must make the best of it. If only there was someone she could talk things over with. Even if she felt able to confide in Dora, her stepmother would tell her she was being silly. But then, James only ever showed his charming side to her, sitting on the side of the bed, holding her hand and feeding her chocolate.

She could write to Sarah, of course, but her sister must be fed up with her outpourings by now. That's probably why she hardly ever replied to her letters. Louise sighed. How she missed the flighty, fun-loving — if sometimes selfish — Sarah.

If only James had been called up like most of the other young men in the town, she thought, immediately chiding herself for her wickedness. Of course, she didn't want anything to happen to him, but at least she'd have some respite from his carping, his insistence that everything be done his way.

She couldn't imagine what the medical condition could be that had exempted him from military service. He had declined to enlighten her and, although she'd tentatively asked the doctor, he had pleaded patient confidentiality. "You must ask him yourself, my dear," he'd said.

Louise was sure that, like her, the doctor didn't really think there was anything wrong. He had unbent sufficiently to tell her that he hadn't examined James himself. "Your husband visited his own doctor," he said. "Whatever he put on the certificate ensured that he didn't have to go through an army medical."

James certainly showed no sign of illness or disability and since wriggling out of conscription he'd become an air raid warden. He was often away at night, patrolling the town to make sure blackout regulations were enforced or manning the ARP post.

Louise enjoyed the respite his absences gave her but even when he wasn't there she couldn't relax. He often came home unexpectedly as if hoping to catch her out in some imagined misdemeanour. And sometimes he'd invite friends for drinks and cards. They would stay very late, filling the drawing room with smoke and alcohol fumes. It wouldn't be so bad if he let her go to bed. But he insisted she act as hostess, clearing the empty glasses and ashtrays, making coffee and polite conversation.

James would pull her to him, an arm firmly round her waist, laughing and telling his friends what a lucky blighter he was to have married her. At last they would leave, or more often fall asleep at the table and she would creep up to bed, listening for James's step on the stairs.

Daytimes weren't much better. She was constantly on edge, going over the house time and again to make sure everything was tidy and clean. James had an eagle eye for a spot of dust or a stray cobweb. He wasn't violent but there was an underlying menace in his eyes and his cutting words could reduce her to tears. Then he would be all apologies and protestations of love. And that led to something else she would rather not think about.

His assaults on her body in the name of love were only endurable for the hope that they would produce what she most longed for — a child, someone of her own to love. But to her sorrow it hadn't happened so far.

Dora seemed to blame Louise for not producing a son for James. "Most young women are pregnant within the first year of marriage," she said. "I fell for Sarah straight away. A son to follow on in the business would make James so happy."

Louise had spoken to Dr Tate, wondering if there was something wrong with her. His eyes twinkled behind his spectacles. "It will happen when it's meant to, my dear," he said. "That fever last year left you completely washed out. It will take time to get your strength back."

"I'm still so tired all the time," Louise told him.

"Not surprising is it? You're looking after your stepmother and this big house, as well as getting used to married life. Not to mention coping with rationing and all the changes the war has brought. Of course you're tired." He had given her a tonic but she didn't think it was doing any good.

She sighed, glancing at the clock. Would James be home for tea, or would he stay out till all hours? She never knew when to prepare a meal these days.

The kettle boiled but she ignored it, instead sitting down at the table and resting her chin on her hand. She thought about Sarah, wondering why she hadn't replied to her last letter. She's probably busy and the post is so unreliable anyway, she thought. Still, it was months since she'd heard from her and Dora was getting upset too.

Dora was another worry. She rarely left her room and Louise now had to help her to the bathroom and assist her in washing and undressing. Dr Tate had assured her that Dora had no physical illness but, apart from a brief spurt of energy while planning Louise's wedding, she'd gone steadily downhill since Stanley's death. It was as if everything was too much of an effort for her.

Now, as well as tensing for the sound of James's key in the front door, Louise was constantly poised to rush upstairs in answer to her stepmother's frantic ringing of the bell on her bedside table.

It was all too much and Louise dropped her head into her hands and allowed a slow tear to trickle down her cheek. She straightened and scrubbed at her face with a tea towel when she heard the front door open. She wouldn't let James see how weak she was.

She busied herself preparing a tray, hoping he wouldn't come into the kitchen. Although she was listening intently, she jumped when he approached, running his hands down her body. "And how is my lovely wife this evening?" he asked, his words slurred.

She moved away and reached into the cupboard for a saucer. "I thought you might be hungry. Or have you eaten already?"

"I'm hungry, yes — for you, my dear." He made a grab for her and the saucer slid out of her hands to shatter on the tiled floor.

She stooped quickly to gather up the pieces.

"Leave that," he said. "We've got better things to do." He grabbed her wrist and dragged her towards the stairs.

"Please, James. I'm so tired," she protested.

"You can sleep afterwards," he said, pushing her in front of him.

At least it was over soon and James slumped down beside her, snoring heavily and breathing whisky fumes into her face. She turned away, her thoughts in turmoil. Why, oh why, had she not been strong enough to speak up in time to stop this farce? Why had she drifted along hoping everything would be all right? And why had she not realized before that, in spite of his superficial charm, James was a bully who was determined to have his own way? As she had once again discovered, it was useless to try and stand up for herself. She only hoped Dora had taken one of her pills and had remained oblivious to the sounds coming from the bedroom.

Determined not to cry, Louise attempted to console herself with the thought that this time she might be pregnant.

She was woken suddenly by James shaking her shoulder. "Come on, you lazy cow. Move."

She struggled upright, confused as she realized it was morning.

"Just look at the time. I've got to get to the office and your mother's been ringing that damn bell for the past half-hour."

Louise looked at the bedside clock and threw back the covers. "What does she want?" she mumbled.

"How the hell do I know? You'd better get in there and sort her out." James grabbed his jacket and left the room.

As Louise dragged on her dressing gown, he put his head round the door. "I'm having some people round this evening so you'd better buck your ideas up. I don't want you mooning around like a wet week in July."

People — his drinking and gambling friends, no doubt. Why should she put herself out for them? She had enough to do. As if in answer to her thoughts, Dora's bell rang again and a plaintive voice called, "Louise, where are you?"

She went into her stepmother's room and began the morning ritual of getting her out of bed and into the adjoining bathroom. Then there was the inevitable discussion as to whether she should get dressed and sit out or go back to bed.

"Dr Tate said you should get up for a while each day. Besides, it gives me a chance to change your sheets and tidy up." Louise repeated the now familiar refrain.

"What does that old man know? How does he know what I suffer? Time he retired. Why didn't that young nephew of his take over when he had the chance? I don't understand him wanting to work in London, especially with all those bombs."

"He's doing his bit, Mother, working where he feels needed." Louise felt the usual stab in her heart at the mention of Andrew. She tried so hard not to think of him. But since the Blitz had started and the East End of London had been so badly hit, she found he was constantly in her thoughts and prayers. She might never see him again but she really couldn't bear it if anything happened to him.

The morning passed in its usual boring round of housework, laundry and preparing food. Louise sighed when she opened the larder door. As more and more food went on ration it was becoming impossible to put together a meal that would satisfy James and Dora's fussiness. They had each been so used to having exactly what they wanted and they didn't seem to understand that she had to work with what she could get.

She would have to go into town and see what was available. The queue at the butcher's would be long and there might not be anything available at the end of it but at least it would get her out of the house.

After settling Dora in her chair by the window and making sure she had everything she could possibly need, Louise put on her hat and jacket and set off into town. As soon as she closed the front gate her heart lightened and she shook off the oppression that was wearing her down.

The sun was shining and, as usual, she took the long way into town. A walk along the seafront could always lift her spirits. The threat of invasion had receded since Hitler had turned his attention to the Russian front but the dragon's teeth and barbed wire remained in place. But she could still enjoy the sound of the waves sucking at the shingle, the cries of the seabirds. The breeze ruffled her hair and the warmth of the sun brought colour to her cheeks.

Deep inside, she clung to the hope that she might at last be pregnant. The thought brought a smile to her face. She wouldn't think about what had happened to bring about the possibility. On a day like today, she could put James, Dora and even the war out of her mind.

The queue at the butcher's stretched along the High Street and Louise sighed as she joined the end; you couldn't forget the war for long, she thought. The time passed quickly as exchanges of news passed along the queue, coupled with the inevitable rumours and the occasional joke.

As she reached the counter the butcher asked the customer in front of her what she wanted. "Two pounds of fillet steak," the woman said, bursting into laughter at the look on his face.

Everyone else laughed too. "A bit of liver and a couple of sausages, that's all you'll get today, missus," he said, joining in the laughter.

Louise laughed too, envying their ability to make a joke out of such trying circumstances.

The butcher allowed her just three sausages and half a pound of mince — dinner for two days if James didn't spot the sausages and insist on having them for his breakfast.

Busy planning the family meals, she started when someone spoke. "Miss Louise — I'm sorry I should say, Mrs Spencer. How are you?"

Louise turned to see someone in WVS uniform. It was Miss Baines, her father's former secretary. "How nice to see you. How is your mother these days?"

"She died a couple of months ago."

"I'm so sorry, I didn't know." Louise felt guilty. She should have kept in touch. Miss Baines had been such an asset to her father's business. Impulsively, she asked, "Why don't you come and have a cup of tea with me?" Before Miss Baines could answer she shook her head. "No, you don't want to lose your place. Another time, perhaps?"

The older woman glanced at the length of the queue. "It doesn't matter. He'll probably be sold out by the time I get to the front. I'd love to have tea. Where shall we go?"

They found a little café near the library and ordered tea and scones. "This is such a treat for me. I'm usually so busy. I miss the office but things have got better since I joined the WVS. It's good to feel useful," Miss Baines said.

"I'm really sorry you had to leave us," Louise said. "But of course we quite understood that your first duty was to your mother."

"It's true she needed nursing towards the end but that's not why I left," Miss Baines said, looking up from stirring her tea. "You didn't know?"

"I don't understand." Louise busied herself buttering her scone, as she realized James must have dismissed the poor woman. She remembered the time she'd come into the office and he'd been so angry that she'd opened his post.

"Your father relied on me, especially when he was unwell," Miss Baines said. "He trusted me, let me deal with confidential stuff. Mr James didn't like that. I was a secretary and should mind my own business — his words, not mine. When I told him Mr Charlton had made it my business, he got angry with me for standing up for myself."

"But why give you the sack? He did, didn't he?"

"He was just looking for an excuse. When my mother had a bad spell and couldn't be left for a couple of days, he said I was unreliable and he had to let me go." Miss Baines gave a little sob. "I'm sorry," she said, dabbing at her eyes with a lace handkerchief. "It still hurts when I think of all the years I gave to the firm. It was my life . . ."

Louise reached out and patted the older woman's hand. "I wish I'd known. I might have been able to do something. I thought you were retiring early to look after your mother."

"That's what Mr James told everyone. Besides, in the end I was glad to leave. Things weren't the same after your father died and he took over. And Mr James was determined to get rid of me."

"But why? You were the mainstay of the firm. I should have thought James, still being new to business, would have been glad of your help."

Miss Baines gave a small laugh. "He didn't think he needed help — knew it all already." She shook her head. "I'm sorry, my dear. I shouldn't be talking about your husband like this. For a moment I almost forgot that you and he were married."

So did I, Louise thought. But it was a relief to realize that she wasn't the only one to see through James's veneer of charm. They finished their tea and stood up to leave.

"I've enjoyed meeting you, we must do it again, Miss Baines," Louise said.

"Yes, we must — and it's Muriel, please."

"I'll look forward to it, Muriel."

Louise walked away smiling, glad to have found a friend. She'd been feeling so isolated lately with Sarah in America and Peggy down in Portsmouth with the WRNS. She missed them — and her work at the hospital. When she'd mentioned volunteering for some other war work, James had discouraged her, saying she still wasn't fit and she hadn't had the energy to argue.

Now she hurried home feeling much better as she made up her mind to speak to Muriel about joining the

WVS. She might not be able to confide in her new friend as she would Sarah or Peggy but at least she'd have someone to talk to. She gave a little giggle at the thought of sharing with Muriel the sort of confidences she would have exchanged with her sister.

Dora was sleeping when she got home, the sandwiches Louise had left untouched on the tray, an opened box of chocolates on her lap. Where had she got hold of those? Louise wondered. She closed the door quietly hoping Dora would stay asleep while she prepared the evening meal. They'd got into the habit of eating in the early evening before James left for the ARP post.

As soon as she went into the kitchen, her good mood evaporated as she realized where the chocolates had come from. There was an unwashed plate and cup in the sink, crumbs on the table, and a note propped up against the teapot.

*Where were you?* it said. *Back at six. Have dinner ready*. It was signed "J" — no endearments as there would have been a few months ago.

Louise screwed the piece of paper up and threw it in the bin. "Do you have to know where I am every minute of the day?" she muttered, enraged by the tone of the note. And why did he keep giving Mother chocolate? Dr Tate had stressed that it wasn't good for her. He was worried that with no exercise and bad diet her health would deteriorate. But James, as usual, went his own way. When she protested he'd said, "Poor old girl doesn't have much fun in life. I only want to cheer her up."

Louise vented her feelings on the washing up, crashing the crockery onto the draining board.

She looked at the meagre portions of meat the butcher had allowed her: three sausages. James could eat all of those himself. She'd cut them up and make a toad-in-the-hole. That would fill the plates up, together with plenty of potatoes and tinned peas. And, the mood she was in, God help either of them if they complained.

She was furiously beating the batter when Dora's bell rang. As soon as she entered the bedroom her stepmother said, "You were gone a long time. It's a good job James came home. I could have died, left here alone in the house."

"Don't be silly, Mother. You're not going to die. Besides, someone has to do the shopping and there was such a long queue at the butchers." She picked up the box of chocolates and put them out of reach, wondering where James had got hold of them. Like almost everything else, sweets were in short supply and there were rumours that they too would be rationed before long.

"I hope you managed to get something decent for dinner this time. Don't let that butcher palm you off with his rubbish," Dora rattled on, as Louise poured her some water and handed her one of her tablets.

"Did James say why he came home at lunchtime? I wasn't expecting him."

"He said he needed some papers and, besides, he wanted to look in and make sure I was all right." Dora simpered. "He's such a sweet boy. Not many young men would take such care of their mother-in-law."

236

Louise didn't reply. She was sure James hadn't left any papers behind this morning. Was he checking up on her? And why did he feel the need to do so?

The front door bell pealed and Dora patted her hair. "That's probably the vicar. Do I look decent? Go and let him in, Louise. And bring up some cake with the tea if there's any left."

The Reverend Ayling called at least once a week and Louise was always pleased to see him if only because he kept Dora occupied for an hour or two, allowing her time to get on with her chores.

She smiled a welcome as she opened the door, only to feel the blood drain from her face when she saw who was standing there. She grasped the door jamb, unable to speak.

"I'm sorry. I didn't mean shock you," said Andrew. "I hope it's not inconvenient. I've brought you a surprise."

"I thought you were the vicar," Louise said.

# CHAPTER
# EIGHTEEN

Andrew ran a finger round his neck. "No dog collar, I'm afraid. And no stethoscope to prove I'm a doctor." He laughed. "Don't you want to see the surprise?"

Louise nodded.

Andrew went to the front gate and beckoned. "Come out, lad."

From behind the hedge, a boy hobbled towards her on crutches.

"Alfie!" she screamed, rushing forward and embracing him.

As he struggled to free himself she laughed, tears streaming down her face. "Is it really you? How you've grown. And you're walking."

As she ushered her guests into the drawing room Dora's bell rang and she called out. "Send him up, Louise. He's come to see me, not you."

Louise laughed. "She's expecting Mr Ayling."

"I'll go up and say hello — give you time to chat to young Alfie." Andrew bounded up the stairs and as Louise watched him go, her heartbeat returned to normal. It was kind of him to bring Alfie to see her but it seemed he didn't want to spend time with her himself.

Alfie discarded his crutches and sat down. Louise sat opposite him. "I can't believe the change in you. Country air seems to suit you. Tell me how this came about."

"It's all down to the doc. He got one of his doctor mates to take a look at me legs. They put these iron things on to straighten them out. And I've been doing these exercises. That Nurse Faversham — she makes sure I keep them up. And the doc's always ringing her up to see how I'm doing. If it wasn't for them two I'd still be in the chair."

Louise's heart sank at the mention of the nurse who'd looked after her during her illness. She knew the young woman had been smitten with Andrew. Did he return the feeling? She bit her lip. What business was it of hers? She was a married woman — she shouldn't be having such thoughts.

She tried to concentrate on her young visitor. "I'm so pleased for you, Alfie. I expect you'll be going home soon then."

A shadow passed across the boy's face. "Ain't got no home now, miss." He punched the arm of the chair. "Bleedin' Germans."

"Your house was bombed? What about . . .?"

"Me mum and me gran — both copped it. Gran didn't like going down the shelter, see."

His shoulders tensed as he fought back tears. Louise wanted to put her arms round him, but she was sure he'd push her away. She stood up. "I must put the dinner in the oven. Mr Spencer will be home soon."

In the kitchen she too found herself fighting back tears. Poor little Alfie, she thought. It certainly put her own problems into perspective. When she'd finished preparing the toad-in-the-hole and put it into the oven, she poured a glass of milk and put a couple of biscuits on a plate. She glanced at the clock — plenty of time to do the potatoes before James came home.

Back in the drawing room, Alfie had composed himself and he grinned up at her when she handed him the biscuits. "Doc says I'm doing well, but it'll be a while before I can chuck those away," he said, nodding towards the crutches propped against the piano. He took a bite of biscuit and a swig of milk.

"It was very nice of Dr Tate to bring you. Do you like it up at Midhurst?"

"Not bad. It's a great big house — better than the 'ospital here. But I miss our walks along the seafront. It's so quiet in the country."

"I wish I could have come to visit but I'm so busy now with looking after Mother. Will you stay at the hospital?"

"Dunno. Can't go back to London can I? Doc says I can stay there a bit longer but I'll have to go to a foster home later." He smiled up at her. "Wish I could stay here, miss."

Why not? Louise thought. There was plenty of room at Steyne House and, now that he could get around on his own, he wouldn't need nursing. He could go to the school round the corner. Was that why Andrew had brought him here? She was about to agree when a cold thought came into her head. What would James say?

She hesitated. "I'll have to think about it, Alfie, talk it over with my husband."

Disappointment clouded his face. "You mean you don't want me," he said, his voice flat.

"It's not up to me. My husband would have to agree, and there's my stepmother. She's not well you know." Louise couldn't bear the look on his face and she excused herself to go and check on the dinner again.

Left on his own, Alfie pulled himself out of the chair. No point in staying. The doc had got it all wrong. He might have known she wouldn't want him. He'd be sent to some children's home until his dad got back from Africa. That's if he got home at all. Bloody war. He brushed the tears from his eyes.

He hadn't realized until now how much he'd banked on being able to stay here with Miss. He liked Nurse Faversham but he didn't like the way she went all moony over the doc. She was bossy too and he couldn't have a laugh with her like he did with Miss Charlton. Suppose he should call her Mrs Spencer now. He felt a spurt of anger. What did she want to go and get married for when she could have had the doc? He was a good bloke.

Alfie stumbled across the room and reached for his crutches. He picked up the framed photo on top of the piano — an older bloke with two girls. It had been taken on the prom near the bandstand. Miss was laughing, brushing her hair out of her face. The other one must be her sister — the one they said was a film star.

As he put the picture back, his hand brushed the piano keys. They were very dusty. He wondered if Miss ever played. He picked out a few notes, wishing he knew how to play. If he lived here, perhaps she'd teach him.

Daft idea, he thought, crashing his hands down on the keys. The noise masked the sound of the door opening and he flinched as a hand grasped the back of his collar.

"What the hell are you doing in my house?" a voice roared. "How did you get in? Trying to steal something are you?"

Alfie's legs began to shake and he would have fallen but for the hand holding him upright. "No, sir. I'm Alfie. Miss let me in. I'm waiting for the doc," he stuttered.

The man shook him until his teeth rattled. "You must be that brat from the hospital. Thought you'd gone for good," he said.

"The doc's trying to find me a foster home," Alfie said. His heart sank. Any hope that he'd be able to stay here fled. Not that he'd want to anyway if this was Miss's husband. He reminded him of their next door neighbour in Stepney — the bloke who'd knocked all his wife's teeth out one night after a session at the pub.

"Good luck to him then," Mr Spencer said. "He'll have a job." He grabbed Alfie's crutches and thrust them at him. "Who'd want to take in a cripple?"

Louise appeared in the doorway. "What's going on? James, I didn't hear you come in."

242

"I caught this young lad bashing around on the piano. I thought we had a burglar." He gave a false laugh.

"This is Alfie. I used to look after him when I worked at the hospital. He's waiting for Dr Tate."

Alfie looked from one to the other, glancing at the door as he heard the doc coming down the stairs. He saw the look on Miss's face, the effort it was for her to smile and say, "I believe you know my husband."

The two men shook hands and exchanged polite greetings but Alfie could tell they didn't like each other. He was glad when the doc touched him on the shoulder and said, "I think we'd better be off if we want to get back in time for supper."

When Miss kissed him goodbye, Alfie blushed and rubbed at his cheek. But as he hobbled down the front path towards the doc's car he was fighting tears once more. Who knew if he'd ever see her again?

Louise watched Andrew helping Alfie into the car, giving a little wave and forcing a smile as the boy looked round and grinned at her. She knew she might never see him again. She'd heard James's words as she came into the room and knew that he'd never allow Alfie to stay with them.

As the boy started his slow walk towards the front gate, Andrew had turned to them and tentatively raised the question. James, all charm again, had explained that Louise couldn't possibly look after a child while looking after Dora.

"You've seen for yourself how my mother-in-law is," he'd said.

Andrew nodded agreement. "I'm sorry to say Mrs Charlton does seem to have gone downhill since I last saw her. Does she keep to her room all the time?"

"Yes. My wife is exhausted with running around after her." James put his arm round Louise and squeezed her to him. "I know you'd love to have the lad here, darling, but I really wouldn't be happy for you to take on anything else."

"Don't worry. Some of the evacuees have gone home — against all advice of course," Andrew said. "I'm sure I'll find a place for him. I just thought it would be nice for the boy to be with someone he knows."

"I'm sorry, Andrew. I hope you understand," Louise said.

Andrew picked up his hat from the hallstand and shook hands with them both. "I'll ask Uncle George to call in and see Mrs Charlton. I can't see anything physically wrong but perhaps he can suggest something. She really shouldn't be spending so long in bed. I'm a great believer in exercise."

James muttered something and Louise thanked him.

When they'd gone, Louise attempted to go into the kitchen. "I must dish up or the food will spoil," she said. "The table's already laid. Why don't you pour yourself a drink and sit down?"

"Never mind the drink. I want an explanation." James gripped her arm and thrust his face close to hers. "What do you think you're up to — entertaining men while I'm at work?"

244

"I don't understand. Dr Tate was visiting Mother, not me."

"Don't give me that. You were upstairs with him. And you left that brat to poke around down here. He could have filled his pockets while you were otherwise engaged."

Louise bit back the retort that rose to her lips. Telling James he was being silly would enrage him further. "I was in the kitchen, seeing to your dinner." She emphasized the word "your". "Dr Tate was talking to Mother. And Alfie was hardly filling his pockets. The poor boy can scarcely stand without his crutches."

"Dr Tate — what happened to Andrew?" James sneered. "Very cosy, calling on my wife, I must say. Bringing the brat with him was a good excuse." He gave her arm a shake and released her. "Now, go and dish my dinner up and you'd better hope it isn't ruined."

It wasn't quite ruined but Louise was careful to cut away the burned edges of the batter. She filled his plate, making sure he had the lion's share of the sausage meat, and took it in to him. He was at the dining table, a half empty whisky tumbler in his hand. She resisted the temptation to point out that it was the last bottle from her father's cellar. Goodness knew when or where they'd get any more.

She put the plate in front of him. "I'll just take Mother's up to her," she said.

"Never mind that. Sit down. I want to talk to you."

She perched nervously on the edge of a chair. Was he going to start ranting about Andrew again?

"I've been thinking," he said. "Perhaps your friend's right about Mother. But if he's wrong and she really needs constant nursing, she should be in a nursing home."

"I couldn't do that to her. I don't mind looking after her. Besides, I gave my father my word."

"I worry about you, darling." His manner changed completely to the false tone of concern which told her he wanted something. "You have so much to do — this house, your mother . . ."

Louise waited. She knew she would never agree, whatever he was about to suggest — not if it meant breaking her promise.

"Listen, darling," he said, taking her hand. "We don't need all this room. It's too much for you on your own. We could sell the house, move somewhere smaller, use some of the money to make sure Mother is looked after."

She almost laughed aloud in relief. "No, James, that's not possible."

Before she could explain, his manner changed. "Why not?" he snapped.

"The house isn't mine. You see, Father stipulated in his will that it was Mother's for her lifetime, then it reverts to me."

A look of fury crossed James's face, gone before she was really sure what she'd seen. Why? Was he really so anxious to get rid of the burden of a bedridden mother-in-law?

He picked up his knife and fork. "I hadn't realized. Oh well, there's no more to be said then." He attacked his dinner, shovelling the food in and for once, not finding anything to complain about.

"Well, you'd better serve Mother and have your own. You'll need to get changed before my friends arrive."

She had quite forgotten that he was expecting friends for drinks and cards. Another long evening of walking on eggshells and keeping a smile on her face while James showed off, she thought. Well, unless they brought their own drink, they wouldn't be able to get drunk this time. The cellar was nearly empty.

They finished their meal in silence and Louise got up to clear the plates away. "I'll just pop up and see to Mother before I wash up," she said.

"Don't worry, I'll go. You get on with things down here. They'll be here soon. Put the card table up and put out some glasses. And I noticed you don't seem to have had time to dust in there today. Too busy entertaining your friends, I suppose."

Louise ignored the jibe and started to stack the plates onto a tray. "I'm sorry James. I'll see to it right away." She hated using such a submissive tone but she just didn't have the energy for another argument.

He nodded in satisfaction. "Right. I'll go up to Mother. I hope she enjoyed the chocolates."

Louise gritted her teeth. "It was very kind of you James. She does appreciate it."

James was whistling as he went upstairs and Louise wondered at his quick change of mood. It was so wearing, never knowing how he'd react or what frame of mind he'd be in when he arrived home. Sometimes she wondered if it was all in her mind. His remarks would probably seem innocent to an onlooker but they often had the power to frighten her. But there was no misinterpreting his anger when he'd come upon Alfie in the drawing room. She was sure that if she hadn't come in at that moment he would have attacked the boy physically.

As she mechanically went about her chores, she tried not to think about Alfie and the disillusioned look on his thin little face when he realized he wouldn't be able to stay. She polished the glasses and took them through to the drawing room, set up the card table and rearranged the chairs. She took the remaining bottles out of the sideboard, noting the low level in the gin and whisky bottles. There was plenty of soda and tonic but no fresh lemons. James would complain but there was nothing she could do about that. No one had seen a lemon for months.

As she returned to the kitchen she glanced up the stairs. James was spending a long time with her stepmother; it wasn't like him to volunteer to do anything in the nature of caring for her needs. He would sit on the side of her bed, patting her hand, flattering her and playing the perfect son-in-law but that was usually the extent of his involvement.

Louise's lips twisted in a wry smile as she wondered if he was trying to cajole Dora into selling the house. He clearly hadn't taken in what she'd said. Dora couldn't sell even if she wanted to. Besides, who'd buy it? The property business, as well as the building trade, had been in decline since the war started. Instead of building new houses, they were relying on the rents from houses they already owned.

Why was James so keen to sell? Was it just to get rid of the burden of an ailing mother-in-law? Or was he desperate for money?

Louise knew it was no good asking. If he was in a good mood he'd pat her hand and tell her not to worry her pretty little head about such things. And if he was in a bad one, his lips would thin and a glint would come into his eyes. "None of your business," he would snap and that would be the end of the matter.

She went back into the drawing room to make sure everything was how James liked it and then went upstairs to change and do her hair. As she passed Dora's room she heard laughter — Dora's light tinkle and James's throaty chuckle. The sound boded well for the coming evening.

She was patting her hair into place when the door opened and she swung round, tense for a word of criticism. Her shoulders relaxed as James said, "Lovely, my dear." He held out a hand and drew her towards him. "You're a credit to me, the perfect hostess. They really envy me, you know. They like coming here for card evenings. Steve and Ed live in lodgings and Roly's wife won't let him have us round there. I told him he should put his foot down." James laughed. "Under the thumb, poor old sod."

Louise didn't like James's new friends. They weren't business colleagues or old school friends. She thought they'd met in the pub or at the race course. She wondered why they weren't in the forces. Like James they showed no sign of being exempt on medical grounds but perhaps they were in reserved occupations. Not that she cared. She just hoped they would all behave themselves that evening. At least, unless they brought their own drink with them, there would be no drunken carousing.

The doorbell rang and she hurried down to answer it. The three men greeted her exuberantly. They had obviously already visited the pub. Louise recoiled at the smell of alcohol on their breath.

When she'd taken their coats and they were seated, she poured their drinks and went into the kitchen to fetch the large plate of canapés she'd prepared earlier.

She returned to a burst of laughter and she caught the words, "Don't know how he does it, old boy."

James was leaning back in his chair a self-satisfied smirk on his face. He tapped the side of his nose. "Don't ask," he said.

She put the plate on the sideboard and caught sight of the new bottle — a very expensive brand of whisky.

As the evening wore on, the room filled with smoke and the game got noisier. James insisted on Louise remaining by his side. "You bring me luck," he said, pulling her down onto his knee. She didn't think so. He was losing consistently.

Louise longed for her bed but James kept his arm round her, resisting her attempts to move away. Her eyes were closing but they flew open as James gave a whoop of triumph, threw his remaining cards down and leaned forward to scoop the heap of money towards him. She seized the moment to start gathering up the glasses. Useless to hope he'd call it a night; a win like that would only spur him on to try his luck again.

A glance at the clock told her it was gone midnight. She hoped Dora was able to sleep through the noise. Perhaps she should go up and check on her.

She was about to slip away when the laughter died down and Roly held up a hand. "Listen," he said.

Into the resulting silence the wail of the air raid siren brought instant sobriety. James pushed back his chair. "So much for a night off. Sorry, boys. Game over. I'd better get down to the post."

He shoved the men out of the front door, grabbed his rifle and tin hat and followed them down the front path. Amid promises to return soon and win their money back, the men parted.

Louise closed the front door with a sigh of relief. It was probably a false alarm. Although their days and nights were often disrupted by the air raid warning, Holton hadn't suffered any bombing so far. The planes were probably on their way to Portsmouth or Southampton. At least the siren had cut the evening short and, with a bit of luck, she'd be asleep by the time James returned.

When the raids had first started, they'd gone down to the cellar to shelter. But getting Dora downstairs took so long that the all clear had usually gone by the time she was settled. After the first couple of false alarms, she had refused to leave her bed, and Louise wouldn't leave her alone.

She went upstairs, hoping her stepmother had slept through the siren's wail. The drone of the bombers sounded much louder than usual and she jumped as she heard the sharp stutter of anti-aircraft fire from the gun emplacement on the promenade. Perhaps she should try to get Dora downstairs this time.

Dora was lying on her back, mouth open, snoring. Louise shook her. "Mother, it's a raid — a bad one," she said.

Dora didn't move and Louise shook her harder, beginning to panic as a loud thump nearby rattled the windows. "Come on, we must get downstairs."

There was still no response and Louise would have thought she was dead but for the loud snores which continued to shake the bed. She sank to her knees, clutching Dora's hand and praying under her breath. How long the raid lasted she couldn't tell but it seemed like hours before the all clear sounded, coinciding with a loud grunt from her stepmother. Louise almost giggled in her relief.

She stood up on shaky legs and once more tried to wake Dora. Why was she sleeping so heavily? The sedative the doctor had prescribed was only a mild one.

The bottle was on the bedside table, not on the shelf where Louise usually left it. She picked it up, noticing that there were only a couple of tablets left. Surely there should be more? Had Dora got confused and taken too many?

She shook her stepmother's shoulder again. "Wake up, please," she whispered. She dashed water from the carafe into her face and struggled to pull her upright. Talking continuously while shaking her and slapping her face, Louise tried to bring her round. Her efforts brought no response and she was contemplating leaving her to go downstairs and telephone for an ambulance when Dora spoke. "What's going on?" she muttered, her words slurred.

"Mother, I was so worried." Louise was almost crying with relief. "How many tablets did you take?" She was sure it must have been a mistake. Dora was not the type to attempt to take her own life.

"James gave me a nice glass of sherry — the dear boy," Dora murmured and fell back on the pillow, asleep once more.

Louise tucked the covers round her and picked up the bottle again.

Surely James hadn't . . .? She shook her head. No, it must have been a mistake. Dora had probably woken and forgotten she'd already taken her medicine. It had happened before, which was why Louise always put the bottle out of reach. If James was to blame for anything it was for leaving the bottle on the bedside table and forgetting that Dora shouldn't mix alcohol with her medication.

# CHAPTER
# NINETEEN

When Louise woke the next morning she discovered that James hadn't returned home after the air raid. Her sleep had been restless; she couldn't quite put out of her mind the tentative suspicion that had arisen when she realized that Dora had taken too many of her sleeping tablets.

Was that why James had kept her so firmly by his side all evening — so that she wouldn't have the opportunity to go and check on her stepmother? She didn't want to believe — couldn't really believe — that he would deliberately harm her just so that he could get his hands on the house.

As soon as she was fully awake she went in to Dora's room, relieved to find her sitting up, her hand on the bell.

"Oh, there you are. My dear, you look dreadful. Did you have a late night?"

"There was an air raid, Mother — a bad one. Didn't you hear the siren?"

Dora yawned. "I didn't hear a thing. I had a good sleep but I woke up with an awful headache. Have we got any aspirin?"

After some hesitation, Louise handed her a pill and a glass of water. Who knew what effect mixing all these tablets might have.

As she went down to prepare breakfast she decided she'd give James the benefit of the doubt. After all, Dora had so many pills and potions arrayed on her bedside table — it must have been a mistake. But she'd definitely speak to him about making sure the sleeping tablets were out of reach. She didn't want to go though another night like last night.

James didn't come home until the middle of the morning. He looked exhausted, his face and hands encrusted with dirt, dark shadows under his eyes. She didn't have the heart to berate him. She made him sit down and poured out the remaining whisky, pleased that his friends hadn't had time to finish the bottle last night. "Rest a while," she said, handing him the tumbler. "I'll run you a bath."

When she came downstairs again he'd fallen asleep in the chair, the tumbler hanging loosely from his hand. She took it away and gently shook his shoulder. "You'll be more comfortable in bed," she said, helping him up.

He was sleeping soundly when she went into their room a little later and she stood for a moment, looking down on him. In sleep she could see once more the boyish good looks that had attracted her. She smiled wryly, telling herself to enjoy the respite while she could. Good looks and charm weren't everything and when he woke he'd soon revert to the demanding controlling person she'd come to know.

She closed the door quietly and looked in on Dora who was dozing in her chair by the window. She had shown no interest in the raid and Louise now realized that she didn't know what had happened either. James had been too exhausted to talk before falling into bed.

She decided to go into town to see for herself. Perhaps she could do something to help. She closed the front door quietly and set off for the town centre.

There was a queue outside the baker's as well as the butcher's today. She nodded to one of the women, a member of St Mark's congregation, and answered questions about her stepmother's health.

"And what about that raid last night?" the woman said. "I was frightened out of my wits. It was quite near me, you know — the bomb. One house completely flattened and the others badly damaged. Three killed I heard."

"Was it your road?" Louise asked.

"The next one over, Alexandra road."

Louise's heart began to hammer. That was where Muriel Baines lived. She had to find out if she was all right. Leaving the queue, she ran up the High Street and past the station.

As she turned the corner she could see that Muriel's house, although badly damaged, was still standing. Beyond it, a gaping crater was cordoned off. A policeman and a warden were roping off the area, while beyond them the rescue squad dug in the rubble.

She ran towards Muriel's house, calling her friend's name.

"There's no one there," the policeman called. "Go along to the church hall. They'll give you any news."

She was about to turn away when she heard a faint cry. Pushing the policeman aside, she tried to look through the shattered window. "Muriel, is that you?" she called.

A movement caught her eye and she heard a groan. Muriel was lying on the far side of the room, the grandfather clock across her legs. Louise turned to the policeman. "She's in there. Help her," she begged.

The policeman caught her arm. "It's not safe. Leave it to the rescue squad."

"It might be too late. We've got to get her out." She shook him off and clambered over the windowsill, edging gingerly towards the still figure.

Muriel groaned and tried to sit up but she couldn't move, her legs trapped by the grandfather clock.

Louise heard a sound behind her and called out to the policeman. "Quickly. We've got to get her out. Help me."

"Careful now," a voice said in her ear.

Louise gasped when she realized it wasn't the constable. But there was no time to speak. An ominous creaking lent her strength and she and Andrew lifted the heavy clock. He held it up while Louise helped to free her friend. They scrambled away as Andrew let the clock fall. He lifted Muriel and deposited her on the ground outside. As he turned to help Louise over the windowsill, the building swayed and brick dust began to rain down. Andrew pulled her away and three of them staggered into the road.

As the policeman helped Muriel into the waiting ambulance, Andrew grabbed Louise by the arms and shook her. "What the hell do you think you're playing at? You should have waited for the rescue squad," he shouted, his face white beneath the layers of dust.

Louise pushed him away. "Suppose I'd waited. Muriel would still be in there." She made to turn away but he grabbed her arm again. "Louise, you could have been killed. I couldn't . . ." His words were drowned by a loud rumble as the building began to collapse.

As the noise died away, she shook her head. What had he been saying? She looked into his eyes, hope flaring at the expression in them. He did care then. She dragged her gaze away and tried to still the trembling in her voice. "I should go down to the WVS centre and tell them what's happened."

"I'll come with you. I might be able to help."

She didn't try to stop him and by the time she reached the corner of the street she was glad of his supporting arm. Reaction had set in and her legs were shaking, her breathing erratic.

At the centre he made her sit down while he went to explain to the WVS leader what had happened.

Someone brought her a cup of tea and she sat with it in her hand, letting it go cold. The hall was full of people, some with shocked blank faces, others speaking volubly as they recounted their experiences. It was the worst raid on Holton Regis so far. Alexandra road wasn't the only area hit and people were still coming in.

She thought Andrew had left until she saw him approaching with his doctor's bag.

"I'd better take a look at that gash, Mrs Spencer," he said, kneeling beside her chair.

Louise hadn't noticed the blood running down her leg. "It's nothing," she said, trying to hide her hurt at his formal tone. What had happened to "Louise"?

"We'll see about that." Quickly and efficiently he cleaned and dressed the wound. He was all doctor now, no sign of the feelings that had almost overwhelmed him earlier. Louise told herself she had imagined it; he'd just been showing the concern he would for anybody in that situation.

While he worked, he told her that Violet Wilson, the WVS coordinator, would find somewhere for Muriel to stay when she was released from the hospital.

Louise thanked him and said, "I ought to be going. Mother will wonder what's happened to me." She stood up. "I'll just have a word with Mrs Wilson. I've been meaning to come down and offer my services."

"I'll wait for you and take you home. You should rest that leg for a day or two."

When she tried to protest he said, "Nonsense. You can't walk through the streets in that state."

For the first time she became aware of her dishevelled hair and torn clothing. "Perhaps you're right," she replied and followed him out to where he had left his uncle's car.

During the short drive to Steyne House Louise was acutely conscious of the man beside her. At the touch of his hand on her arm, feelings she had long tried to suppress came rushing to the fore.

Despite telling herself she'd imagined the anguished concern on his face when they'd escaped the ruins of Muriel's house, she was sure now that he returned those feelings. When his manner had changed and he'd become the professional doctor again, she realized she hadn't been mistaken. But she knew he wasn't the sort of man to act on them. His formal use of her married title was a reminder to both of them that she wasn't free.

Neither of them had said a word since she got in the car and, as it drew up outside the house, she reached for the door, desperate to get away and nurse her wounded heart in private. He leaned across and put his hand on hers. "Wait — please," he said.

"Andrew — I must go." She tried to pull away, panic-stricken as she realized that she had been gone for hours and it was already getting dark. Suppose James had woken and found her gone? He'd never believe she'd just popped out for a loaf of bread.

"Not yet. We haven't had a chance to talk." Andrew gripped her hand. "Please . . ."

"There's nothing to say, is there?"

Andrew groaned. "When I thought you were hurt I wanted to hold you, to comfort you, to —"

"No, Andrew." Louise laid a hand on his arm. "You mustn't talk like that."

He pulled her to him. "What a fool I've been. Why didn't I speak up before . . .?"

She knew she should push him away but she couldn't. Wasn't this what she had dreamed of for so long? She leaned into him and lifted her face for his kiss. How sweet it was to give in to him, to submerge herself in feelings she'd only imagined. She wanted more and she could tell that Andrew did too. He shifted in the seat straining to get closer and, over his shoulder, she saw the front door open.

Frantically, she pushed Andrew away, grabbing for the car door. "I must go," she whispered, "James . . ."

She straightened her jacket and patted her hair, leapt out of the car and ran up the front path, grateful for the deepening dusk. James took a step towards her, peering into the dark as the car pulled away. "Who was that?" he asked.

"Dr Tate brought me home," she said, thankful that there was no need to lie.

"Thought I recognized the old buffer's car," he said. "Why didn't he come in?"

"He had to see a patient," Louse said.

James pushed the door shut and gripped her arms, giving her a little shake. "Where the hell have you been all this time?" He pushed her into the kitchen and snatched up the note she'd left him, waving it under her nose. "And don't say queuing for bread, which is where you said you were going. It doesn't take all afternoon and half the evening does it?" He was still holding her arm and he shook her again.

"I was worried about Miss Baines so I went to see if she was all right. She was trapped in her house. I waited until she was rescued and then went to the WVS centre." It was the truth but he still looked sceptical. Her legs started to shake as guilt smote her. She hadn't lied but it wasn't the whole story. If he suspected . . .

He gave a short laugh and let go of her so abruptly that she stumbled against the kitchen table. "Don't know why you were worrying about that old bag. Besides, you've got your own family to worry about. What about Dora, left alone for hours? She needs you more." He paced up and down the room, stopping in front of her and raising his hand to her face. "If I thought . . ."

"I'm sorry, James," she said quickly. She hated apologizing but she had to calm him down.

He dropped his hand to his side. "I was worried about you, darling, after that dreadful raid last night," he said, with that quick change of manner that always unnerved her. "I woke up and you were gone. I didn't know what to think."

For the first time he seemed to notice the state of her clothes and he reached up to brush a streak of dirt from her cheek. "You are a mess, darling. It must have been quite awful for you."

Louise managed to smile. "No worse than for you. You said it was a bad raid, that's why I felt I had to help. Those poor people made homeless. I wanted to do my bit — just like you, James," she said. "Whenever I ask why you're out so long, that's what you tell me — you're doing your bit. It's what I should have been doing all along but I let you persuade me that my place was here looking after Mother."

"And so it is," James snapped, his mood changing again. "You haven't given her a thought, have you? It's a good job I was here to see to her."

262

For a moment Louise felt ashamed. It was true that Dora's needs had been the last thing on her mind, especially during those few precious moments in the car. Still, she was determined to find time to join the WVS. Mrs Wilson had said they could always use and extra pair of hands.

It was a week after the raid and Louise hadn't had time to go and offer her services at the WVS centre. James had become even more demanding, coming home for lunch every day and insisting on a proper meal. It was almost as if he was trying to find a way to stop her doing anything that would take her away from what he insisted was her duty.

When she tried to protest he said that he was worried about Dora and insinuated that she didn't care about her stepmother. His cutting words struck a little close to home and increased her feelings of guilt. Certainly James's concern seemed genuine. He always found time to sit with Dora for a few minutes before returning to the office. But she was beginning to think that making her feel guilty was James's way of controlling her.

She was putting clean towels in the bathroom and, as she passed Dora's room she heard James say, "Would you really like to go? Are you sure you feel well enough?"

Go where? Louise wondered. Dora hadn't been outside the house for months. Curiosity overcame her and she entered the room. Dora looked up excitedly, holding up the local newspaper. "It's Sarah's film," she said. "It's on at the Picturedrome this week. We must go and see it."

Louise took the paper and glanced at the advertisement for *Guns at Midday*. It was over a year since Sarah had told them she had a part but their little cinema didn't get the latest films. "It's a western," she said. "Do you think you'll like it, Mother?"

"I don't care what it is. I can't miss seeing my daughter, can I?" She smiled. "A film star — my little Sarah."

"We'll go this evening — all of us," James said.

What a dreadful film, Louise thought, shifting in her seat. How could Sarah lower herself to appear in such rubbish? It was all bar fights and shootouts and flashily dressed women egging them on. Normally she would have walked out but she had to admit she was curious to see her sister.

Beside her, Dora gripped her arm as, on the screen, a voluptuous blonde descended the stairs in the saloon, swinging her hips and displaying a generous amount of cleavage. "Is that her? No, it can't be. Where's Sarah then?"

Behind them a man uttered a loud "Shh". He leaned forward and tapped Dora on the shoulder. "Do you mind? Some of us are trying to watch the film."

"But it's my daughter. She's a film star you know," Dora said.

The man gave a derisive laugh.

The film came to an end and, as everybody stood up to leave, Louise lingered, reading the cast list as it

264

scrolled up the screen. But there was no mention of Sarah Charlton.

As they strolled home, Dora gave voice to her disappointment. "I know she said it was a small part but how could we have missed her? Do you think she was one of those *girls*?" She said the word with an expression of distaste.

"Possibly," James said. "They do a lot with make-up. I think she was the dark-haired one with the cute little hat."

"But to play a part like that — my little Sarah who used to sing in church. I hope none of the church ladies see it. I couldn't hold my head up."

Louise bit back a smile at the thought of Mrs Bennett or Mrs Howard sitting through a film like *Guns at Midday*. Besides, if any of those actresses had been her sister, no one in Holton would have recognized her.

In their room later that evening James returned to the subject. "I don't think your sister was in that film at all," he said. "She probably told you that so you'd think she was making a career out there in Hollywood. But if she was so successful we'd have heard. They puff up these new stars, you know."

Louise didn't answer. She had a niggling suspicion he might be right. Was that why she hadn't written lately? Poor Sarah. She'd gone out to America with such high hopes and, for a while, had enjoyed a successful run on Broadway. Why had she given up her singing to try to make it as an actress?

James echoed her thoughts. "There's probably a man at the bottom of it. She's likely got herself a sugar daddy."

"I do hope you're wrong. I hate to think of her in trouble or unhappy." Once again Louise thought how different her life could have been if she'd gone to America too. No James for a start. She frowned, brushing the thought away.

"Don't worry about her," James said, holding out his hand. "Come to bed."

As she climbed in beside him, he said, "That little brunette *could* have been Sarah. She was very pretty." He pulled her to him and nibbled her ear. "But not as pretty as you, darling." He leaned back and looked down at her. "You know, at one time I'd set my sights on your sister. But I realized she wasn't for me — too fond of getting her own way. Not like you my darling, sweet, submissive Louise."

He kissed her and she tried not to pull away. Did he realize how cruel his words were? His hands grew urgent on her body and, as usual, she gave in to his demands. Yes, she was submissive but what choice did she have? Besides, there was always the hope that this time would result in what she longed for. She was convinced that a baby would make up for the disappointment her marriage had turned out to be.

As James turned away from her and fell immediately into a deep sleep, Louise lay awake for hours, her mind a jumble of hope and prayer.

266

# CHAPTER
# TWENTY

# 1943

Despite the disturbed nights due to more frequent air raids, Louise had been feeling much more cheerful these days. She couldn't admit that knowing Andrew loved her had anything to do with it. She told herself it was because her life was so much fuller lately. She'd joined the WVS and enjoyed working with Muriel and Mrs Wilson, either sorting out donated clothing for the evacuees or manning the canteen, which had been set up for the Canadian servicemen who were in training on the sand dunes to the east of the town.

There was another reason for her happiness — something she hadn't dared to confide in anyone just yet. It was too soon to be sure and she'd been disappointed too often over the past couple of years.

But, as she came out of the bathroom on this bitterly cold winter morning, she was fighting back the tears. Once more her hopes were dashed. It was still very early and she could have gone back to bed but she dreaded disturbing James. She hesitated at the top of the stairs. Perhaps she should go down and get the range going.

Instead she climbed up to the room in the turret which had been her sanctuary as a child. She hadn't been up there for months. Earlier in her marriage she had visualized this as a nursery. But years of disappointment had led to a slow acceptance that motherhood was not to be — until recently. This time had been different and she'd really begun to hope. Throughout the preparations for their meagre Christmas she kept to herself the secret thought that this time next year the festive season would have a real meaning for her. Christmas was for children after all. She would tell James on New Year's Eve, she'd thought. A new year, a new beginning for them. They would be a proper family.

But James hadn't been home to see in the New Year with her and she and Dora had drunk a small glass of sherry in her stepmother's room. James had said he was on fire watching duty but she didn't believe him. He'd become more secretive of late, snapping at her when she asked what time he'd be home.

Wait till I tell him my news, she'd thought, with a secret smile.

But now, on this cold January dawn a week later, she was glad she hadn't said anything. He would have looked at her accusingly as if it were her fault. She sat on the window seat and pulled the blackout curtain aside, clutching her abdomen as another cramp attacked her.

Tears rolled down her cheeks and she gazed out at the heaving grey sea breaking against the concrete tank traps on the beach. As the sky lightened she could make out the machine gun post near the bandstand, the men huddled inside their coats.

She shivered and pulled her dressing gown closely around her. She should go down and light the range. Dora would be ringing her bell any minute and James would want hot water for shaving. But still she didn't move, reliving happier days when she would sit up here looking out for her father on his way home from work; days when they would walk along the beach picking up shells and odd-shaped stones; days when she and Sarah would play together on the stretch of sand left by the receding tide.

The tears fell faster as she thought of her sister. Why didn't she answer her letters? The post might be erratic these days but surely one at least should have got through. It had been months since she'd received the last one, but she still wrote every week, hoping that one day she'd hear from her. "Sarah, why did you have to go away?" she murmured.

She stood up with a sigh, taking one last look out of the window. A figure was striding along the promenade, head down against the wind. For a heart-stopping moment she thought it was Andrew. Was he back in Holton? The man turned as a small dog came bounding up behind him. He bent to clip on the dog's lead and Louise saw that it was nothing like Andrew. She shouldn't be thinking about him anyway.

With a determined set to her shoulders she went downstairs. By the time James came down she had coaxed the range into life and was busy preparing breakfast. She finished laying Dora's tray as James sat at the table without a word and began to eat.

Upstairs, she helped Dora to sit up and placed the tray across her knees.

"Did you sleep well, Mother?" she asked.

"I did, dear. Those new tablets work wonders." She picked up a piece of toast and bit into it. "What about you, Louise? You've been looking pleased with yourself lately. I thought you might have some good news for me." She smiled and raised her eyebrows.

"I'm sorry to disappoint you — you're not going to be a grandmother just yet." If ever, she added silently.

"But I thought . . ."

"False alarm," Louise said, her voice almost breaking.

"Perhaps you ought to talk to the doctor," Dora said.

Louise didn't answer, busying herself with tidying the room. She noticed that the bottle of pills was on the bedside table. Surely she'd put them away last night?

James finished eating and wiped his mouth on his napkin. He stood up and went to the bottom of the stairs, listening. A faint murmur of voices came to him and he shrugged, putting on his coat and cramming his hat on. So, the old girl hadn't taken the bait. Not this time anyway.

He picked up his briefcase and opened the front door. "Just off, dear," he called up the stairs and set off down the front path.

A few doors away a neighbour was taking in the milk. James smiled, touching the brim of his hat. "Another cold one," he said. But inside he was seething. It still rankled — the fact that they couldn't sell the house. How could he have made such a stupid mistake, assuming that Louise owned it? Why hadn't she mentioned the condition of looking after her stepmother. But putting the old girl in a nursing home was looking after her, surely. He'd tried sweet talking Dora but she could be stubborn too.

It was after the argument with Louise about the sleeping pills that the idea had come to him. Not that he actually intended to bump the old girl off, of course. But who knew what might happen when she was in pain, unable to sleep and terrified of the noise when that big gun started up so close to the house?

Since that last big raid the town had suffered several near misses. The bombers often flew over on their way to and from their real targets — the big cities and air fields to the west of the town.

Last night there'd been another warning and, before leaving for the ARP post, James had gone in to Dora who was sitting up clutching the bed clothes while Louise tried to persuade her to go down to the cellar as she did every time the siren sounded.

The old girl had been adamant. "I can't manage the stairs you know that," she said. "Don't leave me."

"I won't leave you, Mother," said Louise turning to James. "Stay with her for a minute. I'll go down and get the flask and hot water bottle. Then you'd better get off."

James had sat beside Dora, holding her hand. "Why don't you take a pill, dear? Calm you down."

"I've had one already," she said.

"Take another then. You must sleep, dear. The guns have stopped now. False alarm I expect. You'll feel better after a sleep."

"Dr Tate said I mustn't take too many," Dora said. But her hand was reaching out for the tablet and the glass of water.

"It won't hurt. Better than lying awake all night listening for the planes going over." James watched her swallow the tablet and took the glass from her. "Listen, that's the all clear. You can sleep now. I'll leave the bottle handy in case you wake in the night."

Dora laid back and closed her eyes. "Thank you, dear. You're such a good boy."

When Louise came back with the hot water bottle he put his finger to his lips to stop her coming into the room. "She's just drifting off. Best not to disturb her," he whispered.

Now he strode up the road towards the office thinking furiously. He needed money badly. If only he could sell the house. That would pay off his gambling debt and leave a little to tide him over till business picked up again.

He hadn't been able to believe his luck when he'd been approached by the ministry wanting accommodation for some high-ranking personnel. It was all very hush hush but he guessed it was something to do with the plans for invading France.

As the leading estate agent in the town, Charlton and Spencer were in an ideal position to scout for a suitable property. Straight away James thought of Steyne

House. They were offering a good price — more than enough to solve his financial difficulties.

He'd thought his troubles were over until Louise dropped her bombshell. If he couldn't sell the house, where was the money to come from? What a pity Dora wasn't as ill as she made out. But she was definitely becoming dependent on those sleeping tablets. No one would think anything of it if she took too many one night. With her out of the way he was confident he could persuade Louise that her life would be easier in a smaller place.

He entered the office and threw his briefcase down on the desk. Nancy, his new secretary looked up and smiled. She was a pretty little thing, not very bright, but that was to his advantage. She wouldn't go poking her nose into his files and asking awkward questions like that Baines woman. He'd got rid of her just in time.

He smiled back at the girl and held out his hand for the post. She blushed as his hand brushed hers. Turning back to his desk he hid a grin. He enjoyed flirting with her and he could tell she was up for it. But he resisted temptation. Maybe some time in the future, he thought. But he wouldn't jeopardize his marriage — not until he had his hands on the house anyway.

As he sorted the post his thoughts turned to his wife. Just lately she'd begun to stand up for herself and, instead of always being at home when he finished work, she was often at the WVS centre. Perhaps he should start being more firm with her. But he had to be careful. Only the other day he'd bumped into the Revd Ayling who'd begun singing Louise's praises. And that pompous old fool of a doctor was always saying how lucky he was to have such a dedicated and hard-working wife.

He hated her having outside interests but he couldn't complain that she neglected him or his mother-in-law. Louise always made sure everything in the home was just as he liked it — meals ready on time and a companion there for Dora when she was out.

He sighed and pulled a ledger from a locked drawer in the desk. He went over the figures, hoping he'd made a mistake. But it was a forlorn hope. The business was in trouble and he only had himself to blame. He couldn't manipulate the books any further. But he had to have money — and soon.

He stood up abruptly. "I'm off to visit a client. Hold the fort, Nancy."

"Yes, Mr Spencer. You can rely on me." The girl looked up and smiled.

"I know I can." He winked at her, grabbed his hat and left. There was no client, of course, but the pubs would be open now.

As he sat in a corner of the saloon bar of the Red Lion, he pulled a letter from his pocket. He'd forgotten about it until now. When he'd seen the American stamp he had grabbed it quickly. Usually he threw Sarah's letters on the fire unread but Louise had come into the hall as he picked up the post and he'd shoved it into his pocket.

He usually managed to intercept Sarah's letters as well as some of Louise's to her sister. He had to smile

274

when he'd read those, consisting as they did of passionate pleas for Sarah to get in touch.

He tore open the envelope, curious to see what the little bitch had written. I always knew she was self-centred, he thought. Pages of what she was up to, the famous people she'd met, the films she was starring in. Well, so far he hadn't seen her name on the posters outside the Picturedrome. It was all talk, he thought.

He turned the sheet over. There it was as usual. "Why don't you write? I haven't heard for ages. Is Mother all right? And are you pregnant yet? I want to be an aunty."

James gave a snort of laughter. Pregnant? If only. How he dreamed of having a son to follow him in the business. Besides, if Louise had a baby it would keep her in her proper place — at home. These past few weeks he'd begun to hope, until he'd seen the familiar despair on her face that morning. Well, they could keep trying. He smiled as he sipped the weak beer but, as he thought about his wife, her image was replaced by that of Nancy's sparkling eyes and pert breasts.

Mrs Howard was late. Louise glanced impatiently at her watch. She'd promised to meet Muriel in time for the afternoon matinee at the Picturedrome. Dora thought she was doing canteen duty with the WVS and, although she'd complained as usual, Louise guessed she was really looking forward to an afternoon of gossip with her old friend.

Louise put on her hat and gloves and reached for her handbag, ready to leave the moment the older woman

275

arrived. She didn't dare go out and leave her stepmother alone. The last time that had happened, James had arrived home unexpectedly to find Dora in hysterics and there had been a furious row.

He was adamant that Dora mustn't be left alone. "Who knows what could happen?" he'd said. "She might try to get downstairs and have a fall; she could take too many of her tablets — you know how confused she gets." He had seemed genuinely upset but Louise couldn't help feeling it was just an act. But why? It wasn't as if he had anything to gain by being nice to Dora. Perhaps she'd misjudged him and he was genuinely fond of her. He certainly spent a lot of time in her room and Louise had often heard them laughing together.

She looked at her watch again, tempted to leave anyway. She'd made sure Dora had everything she needed and, if Mrs Howard didn't turn up, surely it wouldn't hurt to leave her for a couple of hours. Going to the pictures with Muriel was her only pleasure these days and she was reluctant to give it up today. Goodness knows, I need something to cheer me up, she thought. She was still feeling depressed and tired after yet again discovering she was not pregnant. Losing herself in what was happening up on the screen would help to take her mind off her troubles for a while.

She opened the front door, smiling with relief as she saw Dora's friend hurrying up the road.

"So sorry, my dear — long queue at the butcher's. You know what it's like," she panted, patting Louise's

276

arm. "Hurry along, dear. You don't want to be late on duty."

"Thank you, Mrs Howard. I'll try not to be late back." Louise felt guilty for lying about where she was going. But she daren't tell the woman the truth in case she mentioned it to Dora. Her stepmother felt neglected enough already but had reluctantly submitted to Louise's absences in the belief that she was "doing her bit" for the war effort. Both she and James would be furious if they knew she was enjoying an afternoon at the pictures.

Muriel was waiting outside the Picturedrome when she turned the corner. The friends greeted each other and studied the posters outside the cinema. "I didn't even check to see what was on," she said. "Do you really want to see this?"

"It sounds a bit risqué," Muriel said, reading from the poster. "Sultry, sizzling, sensual — *The Sultan's Treasure*. Not exactly *Mrs Miniver* is it?" Her face was a bit pink and she stifled a giggle, pointing to the picture of a voluptuous beauty, her face half concealed by a filmy veil. "What do you think — should we . . .?"

Louise hesitated. Wasn't this the film Sarah had mentioned in one of her letters? But her name wasn't on the poster and, if she was in it, the part was probably not as big as she'd hinted.

Muriel tugged at her arm. "Come on. We can always leave if we don't like it."

They settled down in the darkened cinema as the newsreel came on with its scenes of fighting in the desert and bomb damage nearer home, followed by an information film showing people how to make the most of their rations.

At last the main film started and Louise soon became lost in the rather corny tale of a young girl abducted into a harem to become the "sultan's treasure" and her subsequent rescue by the hero. She just couldn't believe it was her little sister up there on the screen. Her acting talent had certainly developed over the past few years, Louise thought. No wonder she hadn't recognized her in that other film. The name had thrown her off too. Why had she changed it?

She glanced at her friend who was totally immersed in the screen. Had Muriel recognized "Sally Charles" as the girl who used to visit her father in the offices of Charlton and Spencer? And, if she had, what would her rather strait-laced friend think of the transformation from child singer to sultry siren of the screen?

Louise didn't care. She was proud of Sarah's success and she'd write and tell her so as soon as she got home. As the film came to an end and the credits rolled over the closing scene of the lovers riding off into the sunset, the name Sally Charles leapt out at her. Louise wondered again why she'd changed it. She had always wanted to sing and act and had always dreamt of being famous. Perhaps she was ashamed of the sort of film she was starring in. Was that why she hadn't written for so long?

# CHAPTER
# TWENTY-ONE

Louise didn't tell anyone about seeing Sarah in the film. At one time she'd have boasted about her film star sister. But when she realized Muriel hadn't recognized her, something stopped her from revealing that Sarah had become Sally Charles. Even when she realized that her friend wasn't quite as strait-laced as she'd always thought, she wasn't sure why she hadn't said anything.

When they came out of the cinema, she'd asked Muriel's opinion of the film.

"A bit risqué, but fun though," Muriel had said. "Total nonsense, of course." She gave a half laugh. "Why don't things like that happen in real life?"

Louise laughed too. "So you want to be abducted by a sheikh, do you?"

"'Course not, silly. But to be rescued and gallop off into the sunset . . ." She sighed.

"Yes, I can just see some handsome man riding along the prom in Holton looking for maidens in distress."

They had both laughed but Louise's thoughts were sombre. While she was at the pictures she could daydream but she had to return to real life. And in real life, no one was going to rescue her from James. Now, she had to go home and face him and her stepmother, and lie about where she'd been — innocent as the outing was.

If she confessed, she was sure that James would put an end to her afternoons with Muriel, if only by playing on her feelings of guilt. But why shouldn't she occasionally escape from the monotony of queuing for food and trying to make the rations go round?

Since seeing her in *The Sultan's Treasure*, Louise had been to the pictures several times but she hadn't seen Sarah in any of the films. This, coupled with the fact that she'd had no answer to her letters, made her wonder how her sister's career was going. She'd been so excited about going to Hollywood and her early letters had been full of references to Ralph Beauchamp, the man who was going to launch her as a star. Her letters since then had become shorter and less frequent. In fact, Louise realized, she hadn't heard from her sister for over a year.

She resolved to write again. Sarah ought to be told about her mother's health. Dora was becoming frailer and her mind was often confused. Sometimes she called James "Stanley" and mistook Louise for Sarah and she'd stopped knitting for the Red Cross months ago.

Dr Tate had prescribed some different tablets but they didn't seem to be doing any good and this morning James had broached the subject of a nursing home once more.

"It's wearing you out, darling, all that running up and down stairs, and the cooking and cleaning, not to mention your WVS work. I worry about you, darling," he said, taking her hand.

"I'm perfectly all right. Other women have far more to cope with than I do. And I don't mind looking after Mother," she protested.

At one time she'd have been touched by his concern but he nagged away at her like a persistent toothache and she realized he was trying to wear her down. He hadn't mentioned selling the house again but she had a feeling that was behind it. Why? Were they so short of money?

Once more she regretted that she hadn't insisted on being involved with the business — after all she owned a share in it. But between looking after Dora and running the household, as well as her WVS work, she'd let it slide.

Besides, after yet another sleepless night, she was too tired to care. There'd been another raid last night and she'd been helping at the rest centre. It was a miracle no one had been killed but so many people had lost everything.

She got back to find that Mrs Howard had just left. James was already home after helping in the rescue. Louise had long since given up hoping that their shared experiences would bring them closer. He refused to talk about it and she couldn't help a sneaking suspicion that not all his absences were due to warden duties.

He'd gone straight to bed and, after checking on Dora, she'd done the washing as well as cleaning out the range and lighting it so that the kitchen would be warm when James woke.

She'd just come in from hanging the sheets on the line when she heard the rattle of the letterbox. She rushed into the hall. Perhaps there'd be a letter from Sarah today. Hope died when she saw there was just one envelope addressed to James. He came out of the kitchen as she picked it up.

"Is that all?" he asked, glancing at it and shoving it in his pocket. "Nothing from your sister?" His voice was sharp and she waited for one of his barbed comments. But he shrugged and said, "About time she wrote. Mother's getting worried."

"I am too," Louise confessed.

"Well, you shouldn't be. She's probably living it up over there while her mother's sick and you're struggling to look after her. Still, she always was a self-centred little madam."

Before Louise could reply, he opened the front door and strode off down the path. "I won't be home for lunch," he called as he reached the front gate.

She stood for a moment looking after him. What was that all about? She wondered. He rarely mentioned Sarah, had shown no interest in the fact that his sister-in-law was a well-known singer and blossoming movie star. Was it really concern for his wife and mother-in-law that annoyed him? Or was it that she'd insisted on consulting Sarah before making a decision on putting Mother in a nursing home?

The insistent ringing of Dora's bell broke into her thoughts and she went upstairs, her feet dragging as she neared the bedroom. If only she weren't so tired.

She pasted a smile on her face and went in to see what Dora wanted.

"My tea's gone cold — and James didn't come in to say goodbye. He's always in such a hurry," she complained.

"You know he's busy with the office and trying to fit his warden work in as well." Louise hated making excuses for him. She knew very well that he often left the office and spent time in the Red Lion.

"I shouldn't complain. I know the dear boy works hard."

Louise picked up the tray, hiding a smile. If only she knew what he was really like, she thought. But Dora only saw the best in him and he was always at his most charming when he sat playing cards with her or telling amusing stories about his day.

"I'll make some fresh tea," she said.

When she returned Dora had fallen asleep but she started up as the door closed. "Oh, there you are. I thought you'd gone out and left me alone again," she said.

Louise didn't reply. Her stepmother was never left alone; if she and James were both out, Mrs Howard or one of the other church ladies always sat with her. But it was useless to protest. If she didn't come immediately in answer to the bell, Dora accused her of neglect.

She poured the tea and put it on the bedside table. "I must wash up and tidy the kitchen. I'm at home all day today, Mother, but I must get some housework done. You'll be all right for a while, won't you?"

"I suppose so. I never thought I'd say this but I do miss Polly. Why did she have to go and work in that horrible factory? She had a good life here. We treated her like one of the family."

Dora had a rather selective memory, Louise thought, remembering the times she'd berated the poor woman.

"She earns far more now than we could afford to pay her," she said mildly.

Dora's lips tightened but before she could say anything, Louise left the room with the excuse that she had a lot to do.

As she mopped the kitchen floor and took the rubbish out, she reflected that she quite enjoyed housekeeping. It was something she was good at and she would have been perfectly content if her marriage had turned out the way she'd hoped. She had never been ambitious like her half-sister. Looking after a home and family with a man you loved must surely be the way to happiness, she thought.

But the longed-for children hadn't come and the man she married had turned out to be someone who turned on the charm when he wanted his own way, but became cold and repressive when thwarted.

In that he was very like Dora, Louise realized as she swept and dusted the little used drawing room. As she worked, she thought once more how much easier her life would be if she didn't have to keep going up and downstairs. But when she'd proposed moving some of the furniture into the dining room and bringing Dora's bed down there, James had vetoed the suggestion. "Mother's comfortable with all her familiar things around her," he said. "Besides, it would be such an upheaval. I can't have you wearing yourself out, changing everything round."

Louise had the disloyal thought that it was he who didn't want the hassle. But when he pointed out that the bathroom was right next to her bedroom, she'd agreed to leave things as they were.

This would make a nice bed-sitting room though, Louise thought as she straightened the cushions and gave a final swipe with the duster. And there's the cloakroom down the hall.

The mantel clock chimed noon. Almost lunchtime. Still, it wouldn't matter if it was bit late. James wouldn't be home today. Dora's bell sounded again. "She'll have to wait," Louise muttered. She'd put the soup on first then go up to see what she wanted.

As she prepared the lunch she tried to ignore the insistent ringing. She really didn't mind attending to her stepmother's needs but sometimes she was a bit too demanding. Perhaps giving her that bell had been a mistake.

"I need my tablet," Dora said as soon as she entered the room.

"You've already had it," Louise said, trying to hide her impatience.

"I need another one. James always gives me one with my lunch when he's here."

"Are you sure?" Louise picked up the bottle. "It says on the label twice a day."

She'd have to speak to James. Dr Tate had insisted that Dora didn't take more than the stated dose. It was one thing to pander to her whims for the sake of a quiet life, but not to the extent of letting her have too much of her medicine. When she'd found the bottle on the bedside table that time, she'd managed to convince herself that she'd left it there herself. But now that fleeting suspicion that James was up to something returned. Perhaps he thought it would be easier to persuade Dora into a nursing home if she became more confused.

After giving her stepmother her lunch and making sure she was comfortable, Louise went downstairs and sat down in Cookie's old rocking chair by the range. She was so tired she couldn't think straight. If only there was someone she could talk over her worries with. Despite her growing friendship with Muriel she wasn't quite ready to confide in her.

She leaned back in the chair and closed her eyes. She ought to get the washing in and start on the ironing but she couldn't force herself out of the chair. Her last thought as she lapsed into a deep sleep was of Sarah. I could confide in you, she thought. Why aren't you here? Why don't you at least write?

Louise woke with a start, conscious that the sound of Dora's bell had disturbed her dreams. But it wasn't that which had woken her.

Footsteps thundered down the stairs and the kitchen door was flung open. She started up from the chair as James shook her by the shoulders. "How could you leave her like that?" he shouted, spittle flying in her face. "Go up and see to her while I phone for an ambulance."

Louise, wide awake now, rushed up to Dora's room. Her stepmother was lying on the floor amid the debris of her lunch tray. The bottle of sleeping tablets was inches from her outflung hand. Relieved, Louise saw that the top was still on it so she hadn't taken any more tablets. Dora had probably been reaching for it when she fell. But I'm sure I put it away, Louise thought.

Kneeling, she gently wiped away the blood seeping from a cut on her stepmother's temple. "Mother, speak to me." Guilt stabbed at her heart as she recalled the ringing of the bell piercing her dreams. How had she slept through it?

Dora stirred and groaned.

"Don't try to move. James has gone for an ambulance. Tell me where it hurts."

Her stepmother's eyes fluttered and closed. Her lips were blue and her breathing ragged.

"Hurry, please hurry," Louise prayed. She had learned first aid in the WVS and knew she shouldn't try to move her. She grabbed a pillow and gently eased it under Dora's head, pulled a blanket off the bed and covered her.

There was nothing else she could do and she sat holding the older woman's hand, her thoughts churning. I know I was tired but how could I have slept so deeply? I've always tried to be a dutiful daughter, to keep my promise to Father to look after Dora.

It was true she'd sometimes felt resentful of the demands made on her, but she had tried her best. Tears began to fall as she prayed that Dora would be all right.

James's harsh voice roused her. "Don't know what you're crying about. It's your fault she's in this state. You should've been listening out for her." He knelt beside Dora and took her hand, pushing Louise out of the way. "The ambulance will be here soon, dear. You'll be all right."

Dora sank into unconsciousness and died later that night in hospital. Louise was inconsolable. She hadn't really loved her stepmother and she knew it was her sense of guilt that caused her grief.

Dr Tate was at the hospital and he advised James to take her home and give her a sedative. "I'll call tomorrow, my dear," he said.

James shook hands with the doctor and put his arm round her, leading her outside with every appearance of loving concern. But when they got home, he turned to her and snapped. "Stop snivelling, woman. If you'd taken my advice over the nursing home, this wouldn't have happened. She would have been properly cared for."

"I did care for her," Louise protested. She might not have loved Dora as a daughter should but she had tried to for her father's sake. Besides, she thought rebelliously, it wasn't all her fault. If James had agreed to move Dora's bed downstairs, she would have heard her and woken in time to fetch help. No one was sure how long she'd lain on the cold floor before he arrived home.

A few days after the funeral Louise was half dozing on the sofa in the drawing room. She was roused by the low murmur of voices from the hall. "I'm worried, Doctor." That was James, she thought.

"Well, it's no good telling her to snap out of it, you know. Grief takes many forms. Sometimes it takes a long time to get back to normal life."

Dr Tate's deep voice sounded a little impatient, Louise thought. Perhaps she should make more of an effort. It wasn't like her to lie around feeling sorry for herself.

"I'm really worried about her," James said, his voice choking on a sob.

The doctor murmured something and there came the sound of the front door closing. When the drawing-room door opened Louise was lying back with her eyes closed. You don't fool me, she thought. She'd known that as soon as the doctor left his manner would change.

He slammed the door and she jerked upright. "You going to lie there all day?" he said. "About time you pulled yourself together and starting acting like a wife. I've been working all day and I come home to find you lazing around. Don't know what you're upset about — you didn't even like the old bag."

Louise flinched as much at the grain of truth in his words as the venom in his voice. She hadn't liked Dora, had often wondered why her father had married her.

But she was Sarah's mother and for her and her father's sake she had tried to love her. Surely no one could doubt that over the past few years she had done her duty as a real daughter would.

James was right though. She should try to start living again, get out of the house, make herself useful once more. If only she wasn't so tired. Perhaps it was the medicine Dr Tate had given her. She had refused the sleeping tablets, remembering how confused they'd made Dora. But he had insisted she needed a tonic to build her up.

She struggled up from the sofa and walked unsteadily into the kitchen. James followed her, pausing in the doorway. "We'll eat in the dining room. I've had enough of living like a common labourer. Now that you haven't got to keep taking trays upstairs you'll have time to do things properly." He went into the dining room and slammed the door.

Louise looked round helplessly wondering what she could cook. She hadn't been outside the house since the funeral and James hadn't been home for his meals at all lately. She opened the larder door, not expecting to see much there. To her surprise there was a pie on the shelf and a covered casserole dish. She remembered then that several of her stepmother's church friends had called round after the funeral. How kind people were, she thought. She must make the effort to go to church on Sunday and thank them all.

But she never got to church. She began to suffer dizzy spells and took to her bed. It was almost like the time she'd had the fever. In a rare moment of consciousness she became aware of James leaning over her. "Take your medicine, dear," he said, holding a small glass to her lips.

She tried to push his hand away but he slapped her face. "Drink it," he commanded.

She choked as he forced her to drink and some of it ran down her chin. Her last thought as she fell into a heavy sleep was that she was turning into Dora. Then she dreamed she was running along the beach, the wind in her hair, the shingle crunching under her feet. She was a girl again and Sarah was with her, laughing and teasing her about Andrew Tate. "Sarah, help me," she muttered. But Sarah seemed to have cut herself off from her family. She hadn't even replied to the letter telling her of her mother's death.

# CHAPTER
# TWENTY-TWO

James was worried and frightened. The people he owed money to weren't the sort to wait and he cursed the day he'd let Roly talk him into visiting that illegal gambling club in Brighton.

The massive bomb that had destroyed most of the houses in a row owned by Charlton and Spencer was the last straw. Even those still standing were dangerous and beyond repair and the rents from them had been almost their only source of income lately.

James groaned and tugged at his hair. He needed money and his only hope now was to sell Steyne House. Thank God the offer from the ministry was still on the table. Everyone knew they were getting ready for the big push and the war department staff needed accommodation. But if he didn't finalize the deal, the property would be no use to them.

Damn Sarah. Why hadn't she signed those papers? And why hadn't Louise made it clear to him earlier that she'd need Sarah's signature? He was sure she'd told him the house would be solely hers after Dora died.

He jumped up and rushed out of the office. There must be a way round it. Louise would have to speak to the solicitor. It was for her own good too, he told himself. Dora's death had affected her badly and she was still suffering from depression. She just couldn't manage that big house. Much as he hated the thought, they'd have to move into one of their small rental properties.

As he rounded the corner he bumped into the Reverend Ayling. He forced himself to smile and respond to his inquiries about Louise's health.

"Please tell her that I'll call round soon," the vicar said.

"I'm afraid she's not up to visitors at the moment," James said.

"Well, be sure to give her my good wishes and tell her the congregation is praying for her."

James nodded. "If you'll excuse me, I'm just on my way home now. I like to pop in and make sure Louise is all right."

He hurried away grinning to himself. It didn't hurt to let people think they were a devoted couple. He'd keep up the act a bit longer — just till he had his hands on the house and her share of the business.

Louise was feeling better. She'd woken early, relieved that James hadn't come home the night before. She'd waited as long as possible before eating her own evening meal and going straight to bed.

She'd slept well for the first time in months. She went into the bathroom and picked up the bottle of tonic that Dr Tate had prescribed — she'd forgotten to take it last night. She shrugged and put it down without measuring out the usual dose. I'm sure I don't need it, she told herself. It's time I stopped relying on medicine to see me through the day. James is right. Sitting around feeling sorry for myself won't help. Besides, I know deep down that I wasn't responsible for Dora's death. There was nothing I could have done. And I must stop blaming James too. He wasn't even in the house when she fell.

She put the bottle back on the shelf, brushed her teeth and went downstairs. After breakfast she set about cleaning the kitchen with more energy than she'd had for weeks. The sun was pouring in through the kitchen window and she opened the back door, breathing in the fresh sea air. Summer had come almost without her realizing it.

I'll go into town today, she thought; maybe I'll see Muriel. She'd been a little hurt that her friend hadn't called to inquire how she was. But then, knowing how much she disliked James, Louise couldn't blame her for not coming round. Still, she could have telephoned.

She washed her hands and tidied her hair and was about to pick up her handbag when the front door opened.

"James, you're home," she said brightly, anxious not to annoy him by asking where he'd been.

"Just making sure you're all right, darling," he said, smiling. "Still, it seems you're feeling better. Where are you off to?"

"I'm off to the shops. Everyone's been so kind, but it's about time I stopped relying on other people."

"Are you sure you're well enough? You don't want to overdo it."

294

She wasn't sure if it was flicker of annoyance or genuine concern that passed across his face. "I was just going to take a gentle stroll up to the butcher's, that's all."

"Plenty of time, darling. Come and sit down. Have a cup of tea with me first. You can't dash off the minute I get home." He took her arm and led her into the kitchen. "Sit down. I'll do it."

She sat in the old rocking chair and leaned back. Why was he being so nice to her? Was it because she seemed to be almost her old self again — ready to be what he called a "proper wife"?

He made the tea and turned to her. "I'll just pop up and get changed, then we can sit and have a chat." He ran up the stairs whistling. A minute later he returned, the tonic bottle in his hand. "You haven't taken your medicine today," he said.

"I was feeling so much better I decided not to," she said.

"*You* decided? Surely it's up to Dr Tate to make that decision." He got a spoon from the drawer and poured out a dose.

She turned her head away as he held the spoon towards her, "No, really, James. I don't want it."

"Drink it," he commanded.

She flinched at his harsh tone and immediately he smiled. "Come on, darling. It's for your own good. You know how much I worry about you."

Reluctantly, she swallowed the medicine, resolving to speak to the doctor about it. She was sure she didn't need it now. James held out another spoonful. "There, that didn't hurt did it?" he said, as if speaking to a child. He put the bottle and spoon down and turned to her. "Now, let's have that tea."

He sat opposite her and asked, "No word from your sister yet?"

Louise shook her head, feeling a lump in her throat. Why had Sarah cut herself off from her family? Was she having such a good time over there? But even if she had no time for Louise now that she was famous actress, she should have written when she'd heard about her mother's death. Of course, Sarah had always been a bit self-centred, especially when it came to her career, but she had loved her mother.

James stirred his tea thoughtfully. "You must write to her again."

"I don't see why I should. If she ignores me why should I bother to write?"

"You must. I mean, with the war and ships being sunk, she may not have got your letters."

Louise leaned back in the chair and closed her eyes. She didn't want to think about it. Her brief burst of energy that morning had dissipated. Perhaps she'd overdone it after all. James's voice came to her through a haze of tiredness. He was saying something about the business.

"We need some capital," he said.

What did he mean?

He shook her by the arm. "Listen to me, Louise. This is serious. I've tried to shield you from my problems. But we have to do something."

"I don't understand. I know you haven't been able to do any building work but we've still got the rents."

"You haven't been listening to me. Those houses — a whole street — hit by that big bomb last week. They were our properties. No one can move back there. And we'll have to pay for the repairs."

Louise forced herself to concentrate. "I thought you got compensation from the government."

"We might, but with all the red tape that could take months, years even. We need money now. And the only way is to sell this house."

"But we can't unless Sarah agrees."

"Exactly. That's why you must write to her again. Tell her she must sign the form you sent her."

Louise sighed. "I'll do it later, James. I'm too tired to think straight just now."

He stood up and snatched the cup and saucer from her. "You were all right earlier. Weren't you just getting ready to go out? Now, when I want you to do something, suddenly you're too tired. Well, you can just pull yourself together and get it done." He grabbed her arm and pulled her out of the chair, propelling her out of the kitchen and into his study.

"Sit down and start writing." He produced paper, pen and ink.

As she picked up the pen, tears began to fall. She scribbled frantically, "Why, why don't you write? Are you all right? I need to hear from you."

James glanced over her shoulder. "That won't do," he said, snatching the paper and screwing it up. "Start again. Write what I tell you."

By now Louise's head was swimming. What was wrong with her? She'd been perfectly all right until she took her medicine. The tonic was supposed to perk her up, not send her to sleep. James's voice hammered in her head and it was easier to write down what he dictated.

"There, that'll do. Let's hope she appreciates the urgency," he said, taking the letter and folding it. He waited while she wrote the address and then sealed the envelope. "I'll post this on my way back to the office." He turned at the door. "Give me the ration book. I'll get something at the butcher's. You're in no state to go shopping." He bent and kissed her cheek, the loving husband again now she had done his bidding. "Get some rest, darling. You'll feel better after a sleep."

Louise couldn't even summon the energy to get up from the desk. She laid her head down and closed her eyes, relieved when the front door closed and she heard him whistling again as he went down the front path. Pleased with himself, now he's got his own way, she thought.

Her thoughts churned as she half dozed. She hated the thought of leaving the house where she'd spent her whole life and which held such happy memories of her early life with Father. Telling James she needed her sister's signature too had only delayed the inevitable. Anyway, perhaps he was right. It was all too much for her to cope with since her health had deteriorated. She thought of the many unused rooms gathering dust, the neglected garden. Life would be simpler in a smaller place, she told herself.

The clock in the hall chimed and she sat up, rubbing her eyes. She stumbled into the kitchen and surveyed the mess. Surely she'd cleaned up this morning. She remembered James making the tea but he hadn't put anything away and the cups were still on the table. As she slowly and unsteadily began to put things to rights, she thought back to that morning. Where had that burst of energy come from?

She picked up the tonic bottle which James had left on the dresser. She'd been all right until she'd taken the medicine. Could Dr Tate have possibly prescribed the wrong stuff? It was true he was getting old and a bit vague but he'd been a good doctor, attending the family ever since she could remember. She didn't want to believe it, but that was easier than entertaining suspicions about her husband. She put the bottle on a high shelf at the back of the larder, resolved not to take any more, no matter what James said. And, as soon as possible, she'd have a tactful word with the doctor.

When she'd finished tidying up, she looked out of the kitchen window. The sun was still shining and a breeze ruffled the leaves of the lilac tree by the back door. "I will go out," she said aloud. Perhaps the fresh air would blow the cobwebs away. I don't have to go far, just down to the seafront to look at the sea. It seemed ages since she'd last taken a walk just for the pleasure of it.

She put on a hat and jacket and picked up her handbag, smiling at the thought of James queuing in the butcher's. He wouldn't of course. He'd get that girl, Nancy, to do it.

At the front gate she glanced up the road and was about to turn towards the seafront when Muriel came round the corner. Before she could speak her friend said, "Oh, you're better. I'm so glad. James gave me the impression you were at death's door. I've been so worried."

"I've just been a bit tired and rundown that's all."

"Thank goodness it wasn't anything serious. James said you weren't up to having visitors or I'd have called. And your telephone's been out of order so I couldn't ring."

"I thought you'd forgotten me," Louise said.

"Didn't James give you my note?"

Louise shook her head.

"Never mind," said Muriel. "Where are you off to now?"

"Just getting a bit of fresh air. It's about time I started getting out and about."

"Come on then, let's get some roses in those cheeks." Muriel tucked Louise's arm into hers and they set off across the road and along the promenade.

Louise's legs soon began to shake from the unaccustomed exercise and she stopped to take a breath. "Let's sit down for a moment," she said.

They sat on a low wall looking out to sea across the tangle of rusting barbed wire. The breeze ruffled the water and seabirds cried as they skimmed the waves in search of food. Despite the sea defences and blurred outline of naval ships on the horizon it seemed very peaceful. Louise sighed contentedly.

"I do love it here," she said. "I always said I wanted to get away from Holton but when I was in London, I longed for the sight of the sea."

"Do you ever wish you'd gone to America with Sarah?"

"I thought about it but Father made me promise to look after Dora." She couldn't tell her friend the real reason she wanted to stay in Holton. Resolutely, she pushed the thought of Andrew to the back of her mind.

"The pull of duty is strong," Muriel said. "I could have married you know. My fiancé was in the diplomatic service. He was posted to India and wanted me to go with him. But I couldn't leave Mother — she'd gone through so much. My father died young and then my brother was killed at Ypres."

Louise didn't know what to say. It was the first time Muriel had confided in her. She'd always been the staid Miss Baines, her father's secretary, and even when they'd become friends they hadn't exchanged confidences.

Muriel gave a half laugh. "Sorry, didn't mean to sound gloomy. It's all in the past and I'm quite content now. I'm more worried about you. Still, James seems to be taking care of you. He's most solicitous."

"Too solicitous sometimes," Louise said. "He hovers over me, makes me take my medicine, stops my friends from calling . . ." Suddenly she became overwhelmed and her eyes filled with tears.

Muriel put her arm round her. "It's all right. Maybe you need a good cry."

Suddenly the words gushed forth, releasing the guilt she felt over Dora's death — feelings she'd kept pent up for too long. "If I hadn't fallen asleep I'd have heard her. I could have got help sooner," she sobbed.

"You weren't to blame. You were exhausted yourself." Muriel tried to comfort her but she couldn't stop.

"It's not just that. I lied to James about the house." In a broken voice, punctuated by sniffs and hiccups she confided in her friend that she didn't want to leave Steyne House and had told James she needed her sister's signature before they could sell. "He made me send the papers to her and now she's going to wonder what's going on."

"Why is he so keen to sell? Nobody's buying houses now."

Louise told her about the offer from the ministry. "James says we need the money but I don't understand. Even if business is at a standstill we still have some capital." Normally, she wouldn't have dreamt of mentioning financial matters. It just wasn't done. But Muriel's long involvement with Charlton and Spencer meant that she'd understand.

"Things seemed to be ticking over all right when I was still there. But when James took over he wouldn't let me have anything to do with business. I was reduced to being nothing but a filing clerk." Muriel's voice was bitter.

"I'm sorry about that. My father always relied on you."

"It wasn't the same after he died. I was glad to go. James and I just didn't see eye to eye." Muriel stood up.

"I'm sorry, I know he's your husband but seriously, Louise, I don't know why you married him."

She gave a wry smile. "I sometimes wonder that myself. Perhaps it would be different if we had children." She shrugged. "It seems it's not to be."

They began to walk back to the house. The time for confidences was over. Not that Louise was ready yet to tell her friend that she suspected the medicine James insisted on her taking was not what the doctor had prescribed.

# CHAPTER
# TWENTY-THREE

When Louise got home she was exhausted, whether from the walk or her outburst of emotion she wasn't sure. Yet, despite the heaviness of her limbs, she felt more like her old self. The chat with Muriel had probably done her as much good as the fresh air, she thought. She'd missed having someone to talk to.

Although she was tired, she thought she ought to prepare a meal for when James came home and decided to make a Woolton pie. There were a few vegetables and plenty of potatoes with the remains of the cheese ration to give it a bit of flavour. She'd become quite good at adapting recipes to use whatever she had in the larder. It was pointless to wait and see what James had managed to scrounge from the butcher as she had no idea when he'd be home.

When she opened the larder door and saw the newspaper wrapped package on the stone shelf she knew James had returned while she'd been gone. She felt a little tremor of unease as she unwrapped the liver, dreading the confrontation when he realized she'd gone out after all.

She reached up to the shelf where she'd hidden the tonic bottle. It wasn't there. Surely that's where she'd put it? Perhaps she'd already thrown it away. She had been getting so forgetful lately.

She shrugged and decided to get on with cooking. They'd have the liver after all — they could have Woolton pie any time. When she went to get a knife from the dresser drawer she saw the note propped up against the tonic bottle.

*Didn't want to disturb you, darling. Hope you had a good sleep. Don't forget to take your medicine, J.*

So, he'd thought she was in her room. A wave of relief washed over her. She wasn't sure why, but she didn't want him to know she'd been out. He made such a fuss about her health. As she'd confided to Muriel, sometimes he was just too concerned, but instead of making her feel loved and cosseted, it stifled her. She wasn't like Dora who had "enjoyed ill health" as the saying went. She hated feeling this way and longed for a return of her old carefree self. She had to admit though, that when she was feeling poorly, James was a lot kinder.

She picked up the bottle and the spoon which James had thoughtfully left beside it. She measured out a dose and then turned to the sink, tipping the spoonful away. Another followed it. She turned the tap on and rinsed it away, then laid the used spoon on the draining board. She re-corked the bottle and resumed preparing the meal. Soon the smell of frying onions filled the kitchen and she realized that for the first time in months she felt really hungry. The sea air really had done her good.

When James came in she was sitting in the rocking chair, her eyes closed. But the dining room table was laid and the meal ready to dish up. He bent and kissed her cheek. "Something smells good," he said. "You found the meat then?"

She opened her eyes and smiled. "Thank you, yes. I didn't hear you come in earlier."

"You must have been sound asleep. I didn't go up. Better to let you rest. It seems to have done the trick." He laughed. "Thought I might have to cook my own dinner."

Louise managed a laugh as well. He'd never cooked in his life. On those days when she wasn't well enough to prepare a meal he ate out or made do with sandwiches or beans on toast.

James poured himself a drink while she dished up. When they were seated he returned to the subject of the house and her father's will. "I hope we don't have to wait too long to hear from Sarah," he said.

"I'm sure she'll send the papers back as soon as she can."

Louise picked at her food, feeling bad about perpetuating the lie but hoping that Sarah stayed true to form and didn't reply. After all, she hadn't bothered to write for months.

James cleared his plate and stood up. "Bring my coffee through to the study — that's if we have any."

"There's a little. I'll clear away first."

He turned at the door. "Hurry up then — and don't forget to take your medicine."

306

She didn't reply. Treating me like a child, she thought, crashing the plates into the sink. Well, I won't take it. The thought made her smile unwillingly. Now who's being childish, she asked herself. But she tipped some of the tonic away as she'd done before, glancing nervously at the door as she did so.

It was a week later and Louise had still managed to avoid taking her medicine, except on a couple of occasions when James had stood over her. She was now convinced that it was the so-called tonic that was causing her confusion and tiredness. But she still wasn't ready to accuse James of adding something to the mixture. She was equally reluctant to blame Dr Tate but he *was* getting old and he could have made a mistake.

The bottle was almost empty and James offered to call in at the surgery and get some more.

"Don't bother, James. I'll telephone Dr Tate and ask him to call. He hasn't been round for ages."

"It's no trouble, darling. Besides, the phone's still out of order."

"Really? I thought you were speaking to someone the other day."

James laughed. "You probably heard me swearing because I couldn't get through." He bent and kissed her cheek. "I must be off. Now, don't overdo it, make sure you rest."

Louise nodded but when he'd gone she ran up the stairs and began to strip the beds. It was getting harder to disguise from James her sudden access of energy. But he hadn't commented on the fact that the house was looking cleaner and tidier than it had since Polly had left them. She still wasn't quite sure why she felt the need to deceive him.

Downstairs she put the linen in the copper and left it to boil, then got the dustpan and brush. She swept the stairs down and as she reached the bottom she noticed that the wire from the telephone was loose. She jiggled it and lifted the receiver. No sound. She jiggled the wire a bit more and was rewarded with the dialling tone. She couldn't hide the suspicion that James had loosened the wire. She was convinced he was trying to cut her off from her friends.

On impulse she dialled the doctor's number. His housekeeper answered, saying he was on his rounds but that she'd ask him to call.

"It's not urgent," Louise assured her. "When he's not too busy will do."

She got on with the rest of her household chores, reflecting once more that when she was feeling well she enjoyed being a housewife. Not for her the life her sister had, although, despite her hurt at being neglected for so long she truly hoped Sarah was happy.

The thought led her to wonder what James would do if Sarah didn't return the papers. He was fully convinced that her signature was needed and as each day passed with no word from her he became more desperate, taking out his frustration on her.

Although James blamed the war for the fall-off in business, Louise couldn't help feeling that if her father had still been around things wouldn't have got so bad.

After all, Stanley had brought them through the slump and the problems caused by the disastrous Winter Gardens fire.

Louise was in the garden hanging out the washing when Dr Tate arrived. He came round to the side gate and called to her. "What a pleasure to see you looking so well, my dear. My tonic is doing some good then?"

When they were seated in the drawing room, he opened his bag. "Your husband popped in this morning and asked me for another bottle. I'm so pleased you're feeling the better for it."

Louise hesitated. How could she explain that she felt better for *not* taking it? "Actually, Doctor, I'm not sure I need any more. I've been feeling really well lately and —"

He interrupted. "Don't be hasty, my dear. Let's examine you first before we decide." He got out his stethoscope and listened while he took her pulse. Then he shone a small torch in her eyes and examined her tongue. When he'd finished he leaned back with a sigh of satisfaction.

"I think you're right — we can dispense with the medication. You must still take plenty of rest though, combined with fresh air and moderate exercise." He put his stethoscope away and stood up. "I knew it was only a matter of time. You hadn't had time to grieve over your father's death before Dora became ill and you were charged with caring for her. You just wore yourself out and when she died your body and subconscious mind told you it was all right to let go. Take it gently though, build yourself up and don't try to do too much too soon."

Louise smiled, relieved that she hadn't voiced her concerns. Now she could truthfully tell James that there was no need for her to take it.

As she stood up to see the doctor out, he picked up the bottle. "I'm so pleased you don't need this any more," he said.

James was furious. Interfering old fool, he thought. Now what am I going to do? He had to keep Louise sweet — and docile — for a bit longer. It had been so easy to mix a few of Dora's sleeping pills with Louise's medicine and then make sure she took enough to keep her tired and confused.

He paced his study, grinding his teeth in frustration. He'd come home with his head reeling from trying to manipulate the firm's finances, only to be greeted by a smiling Louise.

Pleased as punch she was, telling him that the doctor had called. James had told him there was no need to disturb her and that he'd pick the tonic up on his way home. Why didn't he say he was going to call? At least he could have made sure he was there. He slammed his fist down on the desk.

As if that wasn't frustrating enough, there was still no answer from that sister of hers. If he didn't get her signature soon, the deal would fall through. He wouldn't let that happen, though. A sly grin stole over his face. He unlocked a drawer in the desk and took the letter out. It had arrived some time ago and he'd shoved it in the drawer when Louise had come in unexpectedly. He'd burnt the others but never got round to disposing of this one.

He opened the study door and listened. Louise was bustling around in the kitchen. He heard her humming as she worked. He closed the door and took the flimsy sheet of airmail paper out of the envelope. He didn't bother reading it. He already knew by heart the sentimental outpourings and the heartbroken pleas to write. He sat down and drew a sheet of writing paper towards him. Uncapping his fountain pen he began to write, covering the paper with a childish scrawl. It wasn't long before he'd perfected his sister-in-law's signature. Sarah's writing was so easy to copy.

# CHAPTER
# TWENTY-FOUR

Louise continued to feel well and, as her health improved, her suspicions that James had doctored her medicine lessened. How foolish she'd been. What reason could he have for doing such a thing? Besides, if he really wanted to harm her he'd have found another way once she stopped taking the tonic. It was much more likely that the old doctor had made a mistake.

Now that she was more her old self, James seemed in a better mood too. He no longer asked if there was a letter from Sarah or spoke about selling the house and, although she didn't dare ask, she assumed that the financial crisis had now been solved.

After a bout of unseasonably warm weather, it had turned damp and chilly once more but Louise decided to walk to church that morning. James accompanied her and, as they walked up the path to the church door, she said, "I think I'll call in at the WVS centre tomorrow. It's time I started doing something useful again."

James squeezed her arm. "I don't want you overdoing it," he said. "Remember what Dr Tate said."

She laughed. "You worry too much. I'm fine."

James didn't reply. He smiled and raised his hat to a group of ladies, shook hands with the vicar and ushered Louise into her pew. As she sat down she heard whispering behind her. "Such a charming young man. And how nice to see Louise looking so well."

As the organ started to play and the choir came down the aisle, Louise immersed herself in the familiar order of service. But when the Reverend Ayling mounted the pulpit and began his sermon her mind began to wander. Was it her fault that her marriage hadn't turned out well? Everyone liked James. In the early days of their marriage people had commented on what a charming couple they made. He worked hard both at his business and as an air raid warden. It must be her fault that sometimes he was sarcastic and cold towards her. Even when he was being nice there seemed to be an underlying edge to his manner.

Yes, she thought, but not everyone is taken in by him. Father was reluctant to have him in the business and Muriel makes no bones about her dislike.

She stole a glance at his handsome profile. He was looking up at the pulpit, his expression thoughtful, as if he was taking in every word the Reverend Ayling was saying. But she knew that he had no time for the man he described as a pompous old fool. Yet when they left church he would smile and shake the vicar's hand, complimenting him on his excellent sermon.

They stood for the final hymn and blessing before filing outside, where the wind had got up and cold rain had started to fall. As they reached the gate Louise saw

Andrew holding a big black umbrella over his uncle's head.

The memory of their last passionate meeting swept over her in a hot flush and she would have hurried past but Andrew smiled. "How nice to see you, Mrs Spencer," he said. "My uncle tells me you've been unwell, but it's good to see you're better."

Louise winced at the formality. "I'm very well," she said, "thanks to your uncle's excellent care."

Dr Tate took her hand and patted it. "I hope you're taking my advice, my dear. And now, you'd better get out of this rain. We don't want you catching a chill."

"Quite right, Doctor," said James, taking her arm in a firm grip. "Come along, darling," he said.

As he hustled her away Louise couldn't resist looking back. Andrew was staring after them, his lips tight.

The rain started to come down harder and James cursed. "We should've brought the car," he said.

Usually, Louise didn't mind the rain but she was shivering by the time they got indoors. She took off her wet coat and went into the kitchen to prepare lunch. James appeared in the doorway with two glasses. "Better drink this," he said. "Keep out the cold." He handed her a small tot of whisky.

She pulled a face. "You know I don't like that stuff," she said.

"It's medicinal. As your doctor friend said we can't have you catching a chill."

She sipped cautiously. "I didn't think we had any left," she said. Spirits were almost impossible to get nowadays.

"Did a favour for someone — grateful thanks from a client," James replied, draining his own glass.

Louise didn't ask him what the favour was. She was sure it had nothing to do with the firm of Charlton and Spencer. By the time the meal was ready, James had consumed quite a lot of the whisky. She watched him warily as she picked at her own food. He seemed quite mellow at the moment but she knew his mood could change in a flash. He looked up and grinned.

"So nice to have my wife back," he said. "It's no fun being married to a drooping lily."

"I wasn't ill on purpose," Louise said.

"Of course not, darling. Well, now you're better you can start being a proper wife again." He stood up and reached out a hand. "Come on, let's go upstairs."

Reluctantly, she followed him. It was the last thing she wanted. While she'd been preparing the meal she hadn't been able to stop shivering despite the whisky and now her head was pounding. James ignored her protests, determined to exert what he called his rights.

She felt so ill she didn't have the strength to fight him off, even if she'd been brave enough to do so. Although he'd never beaten her, preferring to use words rather than blows, she sensed the underlying violence in him. She often thought that it wouldn't take much for him to lose control.

By the next day, the chill had taken hold. Louise tried to carry on as usual but eventually had to give in and go back to bed. It wasn't like the fever she'd had before but she felt wretched for almost a week.

To her surprise, instead of becoming impatient, James was most solicitous, dosing her with cough mixture and managing to find tempting treats for her to eat. She was in no state to ask how he'd managed it with rationing becoming more stringent than ever. She'd often suspected he was dealing on the black market.

When she started to feel better she struggled out of bed and made her way downstairs. The kitchen was a mess and she wondered how someone as fastidious as James could leave things in such a state. However, if he knew she was well enough to get up, he would insist on her resuming her housekeeping duties. She made a cup of tea and sat down. She'd clear up the kitchen in a little while. It was comforting to lean back in Cookie's old rocking chair and daydream about happier times.

She was jerked back to the present by the sound of the front door opening and she almost dropped her cup and saucer. She knew it was foolish to be afraid of James and she chided herself for her weakness. Hadn't he lovingly looked after her these past few days? But she was always apprehensive, wondering what sort of mood he'd be in.

He looked surprised when he came into the kitchen and saw her and she quailed inwardly at the expression on his face. But it was gone in an instant and he came over and took her hands.

"Are you sure you should be up, darling?" he asked. He turned to speak to someone in the doorway. "She really has been quite poorly, Doctor."

**316**

Louise struggled upright. "How kind of you to call, Doctor. But it's only a summer cold."

"I intended to make a neighbourly call anyway and when James told me you'd been under the weather, I decided to come straight away."

She forced a smile. "I'm feeling much better now. James worries too much."

The old doctor sat opposite and felt her glands, looked at her tonsils and took her pulse. "A bit more than a summer cold, my dear," he said. "You must look after yourself. Perhaps you should start taking that tonic again."

Louise groaned inwardly. She hated being treated like an invalid. She was about to protest when she felt James's firm hand on her shoulder. "An excellent idea — don't you think so, darling?

She nodded, not wanting to argue in front of the doctor. Perhaps he knew best anyway. Besides, she didn't *have* to take the horrible stuff. She'd pour it away as she'd done before if she didn't think it was doing her any good.

The doctor fastened his bag and stood up. As he was about to leave he said, "How is young Sarah these days?"

Before Louise could reply, James laughed. "She's quite the star. We're very proud of her, aren't we, darling?" He shook hands with the doctor and saw him out.

When he came back in he said to Louise, "I didn't want you telling him we hadn't heard from her. We don't want people thinking she's no time for us now she's a big star."

"I don't think that's why she hasn't written, James. I'm worried about her. What if she's in trouble?"

James gave a cruel laugh. "Worried about *her*? Don't waste your time. She's always been self-centred. Probably having such a good time she's forgotten all about her family."

Louise didn't reply. She was sure that Sarah, despite her occasional thoughtlessness, wouldn't abandon her altogether. It was more likely that her letters weren't getting through.

Despite James's protests, Louise refused the tonic the doctor had prescribed. She couldn't help thinking of her previous illness and her suspicions that James had meddled with her medicine. Why else would she have felt so much worse? She was now sure Dr Tate hadn't made a mistake.

"I'm perfectly all right," she told James. "It was just a summer cold. Please don't fuss."

"It's only because I'm concerned, darling." He used the wheedling tone she'd come to despise. She was convinced now that the reason he was nicer to her when she was ill was that he could manipulate her more easily.

Once she'd realized that, it was easier to believe that he'd been keeping her sedated. Well, he wouldn't get the chance again. From now on, she'd be very careful. But why was he doing this? She'd never openly gone against his wishes and her only bid for independence had been her involvement with the WVS. But he could hardly object to that; everybody had to contribute to the war effort.

Now she answered him in a conciliatory tone. "It's lovely that you care but I really do feel better." She didn't think it was the right moment to confess that she'd poured the contents of the bottle away.

James seemed to accept her decision and gave her a kiss on the cheek but his tone was acid when he said, "Perhaps you'll summon up the energy to iron my best shirt then. I have an important meeting tonight."

After he'd gone, Louise remained in the hall for some minutes, biting back her anger. Why had it taken her so long to realize his true nature? Her resentment coalesced into a small rebellion. His shirt could wait. She picked up her handbag and put on her hat and jacket. She'd go down to the WVS centre and do some work. If Muriel was there she might get a chance to blow off some steam. She'd always tried to be loyal, not to run James down to her friend. But it might make her feel better to share her opinion of the man she'd married, especially knowing that Muriel agreed. She wouldn't tell her friend her suspicions though.

In the past few weeks the town had filled up with service personnel of all nationalities — Canadians, Poles, Americans — and there was a feeling of excitement in the air. Something was about to happen — and soon.

When Louise got to the WVS canteen she was welcomed enthusiastically as the soldiers queued up for their tea and biscuits. The hall was noisy with banter and laughter but Louise could sense the underlying tension in their voices.

After a hurried greeting there was no time to talk to Muriel but keeping busy took Louise's mind off her troubles for a while. When the last currant bun had disappeared and the men were drifting out of the door, summoned by a sergeant's whistle, she took off her apron and ran her hands through her hair. She was exhausted but more content than she'd been for weeks.

These young men would soon be embarking on a perilous venture that everyone hoped would put an end to the long war. The realization helped to put her problems into perspective.

Muriel came across and said, "You look whacked. Let's get out of here."

"I ought to go home," Louise said when they were outside, breathing in the tangy sea air. She was thinking of the ironing that waited for her and of James's displeasure when he found she hadn't done as he'd asked.

"I hoped you'd come to the pictures this afternoon. I've missed our outings," Muriel said.

"So have I. I feel so cut off from everything. Not even a newspaper. James stopped the deliveries and buys one on the way to the office. He's always forgetting to bring it home." She took Muriel's arm. "Yes, let's go. Even if the film's not very good, I'd like to see the newsreel."

"There's a Leslie Howard film on today — such a shame about him being killed. I heard a rumour that he was a spy."

"That's 'cause he played a sort of spy in that film, *Pimpernel Smith*."

"I don't suppose we'll ever know."

They hurried towards the Picturedrome, relieved that today there wasn't a queue, and settled in their seats just as the newsreel started. After showing scenes of the bomb damage in Southampton, the film switched to a scene of tropical jungle and "our brave boys in Burma".

The voiceover announced that during brief moments away from the fighting they were being entertained by the latest singing sensation, straight from Hollywood — the lovely Sally Charles.

Louise sat up straight in her seat and gasped. Sarah? Was it really her?

Muriel clutched at her arm. "Is that . . .? Yes it is — it's your sister." She turned to Louise, ignoring the shushing from the seats behind them. "You didn't tell me . . ."

"I didn't know," Louise whispered. When Muriel started to question her, she shook her head. "I'll tell you later."

Tears rolled down her cheeks as the camera moved in for a close-up and Sarah began to sing *Pennies from Heaven*.

When the main film started, she hardly took it in, despite it starring her favourite actor, and she didn't realize it had finished until Muriel nudged her. She followed her friend out of the cinema, her head still reeling from the discovery that Sarah had not only changed her name but had left America. No wonder I haven't heard from her, she thought.

Muriel shook her arm. "Why didn't you tell me Sarah had changed her name? I read something about this Sally Charles in the paper but didn't realize who it was."

"I knew about her name change but I thought she was still in Hollywood." Louise took out a hankie and blew her nose. "I haven't heard from her for ages. I write every week but get no reply. I was beginning to get worried; worse still — I thought she didn't want to know us any longer."

"Don't be silly. Sarah's not like that. It's most likely letters aren't getting through, especially now she's out in Burma."

Muriel's common sense reassured Louise. "You're probably right. But how was I to know where she was? And what happened to her film career?"

They were walking up the high street and Louise suddenly caught sight of the clock over the town hall. "Oh, goodness, I should be getting home," she exclaimed, quickening her footsteps.

As she started to hurry away, Muriel said, "So it *was* Sarah in that film we saw last year? The one about the sultan starring Sally Charles? No wonder we didn't recognize her."

She obviously wanted to discuss it further but Louise said a hasty goodbye. She *had* recognized Sarah and felt bad about keeping it from her friend. She'd thought Muriel might think less of her sister for appearing in a film like that. But why should she be ashamed? Besides, it looked as if Sarah had changed direction and gone back to singing. So long as she was happy, Louise didn't care. But she did wish her sister had told her what she up to.

When she got home James was waiting, the un-ironed shirt dangling from his hand. "Where have you been?" he asked, his face a mask of fury.

"At the WVS centre," she said. It wasn't like her to be evasive but this wasn't the moment to say she'd been at the pictures, still less to tell him what she'd discovered about her sister.

"You're lying. They told me you left hours ago," he said.

"How dare you accuse me of lying," she said, anger overcoming her usual submissiveness. "I *was* there. I just didn't come straight home."

"You've been with another man," James accused, thrusting his face close to hers. "Who is he?"

She stepped back, flinching. "I was with Muriel if you must know — not that it's any business of yours who my friends are. I don't question you . . ."

"It is my business when you're supposed to be here." He flicked the shirt, catching her across the face and stinging her eyes.

She tried to move away but he did it again. Shocked, she began to whimper. "Please don't . . ." He'd never been physically violent before.

"I'm going to teach you a lesson," he said, making a grab for her.

Terrified now, she pushed past him and made for the stairs but he caught hold of her ankle and dragged her down. She fell, hitting her head on the bottom step. It wasn't hard enough to knock her out but she staggered as she scrambled up.

James was beside her, instantly contrite. "I'm sorry. I didn't mean to hurt you. Are you all right?"

She nodded, clutching her head as pain surged through her.

He put his arms round her. "Darling, I hate it when we quarrel. But you make me so angry. Why can't you just . . .?" He choked on a sob.

Louise sighed. He was doing it again. Trying to make her feel as if it were her fault. Part of her wanted to agree, to tell herself that if she'd come straight home from the WVS and ironed his shirt, everything would be all right. The other half of her seethed with rebellion. Why shouldn't she have a little time to herself, time to enjoy being with friends? Why should her life be all drudgery and duty?

James helped her to her feet and kissed her. "There, darling. Thank goodness you're all right. Just a silly misunderstanding that's all." He followed her into the kitchen and said, "Did you forget I was going out tonight? Never mind, I'll pour you a drink while you iron my shirt."

Louise's head was spinning and she felt sick but she did as he wanted. It was easier to give in. As she ironed, she tried to summon up the anger she'd felt earlier, resolving not to be so spineless in future. It wasn't as if James had ever been physically violent before. She shouldn't let mere words hurt her. But then she remembered the contemptuous look on his face as he flicked the shirt in her face and the murderous rage in his eyes as he'd threatened to teach her a lesson. She was sure he'd been about to hit her.

For a moment she'd been terrified but her terror had faded with his change of mood and now she tried to convince herself that he wouldn't intentionally hurt her.

As he came back into the room and held out his hand for the shirt, she forced herself not to flinch away from him. She wouldn't let him see her fear.

# CHAPTER
# TWENTY-FIVE

For a while after the incident with the shirt, James was much nicer to Louise. It was as if he was ashamed of losing his temper and was trying to make it up to her. He'd stopped inviting his friends round for cards and drinks, always came home for his meals and seemed content to spend the evenings he was not on ARP duty sitting with her and listening to the wireless.

Occasionally he seemed restless, getting up and pacing the room, a glass in his hand. But he seldom drank to excess these days — not surprising, thought Louise, as the contents of her father's cellar had long since gone and spirits were virtually unobtainable unless on the black market.

She guessed his agitation was due to money worries but, fearful of breaking the fragile peace between them, she hesitated to ask. The one time she'd mentioned it he'd brushed her off saying, "It's all under control. I don't want you worrying about it."

Wary of setting off another black mood, she let the subject drop. Besides, she couldn't summon up the energy to really take an interest. In fact, she had little interest in anything these days. She hadn't even gone back to the WVS canteen and, since neither Muriel nor

Mrs Wilson had telephoned to ask why, she hadn't felt inclined to make the effort.

She sat opposite James now, pretending to concentrate on her knitting as he turned the pages of his newspaper. But she could tell he wasn't really reading it.

He looked up suddenly and caught her watching him. "What are you staring at?" he barked. "Do you realize how daft you look, sitting there staring into space like that?"

"I was thinking," she said.

"Huh, thinking." His short laugh was filled with contempt.

So, the brief respite was over, she thought. James was back to his normal sarcastic self. When he went back to his paper, her stomach was churning. Why did he have to be so nasty? What had she done?

She began to shake and, to cover her nervousness, she got up and put away her knitting. "I'll go and make the cocoa, James."

He folded his paper and switched off the wireless. "I'll do it. You go on up. You look tired." He bent and kissed her cheek.

She was sitting up in bed, still feeling unsettled by his change of mood, when he came in with the mug of cocoa. "Drink it up," he urged.

He watched as she drank, patted her shoulder and took the mug away. "I'll be up later. Sleep well," he said.

But it was a sleep of troubled dreams. Sarah was calling out to her, begging her to write. When she woke, her brain still foggy from the dream, James was already up. She could hear him moving around downstairs. She stumbled out of bed and went over to the dressing table. "Pen, paper," she mumbled. "I must write . . ."

The door opened and James came in. "What are you doing?" he asked.

"I want to write to Sarah. I'm sure she's in trouble."

"Don't be ridiculous. How could you know that?" James put down the tray he was carrying and came over to her. "Why do you waste your time worrying about her? The selfish bitch hasn't been in touch for months. I can just imagine her out there, surrounded by adoring soldiers. She's having the time of her life, probably never gives you a thought."

Louise put her head in her hands and began to sob. "I don't believe that. Besides, I can't help worrying about her. It's dangerous where she is. How do I know she hasn't been . . .?"

James stroked her hair. "Please, darling, don't get upset. I didn't mean to sound harsh. I just get angry on your behalf." He pulled her to her feet. "Now stop crying and get back into bed. I've brought you some breakfast and a nice cup of tea."

He settled her with pillows behind her back and laid the tray across her lap. "Now, I want you to stay there and have a nice rest. There's no need to get up at all. I'll be out all day and I'll bring some fish and chips home for our supper."

He turned at the door, smiling. "And be sure to eat up your breakfast. You must keep your strength up."

When he'd gone, Louise tried to eat the toast he'd prepared but her mouth was too dry to swallow. She took a couple of sips of the tea but it had gone cold. Deciding to make some fresh, she pushed the tray aside and got up, but her legs were shaking and she sat down abruptly on the side of the bed.

"I will *not* be ill again," she muttered, forcing herself to stand and make her way downstairs. There was nothing wrong with her; she was just tired, that's all. At least she couldn't blame the tonic. She'd gone through the medicine cabinet and thrown out everything, even the little bottle of aspirin she kept for emergencies. Thank goodness James hadn't seen her in this state. He would send for Dr Tate straight away. But Louise had lost confidence in the old doctor since her last illness and she had resolved not to take any more medicine.

Her head was still pounding but after forcing herself to eat some toast and drink a cup of tea she started to feel better. I'll write to Sarah, she thought, the dream still vivid in her mind. No recriminations, she decided, and no whining about her own situation. She'd just write a chatty friendly letter congratulating her on her singing success and wishing her well.

Her hand shook as she sat down at the desk in James's study, but she gripped the pen firmly and began to write. Once she started, she found herself pouring it all out, even her suspicions that James had been trying to poison her.

She laughed a little as she wrote: *What nonsense it was. I even tried to blame poor old Dr Tate. But the fever was making me imagine things. James has looked*

*after me wonderfully. He even brought me breakfast in
bed this morning. I know I told you in earlier letters
that my marriage wasn't really happy, and I suppose
that's still true, but I'm making the best of things.*

She finished the letter and sealed it, wrote Sarah's
name and addressed it care of her agent in America. It
could take weeks to reach her but she felt better for
having written. She'd go to the post office later.

James had said he'd be out all day but, as she put the
writing materials away, she heard the front door open.
She thrust the letter into the pocket of her cardigan and
stood up as he came into the study.

"What are you doing?" His eyes flicked to the open
desk drawer.

Louise wasn't quite sure why she lied. "I've got a
headache; I was looking for aspirin," she said.

"In here?"

"There's none in the bathroom. I thought you might
have some."

James laughed. "I don't get headaches." He came
towards her looking concerned. "You do look a bit pale.
I'll get you some aspirin on my way home."

When he'd gone out again she took the letter out of
her pocket, wondering if she ought to send it or tear it
up and write another. Who else could she confide in?
Muriel would probably believe her but what could she
do?

She lay back in the old rocking chair beside the
kitchen range and closed her eyes, tears seeping out
and running down her cheeks. For now her earlier
suspicions had been confirmed. James was definitely up

to something. She was sure she hadn't mistaken the guilty look on his face when he'd noticed the open drawer, a look hastily suppressed. And why would he look guilty unless he thought she'd spotted the bottle marked "aspirin" pushed right to the back of the drawer? Why had he lied? And why would he want to harm her?

James had come home ready to confront Louise with her deceitfulness. He'd just discovered that she'd lied about needing her sister's signature to sell the house. What was it about this monstrosity of a Victorian villa that made her want to hang on to it? Had she guessed how desperately he needed money? At one time he'd have sworn she'd do anything to please him but now, she seemed determined to thwart him.

As he strode along the High Street he clenched his fists in his pockets. How he'd stopped himself hitting her he didn't know. But he must play the loving concerned husband for just a little bit longer. It would be hard but no one must know how he really felt about that lying, deceitful bitch.

He entered the premises of Charlton and Spencer, ignoring Nancy's smiling greeting, and went into his office. Throwing himself down in his chair, he replayed the scene with David Webster, the solicitor, earlier that day.

"I'm sorry it's taken so long to get back to you," he'd said. "As you know, my sister-in-law is abroad and it's taken a while for her to return the documents." He withdrew the papers from his briefcase, making sure that the envelope addressed in Sarah's writing was on view.

"Your sister-in-law?" David Webster had raised an eyebrow. "I thought your wife inherited the house." He'd dealt with the Charltons's affairs for years.

"Jointly — with her sister," James explained. "They couldn't sell while Mrs Charlton was alive, of course."

David Webster waved a hand impatiently. "I know that — I drew up the will myself. But I don't recall Miss Sarah Charlton being left the house. She had a small legacy from her mother and Mrs Spencer inherited the house, plus a share of the business."

James thought furiously. What was Louise up to? She'd definitely said she needed Sarah's signature. He took a deep breath. "Mr Webster, as you know, my wife has been in poor health lately. As her husband I am fully authorized to conduct her business. She wants to sell the house and she specifically told me she could not without her sister's consent."

"It's not like Louise — Mrs Spencer — to make a mistake like that." David Webster pursed his lips.

"Well, she has been ill. Some sort of breakdown the doctor says — the strain of nursing her stepmother . . ."

"I quite understand." David Webster nodded sympathetically. "Perhaps it would be better if we wait until your wife is well enough to come in and see me. I really need to be sure she understands what she is signing . . ."

Furious, James had snatched up the papers and stormed out, angry that he'd gone to the trouble of forging Sarah's signature when there'd been no need.

When he got home he'd been surprised to see Louise up and dressed; the sleeping pills he'd dissolved in her tea should have left her drugged for the rest of the day. When he'd seen her rummaging in his desk the impulse to grab her and demand an explanation had been almost overwhelming. Had she really been looking for aspirin? Good job he'd come in before she spotted that bottle. She might have swallowed some of the tablets without realizing they weren't harmless painkillers.

He'd held on to his temper with difficulty. Once he lost it, he knew he wouldn't be able to stop himself really hurting her. That wouldn't do. He'd made sure everyone in Holton knew the state she was in. Anything that happened in the future must look like an accidental overdose. But not yet.

# CHAPTER
# TWENTY-SIX

Louise was finding it hard to conceal her suspicions from James. If only there was someone she could confide in. She'd been tempted to speak to Dr Tate when he called unexpectedly, but she hesitated. He'd only say she was imagining things. After all, he'd been treating her for what he called "her nerves" for ages. She had got him to post the letter to Sarah though. Now, if anything happened to her, her sister would be suspicious and would make a fuss.

Could she confide in Muriel? It seemed her friend was her only hope, but she'd need proof.

Since the morning when she'd woken feeling dizzy and sluggish, Louise had become even more suspicious of James. Although he pretended loving concern, she could read the insincerity in his eyes. He had started making their bedtime cocoa and bringing her tea in bed in the mornings. He'd never done that in the early days of their marriage. He was behaving as he had with Dora just before she died.

It was hard to refuse the drink when he stood over her to make sure she drank it. This morning she had woken up feeling groggy and disoriented as she often did these days.

When James had gone to the office, she went into the study and opened the desk drawer. Last time she looked the bottle marked aspirin had gone. Now there was a new one, pushed right to the back behind some papers. She shook a couple of the tablets out. They looked harmless enough. But they were very similar to the sleeping pills Dr Tate had prescribed for Dora.

Cautiously, Louise tasted one. It definitely wasn't aspirin. Her legs felt weak and she sat down with a sob. Why was he doing this to her?

Her tears didn't last long. Here was the proof she needed. She'd go and see Muriel and ask her friend's advice. James was a respected businessman in the town and she had a feeling that if she went to the police they would dismiss her as a hysterical woman who had fallen out of love with her husband.

She really didn't feel up to walking down to the WVS centre but she had to do something. She thrust the bottle back in case James came in while she was getting ready to go out.

She was in the hall putting on her hat when she heard his key in the door. Checking up on her again, she thought, pasting a smile on her face as he came in.

"Feeling better?" he asked.

"A little," she said. "I have to go to the shops."

"I'll walk down the road with you."

Louise smiled and picked up her handbag, cursing inwardly. She'd intended to show the tablets to Muriel. Now her friend would just have to take her word for it.

James waited while she went into the grocer's and insisted on carrying her shopping bag. As they walked up the High Street they saw several acquaintances. James greeted them politely, raising his hat and answering for her when enquiries were made about her health.

She bit her lip. Who, seeing how solicitously he cared for her, would believe he was systematically trying to poison her, or at the very least, send her mad? As they neared his office, she stopped and held out her hand for the bag. "I'm all right now, James. I think the fresh air has done me good. You must have lots of work to do so I'll let you get on."

"Are you sure? I was going to see you home."

"I thought I'd pop into the WVS centre first."

James frowned. "I think you'll be better at home. You mustn't overdo it." He took her arm and almost dragged her along the street. Unless she made a scene, she had no choice but to follow.

He stayed with her for the rest of the day, hovering over her while she ate or drank with every appearance of concern for her health. She couldn't refuse the food he prepared without arousing his suspicions.

As she fell into an exhausted and, she was sure, drugged sleep she wondered why he didn't just finish her off. Did he hate her so much that he preferred to torture her like this?

She dreamed about Sarah again and woke with her sister's name on her lips. Had that last letter reached her yet? Knowing Sarah, she'd probably laugh off her fears. Besides, what could she do from so far away?

Sarah's career was blossoming and she was happier than she'd ever been. She was in love — really in love this time. Greg Lacey was everything she wanted in a man. He wasn't an actor, jealous of every close-up which might eclipse him; he wasn't a director manipulating her for his own ends; he wasn't a rich man trying to buy her affection. He was just Greg — passably good-looking, quiet, unassuming and a brilliant pianist. When she'd given up the silver screen to go to Burma and entertain the troops, he'd come too as her accompanist.

But she hadn't forgotten her sister. She'd written singing Greg's praises, bubbling over with excitement at the new direction her life had taken. She was deeply hurt that Louise hadn't replied. It was more than a year since she'd heard anything.

"I don't care," she told Greg when once again the postbag brought nothing for her. "She's probably jealous of my success."

"Sweetheart. I'm sure you're wrong," Greg said. "Didn't you tell me you were always close, that she always looked out for you and encouraged you in your singing?" He stroked her hair and held her close. "Don't fret, honey. I'm sure you'll hear soon. There's probably a letter on its way right now. You know how the post gets held up — and we've been moving around a lot."

Sarah sniffed. "I expect you're right. I just miss her so much, you know. It's nearly five years since I saw her. And I worry about her too."

Greg laughed. "Now you sound like the big sister. What's to worry about? She's got a husband to take care of her and from what you say, that little town isn't going to be a prime target for Hitler's bombs."

Sarah shook her head. "I still worry. You've seen the newsreels — how people back home are struggling with the rationing and everything. Besides, I don't like her husband and I think she's unhappy. The last letter I had — ages ago now — really upset me."

"I thought she got married after you left England."

"She did and I wish I'd been there to stop her. James was a bully — always teasing the younger ones at infant school. Being the son of my dad's partner we used to see quite a bit of him until he went away to boarding-school." Sarah sighed. "I just hope I'm wrong and that he's grown up and become more responsible."

"Well, you'll be able to see for yourself soon. When this tour ends you'll go back to England." He kissed her and gave a wry smile. "And I'll be with you, honey. I'm not letting you get away."

Sarah laughed, her worries over her sister temporarily forgotten as she melted into his embrace.

Some time later Greg sat up with a muttered exclamation. "Time for the show. Come on, Sarah, get dressed."

Half an hour later she was on the makeshift stage, surrounded by cheering soldiers. Greg, seated at the piano, looked over his shoulder and gave her an encouraging smile. But she needed no encouragement. From the first note she was entranced and her audience was too. She sang all the old favourites, ending with

338

*Wait for me Darling*, a song of love, hope and longing for home that Greg had written specially for her.

She didn't think about Louise at all until the next postbag arrived. Two letters. She tore them open and skimmed though the pages, her heart thumping furiously. What was going on?

Greg found her slumped on her bunk, her face streaked with tears. "I've got to go home," she whispered, holding out the crumpled sheets of paper. "Louise needs me."

# CHAPTER
# TWENTY-SEVEN

James was becoming impatient. He hadn't confronted Louise with her lie, hoping that David Webster would accept her forged signature to the deed of conveyance; he was becoming quite adept at signing her name as well as Sarah's. But the solicitor had insisted that he speak to Louise before agreeing to proceed. He couldn't see the urgency and wanted to wait until she was well again.

"There's no need to disturb Mrs Spencer while she's ill," he said.

James knew that if Louise was in her right mind she'd never agree to selling the house. And he couldn't ask the solicitor to call. It wouldn't do for anyone to see the state she was in, worse still for Louise to start babbling.

But he had to do something. The ministry needed accommodation and they would go elsewhere if Steyne House wasn't available. As James left Webster's office, an idea occurred to him and, instead of turning for home, he walked briskly to the railway station. He'd just recalled meeting a solicitor at the gambling club in Brighton. Perhaps he would be more amenable.

Sarah was on her way home and, as the train pulled into Brighton Station, she was becoming frustrated at the disruption to the trains which meant changing there and then getting a slow train which stopped at every station along the coast.

Although she'd hardly given a thought to her old life in Holton since setting sail on the *Queen Mary* almost five years ago, she couldn't wait to get home now. As she grabbed her suitcase and hurried over to the next platform, she sighed with impatience. As soon as she'd read Louise's last letter, she'd known something was dreadfully wrong. Then there was the puzzle of the forms which Louise said needed her signature. Even when Greg had explained, she was still confused. There was something funny going on. And why did Louise want to sell the house anyway?

She hadn't told her sister she was coming and had booked into a small hotel at the other end of the esplanade from Steyne House. How she wished Greg was with her. She missed him already. As she boarded the packed train and forced her way along the corridor in search of a seat, the train lurched, banging her suitcase against her shin.

"Here, let me." Someone grabbed the case and opened the door of the compartment. The man heaved the case up onto the rack and sat down. Sarah had no choice but to sit beside him. She glanced sideways at his handsome profile and he turned to smile at her.

"Is your journey really necessary?" he said, showing white teeth in a grin and pointing to the poster above their heads.

If she hadn't been so worried about Louise, she'd have laughed. But today her thoughts were with her sister. Had she seriously been suggesting that her husband was poisoning her? But then there'd been that bit at the end, saying she was mistaken and that it was all the product of a mind confused by illness.

Sarah had been tempted to laugh it off. But something had nagged away at the back of her mind. It was true she'd never liked James and had been dismayed when she learned that Louise had married him. But, she'd firmly told herself, it was her choice. Hadn't she herself made mistakes over men in the past?

The train lurched again, throwing her against the man who'd helped with her suitcase. There were resigned sighs from the other passengers as the train slowed to a stop.

The man turned to her. "I'd say no one whose journey wasn't necessary would put up with this. We'll probably be stuck here for hours."

A woman in a WAAF uniform leaned forward. "There is a war on, young man. Troop movements are more important than whatever your business may be." Her look said that she wondered why he wasn't in uniform.

The man just grinned and tapped the side of his nose. "You'll never know," he said.

The WAAF disappeared behind a newspaper and the man turned to Sarah. "Going far?" he asked.

"Just to Holton."

"Me too. Business or pleasure?"

Sarah hesitated. "Pleasure, I suppose." He seemed nice enough but she wasn't about to reveal her life story.

He looked out of the train window. "Looks like we'll be stuck here for hours. Plenty of time for us to get to know each other — I hope. Lucky me to have such a lovely travelling companion." He lowered his voice and jerked his head in the direction of the WAAF who still seemed immersed in her newspaper. "I could have been stuck with . . ."

Sarah couldn't help giggling.

He stuck out his hand for her to shake. "I'm Jim. I live in Holton, been to Brighton on business."

Sarah looked more closely at him, her eyes widening in recognition. But it had been nearly five years since she'd last seen him. So this was her sister's husband, flirting on a train with a total stranger. She shouldn't encourage him. Nevertheless, she smiled and said, "Sally." For some reason she was reluctant to let him know who she was or that she'd recognized him.

"Well, Sally, what brings you to a sleepy little place like Holton Regis?"

"I'm on leave," she told him. "I just felt like having a few restful days by the sea." Although she wasn't in uniform she managed during the course of their conversation to convey that she'd been doing war work in London.

She wasn't the only one telling half truths. James, while hinting that his work was so secret that he

343

couldn't tell her anything, made himself out to be something of a hero. She smiled to herself, picturing his reaction when he realized who she was.

The train started up again and steamed into Worthing where the WAAF and the other passengers got out. Alone in the carriage, James moved closer to her and took her hand.

Sarah smiled, wondering how far he'd go. She didn't mind a little flirtation but when his hands started to wander she slapped them away. He didn't seem in the least put out, laughing and holding up his hands in surrender. "I know; we've only just met. But seriously, Sally my dear, I'd like to get to know you better. How about a drink at your hotel later on — say eight o'clock?"

She gave him a teasing smile and agreed, knowing that by then she'd have seen Louise and exposed "Jim" for the cad he was.

James took the girl's case down from the rack and insisted on carrying it to the hotel for her. As he said goodbye he was looking forward to their assignation later on. But first, there was something he had to do.

Flirting with the girl on the train had taken his mind off things for a while. But now, he seethed with anger as he recalled his meeting with the man he'd thought of as a friend. The chap had refused point blank to help him. His answer had been the same as David Webster's: a signature wasn't enough. He had to meet Louise in person and have her assurance that she agreed to selling the house. "I don't know your wife, James," he'd said. "In fact for all these months we've been playing poker together you've never once mentioned the fact that you even had a wife."

James had been furious. "Are you implying something?"

"Of course not. It's just that in my business, I like to be sure everything's above board."

James had managed to stay calm, to reassure his friend that he understood. But as he strode towards the station he was fuming. While he waited for the train he calmed down and, with cold clarity he knew what he had to do. Louise had been depressed for months. No one, including that old buffer Tate, would be surprised if she took an overdose of sleeping tablets.

Once he'd made the decision his mood lightened. Flirting with Sally had taken his mind off what he planned to do.

Muriel was concerned about Louise and had telephoned several times. But it was always her husband who answered.

She'd never liked James Spencer and, even before Stanley Charlton's death, she'd been suspicious that he was defrauding the business. How she wished she'd conveyed her suspicions to Louise before she'd married the man. Now, she wondered why he was so keen to keep her friends away, fobbing her off with the excuse that Louise was too ill for visitors.

She knew that wasn't true. Mrs Wilson had said she'd seen Louise out with her husband a few days before.

"He told me she was ill," Muriel said.

"Well, she was a little pale and holding on to her husband's arm. But she must be better if she's out and about," Mrs Wilson said. "I do hope she'll soon be back on duty. We need an extra pair of hands."

"I'll pop round to see her later on," Muriel said.

When her shift was over, Muriel walked round to Steyne House, hoping that James would still be at the office. There was no answer to her knock and she went round the side of the house, hoping to find a door or window open. She wasn't going to give up until she knew her friend was all right.

She tried the back door but it was firmly bolted. Looking through the kitchen window she saw that the draining board was piled high with dirty crockery, the remains of a meal on the table in the centre of the room. That wasn't like Louise, she thought. Perhaps she really was ill.

Muriel turned to leave but something made her hesitate and she knocked on the front door again. Still no answer. The curtains were drawn across the bay window but there was a small gap. Peering through it, she saw Louise lying on the sofa. She decided not to disturb her but then she gasped as Louise groaned and one hand flopped down to dangle over the edge of the sofa.

Muriel bit her knuckles, unsure what to do. It didn't look like natural sleep. "Louise, wake up," she shouted, banging on the window. Her friend didn't stir.

"Phone box," Muriel muttered, dashing to the end of the road, only to find she had no change. She looked round wildly, but there was no one in sight. She

346

remembered that Dr Tate lived only a couple of streets away and she began to run, praying that he was home.

Louise struggled to sit up, closing her eyes against the pain in her head. She was going to be sick. There was a sour taste in her mouth and a smell of alcohol in the air. A voice murmured in her ear. "My love, wake up, please . . ."

Strong arms enfolded her and, as memory returned, she fought against them. "No, please don't make me," she cried.

Gentle hands stroked her hair and at last she recognized the reassuring voice. "Andrew," she whispered. "How did you . . .?"

"Your friend fetched me. She was worried about you. Thank God I was there when she called." There was sob in his voice. "I got here just in time."

Louise sat up and pushed him away. "You shouldn't be here," she said. She looked round wildly. "James might come back. He mustn't find you here."

Andrew caught her hands. "He can't hurt you now. We know what he tried to do. It's a good job he forced you to drink the whisky as well. That's what made you sick. The pills didn't have a chance to work."

Muriel spoke from the corner of the room where she'd been rinsing a cloth in a basin of water. "You were semi-conscious when we arrived, muttering and moaning. We were able to make out what had happened."

Louise looked into Andrew's eyes. "You believe me then?"

He nodded and pressed her hands to his lips. "He wanted people to think . . ."

"I would never have believed it, however convincing he was," Muriel said. "I never did trust that man, even when he was a lad. Sly, deceitful . . ." She shrugged. "Sorry, I know he's your husband." She picked up the basin and left the room.

Louise shook her head. "She's right. I don't know why it took me so long to realize . . ."

Andrew was about to say something when there was a knock at the door. "That'll be the police," he said, standing up. When Louise gasped he said, "We had to call them. He tried to kill you."

The door was flung open and Sarah burst in. "Kill — did you say kill?" she shrieked. She threw herself into Louise's arms and burst into tears. "I knew there was something wrong. Oh, Lou, please tell me you're OK. Why didn't I come home sooner? I'm sorry, so sorry."

Now it was Louise's turn to offer comfort. "It doesn't matter. You're here now."

In the midst of the tearful reunion a police sergeant arrived accompanied by a constable. While Muriel and Andrew gave their statements, Sarah went into the kitchen to clear up, saying there would be plenty of time to talk when everyone had gone.

James paced up and down his office, glancing from time to time at his watch. Had the drugs taken effect yet? After leaving Sally, he'd gone home and found Louise resting on the sofa in the drawing room. It had been hard to force her to drink the whisky laced with the sleeping pills. He'd left the glass and pill bottle on the side table, spilled a few of the tablets on the floor and then returned to the office. He glanced at his watch again and the enormity of what he'd done suddenly hit him. Keeping her sedated so that she was confused and amenable was one thing. Murder was quite another. Was it too late to change his mind?

No, he had to go through with it. He needed that money — and he needed a drink too. He grabbed his hat and rushed along to the Red Lion. The landlord knew him well and had his glass on the bar before he could ask for his usual.

He took a deep breath and forced himself to make small talk, reflecting that he might need an alibi later. He finished the drink and banged the glass down for another but the landlord shook his head. "Sorry, Mr Spencer, no more spirits. You can have a beer."

James shook his head. He needed whisky. Perhaps he could get one at the Esplanade Hotel, he thought. Who knows, he might bump into the gorgeous Sally while he was there. Why shouldn't he have a little fun? He'd be playing the grieving widower soon enough and there'd be no chance of fun for a while.

He left the pub and strode along, deep in thought, wondering how soon he could force the house sale and get his hands on the money. Steyne House was on the way to the hotel and he was tempted to check on Louise. No, he thought, better keep away for a bit longer.

As he walked past he noticed that the front door was ajar. Surely he'd locked it when he'd left earlier. He stepped into the hall and put his hand on the drawing-room door. His stomach lurched as he heard voices and he hesitated, schooling his face to register shock, concern, grief.

His grip tightened and he took a deep breath. But as he grasped the doorknob a sound behind him caused him to whirl round.

"You," he gasped. "What are you doing here?"

"I'm visiting my sister," Sarah said calmly.

"Your sister?"

"Didn't recognize me, did you?" Sarah gave a short laugh. "Don't suppose it would have stopped you flirting even if you'd known." Her contemptuous gaze swept over him. "Anyway I should ask what you're doing here. Come to view your handiwork?"

"What do you mean?" he asked, stammering. "Is Louise all right? She's been quite ill, you know. I must go to her." He made to open the door but Sarah stepped in front of him.

"You didn't seem too concerned about your wife earlier on."

"It didn't mean anything — just a bit of fun," he stammered.

"Fun? While your wife was lying here ill?"

James recovered quickly. "I told you, it didn't mean anything. What's happened? Louise was all right when I left home this morning." He tried to push past her again but Sarah stood firm.

"The doctor's with her. He may be able to save her."

"What do you mean?" The hysteria in his voice wasn't feigned. Had Louise been saying anything?

Panic began to set in and he almost regretted what he'd done. It was only because those thugs in Brighton were chasing him. Anyway, it was her fault. She'd tried to deceive him about the house. If she'd agreed to sell straight away this would never have happened.

Louise had still been a little confused when giving her statement but Muriel was adamant that Louise never drank spirits and Andrew assured the sergeant that she'd never been prescribed sleeping tablets. "My uncle will confirm that," he said.

The sergeant closed his notebook with a snap. "I think that's all for now. I'll come back tomorrow, Mrs Spencer. Meanwhile, I'd better have a chat with Mr Spencer." He turned to the constable. "You stay here in case he comes back."

At the sound of voices in the hall, he opened the door. "Ah, Mr Spencer, we'd like a word with you."

James made to push past. "I must see my wife," he said.

"Not so fast. I'm going to take you in for questioning." The sergeant grasped his arm but James shook him off. "Constable," roared the sergeant.

James took one look at the burly policeman and tried to run. As he reached the front door, Sarah stuck her foot out and he tripped, sprawling down the front step. The two policemen were on him in a flash, handcuffing him and leading him away.

Louise looked up as Sarah came back into the room. "I can't believe you're here," she said, smiling through her tears. She glanced across to where Andrew was packing his medical bag. "I'm so lucky to have such friends and family."

Andrew turned to her. "Well, I'm afraid this friend must leave. I promised Uncle George I'd take surgery this evening."

"I must go too," Muriel said. "Anyway, you need time with your sister. I'm sure you've got lots of catching up to do."

"My car's outside," Andrew said. "I'll give you a lift."

When they'd gone, Louise started to cry. Sarah came and sat beside her. "It's reaction," she said. "It's probably only just beginning to sink in."

Louise shook her head. How could she tell her sister she was crying over Andrew? Had he really held her in his arms, stroked her hair, called her his love? Or had she still been hallucinating? She'd leaned on him, accepted the comfort of his arms. And then he'd left, scarcely saying goodbye.

The sisters sat up long into the night filling in the years that had passed. Inevitably the talk turned to James and why he'd done what he did. "I don't understand it," Louise said. "I would have agreed to sell the house if he'd given me a good reason. But I wasn't going to be bullied into it."

"Perhaps he needed money," Sarah said.

As they talked, the sisters realized that, despite their estrangement, the love they'd always felt for each other had never died. There were no recriminations as they began to understand that neither of them was at fault. "It was easy to blame the war for your letters not reaching me. I just didn't want to believe that you'd cut yourself off from your old life," Louise said at last with a sigh.

"I did the same. I kept telling myself you were jealous of my success. Greg told me off. He said there must be a reason you hadn't been in touch. And then, when I got that official-looking letter asking for my signature on those papers, I knew something was up. Greg persuaded me to come home and sort it out. It took ages to arrange."

"Why didn't he come with you?"

"I didn't want him to — in case you refused to see me. I'd have been embarrassed." Sarah gave a nervous laugh. "That's me — thinking of myself again."

"Don't be silly." Louise sat up straight and changed the subject. "When am I going to meet the wonderful Greg?"

"Soon. I've got to go back to London and sort things out. I might get away with breaking my contract on compassionate grounds — it's not every day your brother-in-law is arrested for attempted murder."

Louise bit her lip. "Will they find him guilty, do you think?"

"Sure. That sergeant went though his desk and found some of my old letters still sealed, as well as yours to me — never posted. And what about that paper with our forged signatures all over it? He'd obviously been practising. I should think they've got enough evidence."

"And the pills," Louise said. "I mean, why would he put them in the aspirin bottle?" She shuddered and her voice caught on a sob, "He must have been thinking about it ever since Mother died. I thought I'd thrown away all her old medicines but he must have hidden some away."

Sarah put her arm round her. "It's all over now, Lou. He can't hurt you any more. You can start all over again now — make a new life for yourself."

"New life? Church, WVS, queuing for rations? The only difference is I won't be on pins and needles any more wondering what mood he'll be in when he comes home."

"Don't think about it, Lou. Think of the future."

Louise didn't answer. She didn't dare to think ahead. For those few moments when Andrew had held her in his arms she had dared to hope. But now . . .? Had she imagined the panic in his eyes as he struggled to revive her, his tender words as she responded?

When Sarah turned up, closely followed by the police, he'd once more become the efficient professional doctor caring for his patient. Did he love her after all? And if he did, what difference did it make? She was still a married woman despite what James had done. It would be a long painful process before she was free of him.

A week had gone by and Louise still hadn't seen Andrew. Every time there was a knock on the door she started up, heart thumping. If she could see him, she was sure she'd know instinctively if she'd imagined those tender moments in his arms. But he hadn't been near. She must have been mistaken. Why else would he stay away?

James was still in custody, charged with attempted murder, fraud and embezzlement. David Webster the solicitor had called to inform her of progress. "It seems your husband had been mixing with the wrong sort of people. He'd been gambling and couldn't pay his debts."

"I knew he was worried but I thought it was the business," Louise said. "If only he'd confided in me — I would have helped him."

"I think he'd gone beyond that," Webster said sympathetically. "Just be thankful your friend and your sister turned up when they did."

Louise cleared her throat. "I need to talk to you about something," she said. "It's about James and me." She couldn't go on, couldn't utter the word divorce. It went against all her principles. But how could she stay married to the man who had tried to kill her?

David Webster smiled sympathetically. "I know what you mean. No rush. Make an appointment when you feel ready."

Muriel had gone back to work at the WVS centre. There'd been another bombing raid on the town and she was needed. Louise wanted to go with her but Mrs Wilson had insisted that she recover completely from her ordeal before coming back.

Dr Tate called and told her she ought to be fit enough by the following week. She wanted to ask about Andrew but found herself unable to speak his name and the old doctor hadn't mentioned him either.

She got up from the table and moved around the room restlessly. Her relief at discovering she wasn't going crazy had abated somewhat and she knew she'd have to start living a normal life again soon. One thing was certain; she no longer wanted to stay here. Her childhood home now held more unhappy memories than pleasant ones. I suppose I could go anywhere, she thought. But she'd no idea where. Andrew dominated her thoughts.

Sarah had gone to London to see Greg and sort out her contract. They were hoping to go to Italy where British troops were making progress towards an end to the fighting. Everyone wanted to hear Sally Charles sing and Sarah was in her element entertaining the troops. She'd told Louise that it had been the most fulfilling time of her career and she couldn't wait to get back to it. Perhaps I could go with her, she thought. No, it was a foolish thought. She belonged in Holton. It seemed she was destined to stay in her home town. At least here she might catch a glimpse of Andrew now and then. He'd called her a friend and that was better than nothing. She was still a married woman after all, and even if he did care for her, Andrew was far too honourable a man to do anything about it.

But I don't want just friendship, she cried silently.

She stood up abruptly. She had to get out of the house. It was very windy and black clouds were massing to the west but she didn't even think of putting on a coat or taking an umbrella.

She strode along the esplanade, the wind at her back whipping her hair over her face. There was no one about and she quickened her pace, relishing the solitude and the wild weather. Determined not to dwell on recent happenings, she recalled the walks with Sarah and her father. What fun they'd had picking up shells and stones and strangely shaped pieces of driftwood. In earlier days Louise had kept the prettiest pieces to arrange on her windowsill. They'd all been thrown away when Dora came on the scene. She didn't like her home cluttered with bits of rubbish.

Louise would still enjoy beachcombing if it weren't for the barbed wire barriers preventing access to the beach. Still, it was good to be out in the fresh air, striding along as she used to do, feeling fit for the first time in ages. And free. She hadn't fully realized until now how restricted her life had been, chained first to Dora's wants and needs, then to James and his controlling behaviour. How had she let this happen to her? Was she so weak that anyone could manipulate her?

She shook her wind-blown hair back from her face impatiently. Surely having a sense of duty, of what was the right thing to do, wasn't weak, she thought. James had called her a doormat, but she didn't think she was. Hadn't she tried to stand up to him? She'd have succeeded too if it hadn't been for the drugs.

Forget all that now, she told herself. Start living for today, not in the past. As she walked, she began to make plans. Hard as it would be to leave the family home, the house her great grandfather had built, she couldn't let sentiment stand in the way of being sensible. Besides, the past few unhappy years had completely wiped out the memories of happier days and Steyne House wasn't practical for someone living alone anyway. She smiled at the thought of James's reaction when he heard she was selling after all.

The wind had grown stronger and she was about to turn back when a squall of rain pelted her with large cold drops. By the time she reached the nearest seafront shelter, she was soaked. Before the war the wooden shelters had been well maintained, repainted every year in time for the holiday makers. Now the paint was peeling and several of the glass panes were broken.

The wind whistled through the gaps and drops of rain trickled down Louise's neck. Shivering, she huddled into a corner, hoping the rain wouldn't last.

She didn't hear the man approach and jumped when he spoke.

"Andrew," she gasped.

"I called out but you didn't hear me." He took his coat off, draping it round her shoulders, and sat down beside her.

"Thank you," she whispered, hardly daring to look at him. Could he hear the thunder of her heart? Did he realize she wasn't just shivering from the cold?

When he put his arm round her she tried to pull away but he drew her closer. "Louise, I know this probably isn't the right time, but you must know that I . . ." He moved away from her. "I shouldn't, you're still married, but — I can't go back to London without knowing . . ."

She looked up at him, tears trembling on her lashes. "Knowing what, Andrew? That I love you?" She smiled.

"Oh, Andrew, if you only knew how hard I've tried to hide it, to pretend to myself that I didn't care."

"I could understand that after you married but — before?"

"From the moment I first met you," she said. "But you went back to London and I didn't hear from you. Your uncle said you had all the nurses after you." She gave a small laugh. "I didn't think I could compete. And when you came back to Holton again, you were so cool towards me."

"Oh, yes — that church social." Andrew's lips twisted in a bitter smile. "You seemed to be having such a good time and James was so possessive of you. Your stepmother told me you were about to become engaged. That's why I backed off."

"I was only happy because you were there . . ." Louise's voice broke.

Andrew put his arms round her and she nestled against him. He sighed. "So much time wasted. If only I'd spoken before. But I was so afraid of rejection. I'd just been jilted you see and I was reluctant to risk being hurt again."

"Did you love her?" Louise had to ask.

"I thought so at the time. Later I realized it was for the best. She wasn't the person I thought she was. Her father was a Harley Street consultant and she thought my ambition matched his. She didn't relish the thought of being married to an impoverished doctor working the back streets of London. When I made it clear I wasn't going to change my mind she . . ." He shrugged and smiled down at her. "Seems like we've both made mistakes," he said.

Louise nodded. Her mistake was greater than his, she thought. She'd actually married the wrong man. Was it too late for them?

Andrew echoed her thought. "Can we put those mistakes right?" he asked.

"I hope so." But she wasn't so sure and she moved away from him. A doctor marrying a divorced woman would cause a scandal and having an affair while still married would be even worse.

"I know what you're thinking," he said. "But I don't care. I love you and I want to be with you." He drew her towards him and kissed her, gently at first, then with mounting passion. She melted into him, her hands in his hair, murmuring his name between ever more ardent kisses.

The rain still pelted down and thunder rumbled overhead. The wind rattled the broken glass. But neither of them noticed.

At last Andrew released her and she reluctantly moved away, laughing a little. "You don't know how long I've waited for that," she said breathlessly.

"Me too, and not just kisses either." His blue eyes sparkled.

Louise blushed a little but she smiled and said, "I can't wait."

He frowned. "Louise, my love, we can't — not yet. I couldn't bear it if you were involved in a scandal. There'll be gossip enough as it is when James comes to trial. We mustn't see each other until everything's settled. You should have no trouble getting a divorce after what James did."

"But Andrew, that could take months," Louise cried.

"We've waited this long, we can wait a bit longer. I want everything to be right for us. Besides, we've got our whole lives ahead of us."

"You're right of course. I don't care about myself but you have your career to think of." She smiled as a thought crossed her mind. "But we can still see each other — you are a doctor after all, and I have been ill."

He laughed and pulled her to him one more. "I don't think that would be wise. I'm not sure I could trust myself to behave as a doctor should."

"You're probably right," she said, laughing.

"Just one more kiss and then you must go home. I don't want you getting another chill."

The kiss lasted a little longer than perhaps it should, but eventually Andrew pulled away and took Louise's hand. Reluctantly she stood up and they walked out of the shelter onto the esplanade. The storm had passed and to the east a rainbow arced over the sand dunes. Bright sunlight reflected in the puddles and whitecaps danced on the sea as, hand in hand, they walked back along the esplanade.

# Epilogue

# 1946

A small crowd had gathered at the entrance to the former Steyne House to watch Sarah cut the ribbon and declare the Charlton House Convalescent Home open. Louise and Andrew stood beside her, their eyes shining with pride.

Introducing her, the mayor said how proud they were of their famous former resident and the work she'd done raising money for the home. "Doctor and Mrs Tate, too, have played their part in getting this project off the ground — Mrs Tate by making over her lovely house to the Trust and Dr Tate by freely giving of his services."

There was a burst of applause and a few cheers, loudest of all from the thirteen-year-old boy, standing tall and proud beside them.

Andrew's hand rested on the boy's shoulder and he gave it a squeeze. Alfie looked up at him, grinning. "When they gonna serve the grub, Doc?" he asked.

Louise shushed him but she was finding it hard to suppress her laughter. How different he was from the peaky little boy she'd first seen huddled in his wheelchair. And how fortunate that they'd been able to take him in after his father had been killed in the D-Day landings. When the adoption was complete, Alfie would truly be their son.

She looked down at her swelling stomach. Soon there'd be a brother or sister for Alfie. She caught Sarah's eye and smiled. Her sister too was now married and had a child on the way. She and Greg were still touring, though — nothing could stop Sarah from singing. But they would return often to Holton. The children would grow up together.

We'll be a proper family, Louise thought, reaching for Andrew's hand and smiling up at him.